Robert Forster is a Brisbane-born and based musician and writer. In 1978 he co-founded with friend and fellow singer-songwriter Grant McLennan the internationally acclaimed rock band The Go-Betweens. Their sixth album, *16 Lovers Lane*, was placed at number 12 on the 100 Best Australian Albums list, and their ninth and last, *Oceans Apart*, won the 2005 ARIA award for Best Adult Contemporary Album. In 2010, Brisbane honoured their cultural influence by naming a new river bridge the Go Between Bridge.

Robert's parallel career as a writer began in 2005 when he was appointed music critic for *The Monthly*, and a year later he won the Geraldine Pascall Prize. A collection of his journalism, *The 10 Rules of Rock and Roll*, was published in 2009. In 2015, his alma mater, the University of Queensland, awarded him an honorary Doctor of Letters. Robert's memoir, *Grant & I*, was published in 2016.

Also by Robert Forster

The 10 Rules of Rock and Roll
Grant & I

ROBERT FORSTER

SONG WRITERS ON THE RUN

PENGUIN BOOKS

UK | USA | Canada | Ireland | Australia
India | New Zealand | South Africa | China

Penguin Books is part of the Penguin Random House group of companies whose addresses can be found at global.penguinrandomhouse.com

First published by Penguin Books in 2026

Cover images: Adobe Firefly © Penguin Random House Australia Pty Ltd
Cover design by Adam Laszczuk © Penguin Random House Australia Pty Ltd
Typeset in 11.5/17.7 pt Adobe Caslon Pro by Midland Typesetters, Australia

Printed and bound in Australia by Griffin Press, an accredited
ISO AS/NZS 14001 Environmental Management Systems printer

A catalogue record for this book is available from the National Library of Australia

ISBN 978 0 14377 773 1

We at Penguin Random House Australia acknowledge that Aboriginal and Torres Strait Islander peoples are the Traditional Custodians and the first storytellers of the lands on which we live and work. We honour Aboriginal and Torres Strait Islander peoples' continuous connection to Country, waters, skies and communities. We celebrate Aboriginal and Torres Strait Islander stories, traditions and living cultures, and we pay our respects to Elders past and present.

'I write the songs that make the whole world sing'

Bruce Johnston, 'I Write the Songs'

To Karin
Dass du da bist

Contents

CHAPTER 1

‘We’ve been here before.’

‘You always say that.’

‘We’ve either been here before, or a place very much like it.’ Drew stops, arching a dark eyebrow. ‘I wonder where that was?’

‘And it counts as us being here . . .’

‘I recognise the bull.’

The bull is a two-metre-high rusty metal frame with a head and tail, which the service station owner presumably had knocked up by a welder mate and placed near the road as a tourist attraction. Mick and Drew are walking to their car, a red 1983 Falcon XE station wagon, with burgers and soft drinks in their hands. Drew is turning to see what other signposts of the past he can find. Mick is withdrawn, yet always willing to fence with his friend. *Talking.* People tell them it’s part of their magic.

They are in their early thirties, tall and skinny, rock-star-wrecked handsome and in denim. Drew has the finer features – a thin nose and liquid eyes – while Mick possesses a brutish set of good looks able to curl into a heartbreaking smile or storm up into a potentially arm-breaking scowl. Both men sport shoulder-length hair crushed into shape by stage sweat and early-morning wake-ups in cheap hotels.

In the front seat of the car, behind the wheel, Swifty, his full-moon face ringed by ginger curls, is eating while flicking through a street directory.

'I've found it,' he says, as Drew slides in beside him, Mick taking the back seat – their regular spots. And with his sandwich still in hand, a Coke between his legs, Swifty guides the car back onto the highway.

Tom runs the Durango Bar – a long venue at the top of a steep staircase, with a stage at one end of the room and a bar at the other. The decor is a brave stab at Mexican: empty tequila bottles hold dripping candles, a sad sombrero hangs over the bar. Stuck to the ceiling, with brittle strips of tobacco-stained sticky tape, is a poster of Kris Kristofferson and Rita Coolidge, the Durango Bar's patron saints. It's the only place in Rockhampton where you can play and be guaranteed to get paid.

Tom is a former navy engineer with a beer gut and a grey-streaked quiff; his love of country music ignited through good times with US marines when stationed in Manila. Today, he is where he often is, behind the bar, offering drinks to Mick and Drew, who are perched on barstools, lighting cigarettes.

'Beer, thanks,' says Drew. 'Oh, you got Dos Equis. Lovely, I'll have one of them.'

'It's early mate, J-e-e-z . . .' exhales Mick. He glances at Drew in mock despair. 'A vodka and orange. You got Stoli?'

'Sure do,' says Tom. 'How was last night. Brisbane, right?'

'Yeah, okay,' says Drew wearily. 'Sold out.'

'Hometown crowd?'

'Well, it is for me. Mick's from Casino.'

'I never knew that,' says Tom, handing Mick his drink. Mick, for all his brawn, has a dainty way of drinking. He sips with satisfaction, he doesn't slurp.

'Left when I was twelve,' he says, his bottom lip reaching up for the alcohol's sting.

'I've never been,' says Tom. 'The wife and I have often thought of going down that way.'

'It's worth a stop, I guess. When are we on?'

'Nine. That alright?'

'Great,' says Drew. 'Time to sound-check, go to the motel, freshen up and come back for the show. We've got a big drive tomorrow.'

'Where to?'

'Cairns.' Drew glances at his partner, blank-faced. 'It's only about a thousand kilometres.'

Mick takes another sip of much vodka and orange. It's 4pm, and he and Drew are just sliding into their day. 'I can't remember much about anything anymore.' He rubs his fingers over his brow, as if trying to smooth the ache of a troubled mind. 'We've been on the road for a year and a half promoting our album . . .'

'*Bridges And Vestiges*, fantastic record,' interrupts Tom. 'We play it all the time and local radio are right behind it. They're flogging the single. You'll get a hundred people here tonight.'

Drew is disappointed.

'Yeah, but they're your crowd, *listeners*,' enthuses Tom, 'hanging on every word. And we'll look after ya, don't worry about that.' He raises a finger triumphantly, a greasy lick of hair falling into his eye. 'And it's a Friday night of a long weekend. How about that? So expect some serious walk-up. A hundred and fifty easy.'

'We've been to New Zealand three times. Japan twice.'

'Other way round,' murmurs Drew.

'Two massive European tours. Lots of festivals. Played Poland. Dublin was a two-day party. Greece. Slovenia. Spain. Oh man, the women there.' He dry-laughs on the memory. 'You've got no idea.'

Drew cuts in. 'A Dutch festival with The Pixies.'

Tom looks blank.

'Bohemian women with fire in their eyes.'

Drew realises his mistake: Alternative Rock not on the bar owner's radar. 'Another festival, forget where, Waylon Jennings was on the main stage. We were in a tent the day after.'

'Waylon, huh.'

'And this is our fifth and last time around Australia.' Mick slices the air with his hand. '*Finito*. We've told our manager we want our nest-egg money, and then we're going to take a *long* holiday, man.'

'That's Alastair, right?'

'We call him Bingo.'

'He was polite on the phone. Some people booking their bands are pigs.'

'Oh, that's nice to hear,' says Drew, stubbing out his cigarette. 'We haven't got a pig.'

There is a loud bang downstairs. The musicians jump. Tom brings them back. 'Done America?'

'Not yet,' says Mick, looking out the first-floor window. Locals in flannelette shirts and thongs walking by. 'Tell him.'

Drew leans in, dropping an elbow on the bar, his left hand dangling, ready to form the shades of emphasis he will employ when laying out a plan he and Mick refer to as 'The American Dream'.

'Bingo recently made contact with someone high up at Asylum Records in LA. That's the label of Joni Mitchell, Jackson Browne and Tom Waits. At the end of this tour, we're going to make a demo of some great new songs we've got, and Bingo's going to get them to his contact. Hopefully, we get signed and move to LA. Our first gig will be at The Troubadour.'

Tom's lost again.

'It's a club on Sunset Boulevard. The Eagles, who we're obviously not fans of, got their start there. A lot of people and bands did. It was a hangout and it still is *the gig*.'

'You got it all worked out.'

'You betcha,' says Mick proudly.

'The touring, though. I mean, it must be hard on your partners. Val bitches about me being down here all the time, and I'm only a mile away.'

Mick's face hardens. Drew wants to put his arm around his friend's shoulder and say, 'It's okay, mate.' But he doesn't.

'My wife left me,' says Mick quietly. 'Which means we've got quite a few break-up songs.'

'Too many for me,' says Drew.

'Song title.'

They say this to each other whenever an appealing phrase or word pops up between them. Filed away, a lyric idea for any incoming new tune.

'That's the thing with the road, Tom,' says Mick, emptying his glass with a knock on the bar. 'When you're at home you want to be out there, and when you're on the road you want to be at home. It makes no sense and it's fucking hard work.'

'Hey, guys, where do you want me to put the gear?'

Swifty, having staggered up the stairs, is standing before the stage with a guitar case in each hand; a pair of guitar stands tucked under one arm, a carrier bag with guitar leads jammed under the other. And on his back, an opened bag is spilling band merchandise onto the floor.

*

While the songwriters are sound-checking, Swifty, on Tom's office phone, calls Bingo to report on the door takings from Brisbane and their arrival in Rockhampton. Always the gig upfront and the one behind when on tour.

'Oh . . . and don't forget the radio interview at five.'

'Yeah, got it,' says the roadie, bluffing.

'It's a community station attached to the university – the address is in the itinerary. Marjorie is the announcer's name.'

'I've seen it. But after the day's drive, the guys are tired . . . they mightn't –'

'Mightn't what?'

'Be up for it. Too happy about it.'

'Just tell them.'

'They think we're going back to the hotel.'

'So you didn't know?'

'I did.'

While talking with Bingo, Swifty has been glancing idly around the office. Durango Bar gig posters wallpaper the room, advertising local bands mostly. None of them he's heard of.

'It's just going to be difficult,' adds the roadie. 'They're not keen on doing press between sound-check and shows. They hate it.'

'I've heard that. But if they want an audience tonight, they'll do it.'

'It's like a sacred time for them.'

'*Sacred.* That's Drew, isn't it?' A snort. 'I can imagine the delivery. Everything is "beautiful" or "precious" or "a pleasure", especially if it suits him.'

'I'm just telling you what they're telling me.'

'What they've got to understand is that this isn't Sydney or Melbourne, where the word is out. We're in a country town. That's why I got this little radio station to push the show. It's all I could get and the guys should do me *and* the station the courtesy of turning up. Fifteen minutes, everyone's happy.'

'I'll get them there.'

'You're a trooper.'

Swifty comes out of Tom's office. Mick's singing 'Vagabond Days'. The local mixing guy has got them sounding good. Not too loud in the room, vocals up in the mix. Tom is ringside enjoying this small private show with a joint and beer in hand. Whatever happens between sound-check and the motel, it's going to be a good night.

As it turns out, the radio station is not far from the motel.

Arriving to the sound of barking dogs, a young woman with a side of her head shaved opens the front door, leading them down a tight winding corridor, gig and band posters lining the brown hessian walls to the studio.

A red light glows above the door. Peeking through the thick glass, Mick and Drew can see, but not hear, two announcers behind microphones. One is a woman with a pageboy haircut in her late twenties. The other is a scrawny boy in a buttoned-up dark shirt; a pair of cheesy sunglasses stuck in his short fuzzy hair: Lyle Lovett meets The Jesus and Mary Chain.

Opening the studio door, Michelle Shocked's 'Memories Of East Texas' fills the room. It's a favourite of the songwriters. Taking their chairs with nods and smiles at their hosts, they are ready to talk.

Marjorie says the song will finish in thirty seconds. Then they'll be on air.

'With us in the studio this afternoon are Drew Lovelock and Mick Woods, who are playing tonight at the Durango Bar. Welcome. Is there enough room for both of you?'

'We're fine,' says Drew, shuffling in his chair with a grunt.

'Mick and Drew are very tall and we're in a small space.' She addresses Drew, who is closest to her. 'Is this the first time either of you have played in Rocky?'

'We were talking about this on our way in. It is . . . and considering how often we play the same places, it's nice to be somewhere new.'

'I won't ask you what the audience can expect tonight. I'm sure it's going to be fabulous.' Marjorie's voice is confident and warm.

She could be on a big commercial station, thinks Drew. The drive-time show, perhaps. 'But what are you both expecting tonight?'

'Ah . . .'

Mick interjects. 'A full house.'

'That's right.' Drew grins at the one-liner. The mood in the studio lightening.

'You'll get that, I think,' she smiles. 'You're promoting your second album, *Bridges And Vestiges*, which came out last year. How would you describe your sound, Mick?'

'It's acoustic. We do have drums and bass and other shit – sorry – on the records. But live, it's just me and him. That's all we need, isn't it?'

'Which I know is a bit old fashioned,' chips in Drew. 'But that's where we shine. Where we stand out . . . or hope we do.'

'Mick, your first band was called A Terror Decides.' It's the Kid. 'That wasn't old fashioned, was it?'

Mick drags a luxuriant wave of dark hair back from his farmyard face to reveal the glare of a dangerous set of eyes. 'My first band was called Long Gone Train. And I don't think of fashion anymore. What's in, what's out, what's cool. I'm *way* past that, man.'

'And Drew,' says Marjorie brightly. 'You were in The Shells, which I'm sure some people will remember very fondly.'

'You make it sound like we were around in the sixties,' he chuckles. 'It's not that long ago.'

'Well, there was a touch of the sixties to those guitars.'

'We thought we were The Byrds.'

'Do you play any Shells songs?'

'No.'

'Yes, we do,' Mick interjects again.

'Oh yeah, that's right . . . occasionally we play "Pretty Girl, Pretty Star". In an encore, if it feels right.'

'It *was* a hit.'

'It wasn't, actually.' He likes Marjorie, but people thinking his previous band was bigger, or more commercial, than they were gets under his skin. They'd broken up four years ago and some serious rewriting of history is already underway. 'It went into the top forty for one week at thirty-eight. A real hit goes in the top twenty for at least a few weeks and stays there. Goes top ten, maybe. Then things change. *Then* you can order the limousines and champagne.'

'Let's play a track from the album. With us in the studio are Mick Woods and Drew Lovelock and *this* is "Emergency".'

*

'We were talking before,' continues Marjorie, 'about the groups you guys were in. For Drew, it's The Shells.'

'His first band was Toy Crime,' interrupts the Kid, daring to look at his hero. 'They put out one great single in 1979 called "Don't Ask Me How".'

'Merci,' says Drew, pleased.

'Mick, you were in, and this is a list Richie very kindly made for me' – she holds up a perforated page torn from a notebook – 'A Terror Decides, Splinters Of Blood . . .'

'I plead guilty, Your Honour.'

'My point is . . .'

'To being the lead singer of a number of bands with confronting names.'

'My point is . . .' – she admonishes him with a glare, the cheeky boy in class – 'with your very different musical backgrounds, how did you come together to form a band?'

The songwriters glance at each other. It's the question they get every interview. Who is going to tell the story this time?

'For us,' says Mick, 'it's no surprise. We'd known each other since the early eighties.'

'Our paths crossed,' says Drew, still possessing a fan-like awe in the roots of his own group.

'We were at the opposite ends of the same underground scene. He was doing his thing, I was doing mine. And then about four years ago, in the middle of '87, our bands and our' – an eye roll – '*careers* stopped. We bumped into each other at a party in Surry Hills in Sydney and got talking – about what we were thinking of doing next. And the more we talked about it, the more we realised it was pretty much the same thing. It grew from there. The things we had in common.'

'Acoustic guitars,' says Drew wistfully.

'Songs you can *play* on acoustic guitars to an audience and hold them.'

'An honesty to what we do and no disguises.'

'No distracting rock noise.'

'We're troubadours, aren't we?'

They're talking to themselves now.

'And it's this music,' says Marjorie, cutting in gracefully, 'that has brought you to Rockhampton for the first time. Isn't that wonderful? Thank you for coming in. I do some performing myself, and I know it can be hard squeezing in a radio interview between sound-check and a show.'

'It was an absolute pleasure,' purrs Drew.

*

The gig that night goes well. They all do. After eighteen months on the road, the show simply happens. The songwriters tell themselves they are like master gamblers; their songs, aces, kings, queens and jacks, cards they lay one at a time before an audience, who, at the end of their performance, can only conclude that these two singer-songwriters are holding one of the best hands in rock and roll. A few influential music critics think so too.

The variation to each night is the between-song patter. Drew does most of this; Mick offering a few dry, informative introductions to his songs that, to his thinking, help to ground the comic planets Drew can take off *to* – and sometimes not come back *from*. It can't become a comedy act.

Drew is good on the local stuff, and tonight in Rocky he is sure from his first lines, 'Lovely to be at the *cantina*.' A few laughs. 'Never thought we'd find one in downtown Rocky.' The crowd, 131 payers, enjoy the songs and the humour in their rightful place, bringing the songwriters back for three carefully staged encores.

Returning to the stage, a voice calls from the audience, 'You're geniuses!'

Drew, waiting for the laughter in the room to die, utters seriously, 'Mick and I don't regard ourselves as geniuses.' The crowd remain silent, and after a fiddle of his guitar strap, he adds, side of mouth, 'We're just extraordinarily talented, that's all.'

The loudest laugh comes from Mick.

Thirty seconds after their final song, Tom pops his head around the backstage door, flashing a thumbs-up sign. 'Great show, gentlemen. Right for drinks? I'll let people in in five.'

This is in part what they do it for; this feeling of exhausted ecstasy soothed with the first cigarettes in two hours, a refresh of the bourbon, the two of them having brought the one thing no-one can ever take away from them, their songs, to the one place they belong utterly to the songwriter – the stage.

Drew and Mick don't verbalise any of this. The most you will hear is a contented, 'Good show, man.' Or some delicious fussing on small bits of craft. 'Nice solo on "Life Is A Wheel".' 'Sorry I missed the harmony on the last chorus of "Lorraine".' 'Know what? We should shorten the introduction and bring the first verse in earlier.' That kind of stuff.

Cigarettes smoked, bourbon low, Swifty on stage casing the guitars, the first visitors sheepishly enter the dragon's lair that is the dressing-room.

There are two young women with spiked angular haircuts, hairdressers no doubt from the town's one groovy hair salon. A couple lugging camera gear, reminding Drew that he and Mick had stupidly agreed to do a photo session after the show. A tall sweaty guy, sporting a thick black beard that grows back over his head to be gathered in a ponytail at his neck. And behind him, lingering, are two guys in smart casual gear.

Ponytail approaches Mick.

'Hi, I'm a friend of Tom's . . . and he said you were . . . after something?' His voice trailing off the further the sentence travels.

Mick looks up at him innocently. 'After something?'

'Umm . . . you know . . . grass.'

Mick lets the last word hang, and then, with a sweep of his hand, gestures to the chair beside him. 'Sit down, my friend.' Putting his thumb into his jeans pocket. 'I've got fifty bucks.'

Ponytail unzips a rucksack at his feet to pull out a large plastic bag of marijuana.

'*Ho*-ly shit.'

'It's a gift. I'm a fan.'

'You truly are.'

Mick opens the bag and sniffs. 'Homegrown?'

Ponytail nods.

Mick sniffs again, and, pulling his nose from the bag, he pouts in the way a wine connoisseur would after a mouthful of a particularly fine vintage.

'Near Gympie?'

'How the hell did you know that?'

Mick hands the bag back with a smile. 'Start rollin'.'

The hairdressers have opened a bottle of white wine from a large tub of iced water in the middle of the room. Drew is talking to them and the photographers – adept as he is at running separate conversations backstage. He has noticed three guys creeping into the room; local musicians by the look of them. They'll hang against the wall, hoping to make contact with out-of-towners with careers. An invitation to a party will come, and at 3am he and Mick will be trading songs with them in a trashed lounge-room somewhere. The long march of the night is gathering its troops.

The effect of the dope on Ponytail is apparently nil. Mick is red-eyed, dry-lipped and happy in his cups. If only Ponytail would fucking shut up.

'You know those lines in "The Dark Side Of Town", *The river is wide, the river is long / The dredges do their work, they carry me along / Come on, time, do your magic trick / Take this all away from me, make it quick.* And accepting the distance an artist has to have on his or her work, are these lines – and you don't have to tell me if you don't want to – taken from the perspective of someone caught in despair and unable to get away, or is it a person wanting to give up the despair, wanting to let everything float away.'

Mick wants to say it's none of his business.

'That's a big question, man,' he coughs. 'I think I . . . I got it from a poem.'

'A poem, interesting. There's a version of the song from a bootleg cassette of a Swedish show. I trade with a guy from Malmo, who sends me obscure stuff. You introduce it as a medieval mystery play.'

'Sweden? I said that? That was very pretentious of me.'

A shadow falls. Mick's light is blocked. The two guys in casual gear have crossed the room and are standing before him. The shorter of the two, in a menacing lisp heard above the volume of the room, asks, 'Are you Michael William Woods?'

Mick hesitates. 'Who wants to know?' He smirks, catching Ponytail's distressed eye. 'I could be a visiting spirit. I'm anyone you want me to be, man.'

'We're from the Rockhampton Police. I'm Detective Sergeant Bishop and this is Constable Elroy.'

Behind his inquisitor, Mick watches the room empty. People fleeing like cockroaches from a kitchen when a light comes on at midnight. Even Ponytail has slid out. Bishop turns to Drew.

'And you're Drew Randolph Spencer Lovelock. They sure hung one on you, mate,' grins Bishop.

Petrified Drew, unable to grasp any humour in the remark.

*

Mick had sucked most of the joint – he's a notorious joint hogger. Drew had had a few tokes. The lighting in the backroom of the police station is harsh; the two fluorescent tubes overhead emitting waves of heat. It feels like their necks are being dry roasted over a spit. The cops, shimmering figures in the murderous light, are comical figures of authority. The stout one in the chair behind the desk is a frog. The slim guy standing beside him in a tight cream cardigan is the most handsome man the songwriters have ever seen. He should be modelling in Paris, thinks Mick.

The frog speaks.

'So . . . we have a bag of marijuana on your person and twenty-eight tablets of unknown origin in your luggage.'

'They're prescription,' insists Drew. 'I have a documented fear of flying and I suffer from vertigo. My doctor prescribed . . .'

'And the car – where did you get that?'

'Sydney,' says Mick, focusing, intent on taking the detective's questions.

'How?'

'We paid for it.'

'Oh yeah.'

'With cash.'

'And who did you buy it from?'

'A friend of our manager's. He . . . the manager, ah . . . gave us the money and told us where to go. Gary owned the car and we bought it from him. Simple, officer.'

'Where does Gary live?'

'We met him in a car park. Ah . . . Woolies at Marrickville.'

'Woolies at Marrickville,' remarks Bishop. 'You didn't think that was suspicious?'

Mick says nothing, believing he's done pretty well up until now.

'In a way it is our car.' Drew has sensed an opening. That ownership of the vehicle may increase their standing with the law. They may be drug addicts, but, hey, they're car owners too. 'The way our business works,' he says, slipping into a matey tone, alarming to Mick, 'is that our manager collects our concert fees and after taking his commission – which is twenty per cent, I believe – pays us the profit at the end of every tour. This time, he advanced us money at the *start* of the tour to buy the car.'

Bishop eyes Mick. 'Who's your manager?'

'Alastair Duncan-Smyth.'

'Another fancy name.'

'He's known as Bingo. He runs a booking and talent agency called Open Door Management.'

'Where does this Bingo character operate out of?'

'Melbourne.'

'You can give us his address and number?'

'Yeah, easy.'

Bishop hitches his thumb to his chin. His fingers covering his mouth won't dull what he has to say.

'The car's stolen. Gary Getty sold you a dud. Good car. But it wasn't his to sell.'

Mick and Drew keep their eyes on the detective.

'As for the credit card . . .' He tosses it onto the table. 'You've been using that for some time?'

'Ah . . . for a while, sure,' says Mick. 'Hotels, petrol, you know. Expenses on the road is what they're called.'

'How long you been on the road?'

'This time, a week – six days, maybe – since we left Sydney.'

'It's owing eighteen thousand, four hundred and sixty-two dollars and fifty-six cents. Now, I know musicians like to splash money around. You spent that since leaving Sydney?'

'Well,' chuckles Mick, a lick of spit landing on his bottom lip, 'you'll have to ask Bingo about that.'

A smile cuts into the detective's sleepy-eyed features. 'Our interstate colleagues have been doing their homework on you two bozos. The card's in your names. You've been scamming hotels and whatever else for longer than a week.'

Drew throws his head back with a groan. Mick raises a clenched fist to his face, giving himself a slow-motion punch to the jaw.

*

Scared and exhausted and still a wee bit stoned, this is way beyond any previous trouble the songwriters have encountered on tour. The other mischief – caught filling the van with petrol and driving off without paying; busted for a chunk of hash on the ferry from Amsterdam to London; a jealous boyfriend chasing Mick with an axe – amount to *nothing* compared to the shit they are in now.

And they're alone. That's the worst of it. Out of the conviviality and rock-and-roll rules of the Durango Bar, the real world has crashed in and it's brutal. A place and a state of mind to be avoided at any cost. It's a reason Mick and Drew became musicians in the first place.

Two elderly drunks had been admitted to their holding cell. One of them needing an elbow to the chest from Mick after taking a swing at Drew – he had stared too long at the fixed menace in the guy's face.

'Don't do that,' Mick had admonished his partner, his blow sending the drunk sprawling onto a corner bunk bed and off to sleep. 'It freaks out weird people.'

That done, Mick speaks in a loud whisper to Drew perched on the edge of his bunk. Clasping his fingers, nostrils flaring, as he paces with bow-legged strides his tiny stage of jail-cell floor.

'We have to have this together so when I speak to Bingo in the morning we can fix it and get back on the road. He'll be able to explain the credit card. That it's an administration or bank error.' His eyes, tucked under his prominent brow, darken. 'Bingo does need someone in the office doing the books. Swifty's been telling us.'

'Dear, dear Swifty,' says Drew wistfully.

'An accountant, so we don't get caught out like this again.'

'He could just pay it off and we work it out with him later.'

'You're right,' nods Mick. 'And we don't have to worry about the car.'

'I'm surprised Bingo didn't suss the guy.'

'He seemed okay. And meeting him at Woolies I don't find suspicious. All they *really* have on us is the drugs.'

'And my valium.'

Drew would love one or five now, washed down with a big glass of red wine.

'I've been thinking.' Mick stops and faces Drew. 'It could be a set-up. The guy with the beard could be in on it.'

'Uh-huh.'

'Some kind of relationship between this guy and the cops that we don't know about. Know what I'm saying?'

'Kind of. I didn't meet him.'

'He seemed like a genuine fan. Knew more about the band than I did. I could ask Bingo to phone Tom.' Mick's voice rises above the laboured snores of the drinkers. 'I remember the guy saying Tom had told him we wanted to buy weed.'

'So you're saying Tom told the bearded guy to bring the weed to the show and he was a fan too?'

'I'll tell Bingo to phone Tom, and either he or the bearded guy will feel obliged to help us. This is some small-town crap we've walked in on, I reckon.'

Drew feels better. Mick has worked some magic. No, it was the two of them. Heads together, they can get out of anything.

*

His nightmare is a familiar one, visions that have been chasing and tormenting him for years. The Shells are playing a big rock festival in an open field. Thousands of fans are gathered on the other side of a barricading fence before the stage, and Drew is the only person backstage preparing for the show.

Can't you see we're on in five minutes! he screams to the band.

But no-one responds. Desperately he tunes guitars, yet given the haste, everything he does is in slow motion and botched. Time is water running through his fingers. Why isn't someone carrying an amp? No-one has bothered to write a setlist. The crowd is restless. He's frantic. Distraught and dismayed, he thrashes, his legs caught in the folds of his thin blanket as he pulls himself up from the depths of his dream like a diver, waking to the shock of a presence in the room.

Kicking his bed with a heavy boot. Kicking Mick's bed now. A voice in the dark telling them to get up and get dressed. 'And don't forget your bags and banjos.'

There's a new guy behind the desk at the front of the station. Not the dimwitted constable who'd greeted the songwriters and Bishop at midnight with a yawn. Sergeant Ralf Messenger is in his mid-fifties, ruddy faced, tufts of sandy coloured hair across the scalp, eyes that somehow defy all they have seen and heard to emit hints of human kindness.

'We're rustling you blokes up some breakfast,' he says. 'Put your stuff down there.'

'She'll be here soon,' he adds to Senior Constable Ross Watkins. Watkins resembles Mick. Tall, intense, dark features, feral handsome. His black hair worn short like a skull cap. A face that has never known laughter.

The sergeant returns to his paperwork, busy scrawls of his pen, a sip of tea.

Mick can only wait so long. 'You've heard something?'

'You're being moved,' says Messenger, looking up. 'Where are you boys from?'

'We're on the road mostly,' says Mick carefully. 'We're based in Sydney.'

'I'm from Brisbane,' adds Drew.

'We won't hold that against ya.'

A wan smile from Drew.

'What name do you play under? I've got to put that in here.'

'Our own.' He feels foolish saying it. 'Mick Woods and Drew Lovelock.'

'Never heard of you. Not that that means much.' He grins at Watkins. 'A lot of the younger folk like this guy called Sting. What do you think of him?'

'Yeah,' says Drew gamely, 'he's got some songs.'

'Wait,' says Mick. 'Moved? Aren't we entitled to a phone call and legal representation?'

'There's a phone in the next room. Take him through, Ross.'

'And what if the person I speak to – our manager, who organises all our finances and, you know, what happens to us on the road – can explain the credit card.'

'If he does organise everything, there's still a charge for possession of marijuana.'

'Yeah, okay, that's not him, that was me. I asked because –'

'In our jurisdiction, marijuana is classified as a schedule one drug. The quantity you will be charged with possessing amounts to dealing.'

'You've got it worked out,' says Mick, shitting himself.

Watkins bristles.

'I'm not trying to be difficult,' Mick continues, in a register Drew has never heard before. He is proud his partner can change gears like this. 'If you can see it from our side for a second. We came into town to play a show and leave. Then a bloke we've never seen before comes backstage and gives us – we don't even have to pay for it – *gives us* the drugs. Minutes later, in walk the police. Now what would you think?'

'Hold on, son, I'm being good to you. There are substantial charges against you both and there's no magic wand to wave them away.' He flicks his head to Watkins. 'Make your call.'

As one door closes, another opens, letting in the welcoming rays of morning light and Constable Christine Hill. If she is surprised at the appearance of a lanky musician with shaggy hair and clothes her hippy Uncle Bob wore twenty years ago, she doesn't show it.

She is in her mid-twenties, medium height with short blonde hair. With her back to him, Drew watches her chat with the sergeant, who has a fixed smile and a bashful blink to his eyes. He's apologising for waking her early and asking her to come in on a Saturday morning. Their conversation drops to a mutter. Drew is leaning forward, cocking an ear, when Mick and Watkins re-enter.

Mick's face is white-sheet blank, utterly unresponsive to Drew's hopeful stare. Bingo has apparently not woken to take his call. They are alone and will be alone for however far they are being taken. Out of contact with management is bad.

'Can I write a fax?'

Messenger places a sheet of paper and a pen on the counter with a snap. As Mick and Watkins lug the guitars and bags through the door, Drew scribbles to Bingo, knowing it will be read before it is sent, used as evidence probably, a cry for help.

*

This isn't the road that brought us into town, thinks Mick, rousing himself from a back-seat nap – that was the coast highway with flashing views of the surf and a steady roll of traffic. Elderly Victorians towing caravans to escape southern winters, and truck after truck after truck. He dropped off to sleep soon after they left Rockhampton: the town spluttering out into corrugated-iron shacks and weatherboard homes; junk cars and junk machinery scattered in their yards. At a letterbox, an elderly woman in a singlet and work pants gave the passing police van the finger.

Waking more, Mick feels the bite of the handcuffs at the pit of his back. In front of him, the policewoman with two fingers on the wheel is doing as much driving as needs to be done when travelling down a barrel-straight road with no oncoming traffic.

The landscape reminds him of something he saw in a David Bowie documentary. He and his dad were bunking with Uncle Geoff's family in Newcastle. There was a TV room, and he was watching the screen from the floor, his head cupped in his hands: he would have been fourteen. His dad, he could tell, had his doubts about the 'Thin White Duke'; mercifully, he said little from his lounge chair behind Mick's back. And there was this scene with Bowie, stick-thin, wearing a black fedora and drinking from a carton of milk, in the back seat of a limousine being driven through the desert, Arizona, perhaps – the flat broad plains of bright sand and cactus out the window that brings Mick to this moment. The countryside is not exactly the same. This is endless scattered bush and cracked baked dirt, and he's not Bowie.

'Interesting territory we're travelling through,' observes Drew.

'You think so?' answers Constable Hill, a dropped beat in her reply signalling she isn't up for a chat.

Drew is a city boy. His one trip west of Brisbane – the hour-and-a-half drive to Toowoomba to play a game of schoolboy cricket. 'Well, maybe not.'

He leans forward, his chin resting on the back of the front seat, his cuffed hands inching up his back. 'And nothing would grow out here, would it? It's too dry for plant life.'

'No chance,' says Mick, happy to join in. 'There's no vegetation in hell.'

'When you were asleep, we passed some sugar-cane fields. Livestock?'

No word from the front seat.

'It would be difficult. The horses galloping across the uneven ground during the round-up.'

'There's no cattle,' murmurs Hill.

The police van bumps violently, throwing Drew back into his seat like a puppet. Returning the vehicle off sliding gravel to the grip of the highway, Hill brings it under her tight control.

Panic over, the passengers settled, yet shaken. Another one of life's little blips, reminding you danger is always near.

Drew has a series of questions in his head. Some are practical. *Where are we going? How long till we get there?* Others might impinge upon the constable's personal space. *What's it like being a woman in the police force? Were there other career options or is it a family thing? Law enforcement passed down like a piece of furniture or a treasured photograph through generations?*

He is a curious person. Unfortunately, when he speaks with people, even friends, it can sound like he's interviewing them. It isn't a strategy to hide his own story; it's just that an interest in people's lives overrides the wish to tell his own. There's also a touch of social anxiety to his questioning; if he keeps talking, the conversation won't lag.

Curiosity has certainly got the better of him through the years. At fifteen, it opened the channels away from the suburban life he was being groomed to follow. Curiosity led him to the Velvet Underground. To learning guitar in a home where no-one played a musical instrument. To form a band. To write songs, curiosity driving him to finish each one. To women – it wouldn't be the girl next door. Never content in one place, willing to walk to the end of every street and peek around the corner. The whole caper, really, to this moment in time – Saturday, 8 June 1991; handcuffed, heading west to God knows where – has been fuelled by curiosity.

With the driver hunched, Mick in an odd mood, he turns to his window, contemplating what kind of wildlife could survive the summer heat and winter chills, and what direction Neil Young will take on his next album after the triumph of *Ragged Glory*.

Mick has been brooding on the phone call, the predicament he and Drew have let themselves be sucked into. His consolation is knowing Bingo will be up by now, and the wheels of justice are turning. Who knows, they could be met by contrite faces and apologies at their journey's end. Sandwiches and beer. He allows himself to imagine a plum-voiced Melbourne grandee barrister, a close acquaintance of Bingo's parents, methodically tearing strips off Detective Sergeant Bishop and the entire Rockhampton policing system, some of it bellowed down the phone in Latin.

There'll be bargaining; after all, that's what the law is. Trade-offs. If you plead guilty to one charge, an adjustment can be made in relation to the others. Take into account the miscarriage of justice – the shit he and Drew have been put through – and the marijuana could vanish in the horse trading.

A smile coming to his lips, he glances over to Drew, who nods back. They're good again.

The songwriters have been quiet since the bump in the road; dozing on and off, the slowing of the police van has gone unnoticed. Gradually, they become aware of the change. Masking their perplexity, they tilt their heads in search of a road sign or a side road. But there is nothing new to see. And now it feels like the vehicle is running out of petrol, but it couldn't be. Then veering off the road, the car stops.

Stranded in the back seat, their driver having walked off into the desert without explanation, Mick and Drew go Zen. It has been their experience that some situations they encounter are so bad or bizarre, the chatter has to stop. Sometimes it's best to let the world do its business. Sort out its own karma. Like the time in Adelaide when they were sharing a room and woke to find the television on fire. The hotel manager was screaming, and the fire brigade, having busted down the door, had their extinguishers blasting the TV, just as Gus (mate of Mick's, drummer in Pfud), who'd been sleeping in the bath, walked out nude, his cock in his hand, asking the manager angrily what the hell was going on. The songwriters had known to go quiet. Silence is golden, a sixties group had sung in high-pitched voices – and they were right.

They watch her; it's all they can do. She has turned from her desert contemplation and is reaching the car. She unlocks both back doors, inviting the songwriters to follow her. Wriggling out, they walk to the spot where she's been standing. Looking out from a ledge of jutting rock, their minds are blown in broad daylight.

They are perched high above a crater. A broad bowl of bright red earth ringed by treeless sloping hills. Positioned at the centre of this immense barren expanse is a square, high-fenced compound, penning in rows of low-set buildings. A watchtower with an observation box at its peak guards the barb-wired front gates.

'Welcome to the West Rockhampton Hilton,' murmurs Drew.

'What is this?' squints Mick. 'I never knew these kind of places existed in Australia.'

'It's a private prison,' says Hill. 'The first in the state.'

'They don't have room for us in Rocky, eh?'

'They're full.'

'I bet they are,' says Mick under his breath.

'My eyesight is not what it should be, unfortunately,' remarks Drew. 'Along the top of the gates there's something written in steel.'

'Capricorn Correctional Facility,' says Hill, distinctly.

'Alright, so . . . CCF, not CCR?'

'You're incredible,' says Mick, shaking his head.

Drew shrugs. It's how his mind works.

'What's CCR?' asks the constable, concerned. 'An organisation?'

'You could say that. Creedence Clearwater Revival. One of the five best American bands of the sixties.'

Two black birds, their plumed wings arched wide, glide up the rock face on their way to Perth. The day's fluffy clouds are yet to appear. The outlook from the ledge is hypnotic; like viewing a cathedral in a small town or a stretch of deserted beaches leading off to infinity.

'Why did you stop?' asks Drew.

'I wanted you to see it. The turn-off is just ahead. It can be a bit of a shock if you don't know it's coming.'

'I can imagine.'

'Some prisoners get agitated.'

'We're not prisoners,' says Mick. 'We're musicians in transit.'

She returns his frosty smile. 'I'm going back to the car.'

*

Having crossed the treeless plain, Mick sits erect in the back seat, while Drew has dipped his head and shoulders to look through the windscreen. Before him, the towering iron gates swing open – it's like they're entering a temple. They could be in Afghanistan. Glancing at the side rear-view mirror, he watches a guard in a grey uniform, long-sleeved shirt and pants, push the heavy gates shut. They're inside the prison now, parked, Hill leaving them again, walking the stairs into a louvre-windowed administration office.

The woman behind the counter, a South Sea Islander with the gait and strong arms of a champion swimmer, is helpful if a little flustered, hitting back the songwriters' questions with quick jabs of information. Nothing has come from Rockhampton or Melbourne, no phone call or fax. She has been here all morning.

'But there must be something,' insists Drew.

'Let's get you settled,' she says, adding, 'if something comes in, I'll pass it on.'

Mick, too upset to speak, is able to cap his temper and stop an explosion that may produce one piece of news, but most probably cause an earthquake of grief. To distract himself, he looks out the window, to see an impatient Constable Hill waiting by the van.

*

Their 'cell' is a makeshift space in the laundry. The guard opens the door to two single iron beds on wheels by a row of industrial-sized washing machines. Entering their new place of incarceration, the smell of disinfectant and bleach permeates the white-tiled room; the songwriters realising that within the steel fortress there is improvisation. Their accommodation, the flute solo in a dark metal ballad.

Too depressed and baffled to unravel Bingo's silence, their suitcases and guitars stacked against white plastic laundry baskets filled with filthy towels, Mick and Drew sink into their squeaky beds. They're woken by a bang on the door, a call: their food is ready.

They take their evening meal in the canteen. As the songwriters are guided to a table away from the other prisoners, they gauge the mood of the room as it gawps back at them. Two long-haired blokes in florid cowboy shirts, clinking to their stewed chops and mash in heeled boots. The inclination of both musicians when entering a public space is to flounce a little. On this occasion it is resisted.

There are twenty or so tables, seating groups of four or six men; their uniforms tending to minimise their differences and herd them into a set of characteristics – older guys and fairly docile in temperament. They follow the arrival of the two new boys with suspicion, but no-one screams or licks a knife while holding eye contact. Mick and Drew make it to their table.

A chatty guard roams the room and leads most of the men out after the meal. One table remains, and as soon as the canteen door closes, two of the seated men scramble over and sit with Mick and Drew. Because they are grey-haired, hunched and in their mid-sixties, they look the same. The cook, standing behind the hot-food counter in a stained white t-shirt and chef's cap, looks on.

'I'm Ron, this is Murray. We gotta talk quick.' Ron has an English accent. Manchester, the musicians guess, a city they have played twice.

Mick and Drew introduce themselves.

'What ya in for?' butts in Murray. 'You look like a couple of poofs.'

'We're singer-songwriters, mate,' declares Drew. His defiance undercut a little by the camp inflection of his voice. A tone that has led a few Australians to ask if he's English.

Ron quietens Murray with a palmed hand. And then repeats his question.

'A few things,' says Mick.

'Come on.' Ron glances in the direction of the departing inmates. 'It could help.'

'Credit-card fraud we didn't do and a bag of weed that was given to us,' says Drew.

'How big?' asks Murray.

'A b-a-g.'

Murray cups his hands. 'Was it this big? Or this big?' His eyes flare, taking on a phosphorescent glow. 'Or was it Thai sticks? Juicy heady sticks.'

Mick's hands shape the size of a small pillow.

'Then you're up for dealing,' asserts Ron. 'That's dealing in Rocky. Two years both of you.'

'Oh, shit,' says Drew.

'Any powders or tablets?' asks the bloke from Manchester. He's able to mix the care of a counsellor with the ire of an interrogator.

'Twenty,' says Mick, less certain of himself now.

'Lysergic Acid Diethylamide?' announces Murray proudly. 'That's the proper words for LSD.'

Drew shakes his head. Ridiculous.

'Are you sure? You might have taken one and forgotten what it was?'

'Tablets. The cops swap 'em,' adds Ron.

Mick has had enough of this drug bullshit. Looking at them both. 'What are you in for?'

Silence.

'Alright,' snarls Mick. 'How long you been in?'

'Two serving four,' says Ron briskly. 'Murray's in for three and done one, ain't ya? It's not bad in here. The guy who runs the joint is tough but fair. You might have seen him when you got here. "Big" Bob Knowles? No? The big fat bastard who got into the car driven by the lady cop, with another guy, Brennan, his number two.'

The songwriters look blank.

'The lunatics are running the asylum,' says Ron, his long gaunt face breaking into a smile. 'Ya didn't see him?'

'He's hard to miss,' giggles Murray.

'They've gone to Rocky, haven't they?'

Again, the songwriters draw blank.

'Rockhampton Reef. A three-day fishing trip off the coast. Happens every Queen's Birthday weekend . . .'

'We love our queen,' wheezes Murray. He's smaller than Ron with a round bowling-ball head.

'Lots of cops go. Why not? Fishing. Grog. It's a piss-up on water.'

'Is that why they sent us here?' asks Drew.

'Maybe. They'll bring Knowles and Brennan back on Tuesday.'

'Then we'll go back to Rocky?'

'Who knows.'

There's a pause. Murray fiddles with his fingers. Ron looks away, then quickly back.

'You got a manager?'

'Of course,' says Drew.

'What's he like? Lives within his means?'

'Yeah,' splutters Drew. Bingo and Simone have just bought an apartment in Albert Park and are renovating.

'He'd run the credit card at a guess. How many bands does he manage?'

'You've got a lot of questions. Umm . . . four.'

'Big stars?'

'Not exactly. *Not yet.*'

'Interesting. I used to drive a cab in London, and one day –'

'Sorry to interrupt.' Drew waves a finger. 'Did you sit for the test? You know the one where you have to know every street in the city?'

'I know my Marble Arch from my Elephant and Castle, if that's what you mean,' cracks Ron. 'As I was saying, one day I picked up this guy and we got talking. He was in a famous sixties band. If I told you some of their hits, you'd know who I mean. After his group broke up – the singer joined a religious cult or some fucking thing – he went to see the manager. You see, he was wanting to start a business after the band.' Ron stares off. 'A travel agency, I think. They'd done all these tours on the Continent. Greece, Germany, Spain. Television Christmas specials with Lulu and Tom Jones, the whole lot.'

They hear the sound of footsteps.

'When he got to the office, the manager was gone. Pretty soon he discovered the truth.'

The canteen door opens. The chatty guard returns.

'All the debts were in their names and all the profits were in his. There's a lesson in that.' Ron eyes the musicians. 'Nothing is ever straightforward. Don't forget it.'

He gets up from his chair. 'Come to the chapel service in the morning. We can talk more, if you want.'

Mick and Drew watch them go. Their new best friends.

The guard returns to escort the songwriters to their cell. Walking out into the night, en route to the laundry via a drab courtyard, they are struck by the breadth and beauty of the sky.

Looking at the faraway moon, Mick can believe it is the Earth and he is on the lunar landscape, creeping over dry rocks and dirt, experiencing the stillness of the planets. Single spotlights illuminate the prison's high fence, the rolls of barbed wire cresting the top like frozen waves of silver surf. The darkness has taken out the day's distance, the desert, the blandness of the baked land, leaving what is lit – a lonely space station parked under a banner of stars.

They are on their beds. Drew sitting in a corner where his mattress meets the wall. Mick is lying on his back, hugging his pillow to his chest. Drew has seen him do this before in hotel rooms. It's a comforting thing; whether his partner was in need of comfort or comforting himself, he could never tell.

'My parents are going to kill me if they ever find out I've been in jail.'

'Correctional facility,' says Mick dreamily. 'What do you think of what Ron said?'

'Authentic. Probable.'

'You think Bingo's capable of it?'

'Hard to tell. He's been good for us and I've always felt we're in this together.'

'Same here.'

'But Melbourne . . . it could be tempting if he needed the money. He does have a lifestyle to maintain.'

'That he was born into. Only child too. I'm always suspicious of them.'

'Then again,' reflects Drew, wishing to appear reasonable, knowing it could provoke his partner, 'it could be our fault for not selling enough records.'

'We are who we are. There's nothing we can do about that.'

'If it *is* him . . .'

'His other bands are the scene chasers, not us.' Mick turns his head, his eyes straining to reach Drew. 'In The Tropics, your old mates.'

'I only know Troy,' he pleads. He's diverted Mick down the wrong road: his friendship and rivalry with former pop star Troy Kennan: In The Tropics changing their sound to the whims of Troy's record collection. 'If it is Bingo with the credit card, and he's not answering Bishop's calls either, then we're on our own.' Drew gets fidgety. 'Where's Swifty? He would have gone to the cops this morning and asked about us, surely.'

'Even without a car, he'd find us. And if Bingo's not answering us, Swifty won't be doing any better.'

'This is sickening.'

Mick's voice is shedding his dreamy lilt. 'Let's go to the office in the morning and see if anything has come through. If not, we demand a call. Ron can help us.'

Drew gets up to brush his teeth. Standing at a large laundry tub, he turns to Mick. The pillow is still on his chest – his long bony feet, threaded with black hair, poke out from the end of a sheet. He looks like a patient about to be wheeled off to surgery. Then, in a voice that is often the authoritative one between them, the living corpse says, 'If we haven't spoken to him, we can't go back to Rocky.'

*

As of the 1987 census, Thamalgah is a town of 2976 people: on its one bump of ground sits Our Lady Of The Rosary Catholic church. When he retired two years ago, Father Timothy Ahern had been the residing parish priest for nineteen years. He is an Irishman of medium height, with a head of white hair and a softness to his skin that the long outback summers had failed to burn or coarsen. Remaining, too, is a lyrical home-country accent that had soothed his congregation through floods and droughts of biblical dimensions.

Upon his retirement and to ease the workload of his successor, he has kept one clerical duty for himself. Each Sunday morning he drives the 180-kilometre round trip to deliver mass to a group of prisoners at the Capricorn Correctional Facility. Some of the men he knows through the web of baptisms, weddings and funerals that bind a country town and its neighbouring communities. Bob Knowles, liking the Irish priest, who officiated at his daughter's wedding, had permitted the building of a small chapel at the rear of the facility – not far from Mick and Drew's 'cell'.

A dozen or so inmates attend the service, and with most of them circling the sunny priest, a tea urn and two cinnamon-topped apple cakes, the songwriters have drawn Ron and Murray aside.

'I could have told you last night,' says Ron dismissively. 'The office is closed on Sundays.'

'We're desperate,' says Drew. 'Our manager is not responding to anything we send him.'

'I'm not surprised. And the cops?'

'Nothing.'

'Well, then, I'm tempted to say you're fucked.'

The songwriters are stung. Ron is long out of practice communicating with folk from the outside world. Musicians being sensitive; singer-songwriters as fragile as Viennese glass. Touched by their defeated faces, he asks, 'How desperate are you?'

'Could we get a lawyer?' suggests Drew. 'That would be a start. So when we go to Rocky . . .'

'A lawyer, if you got one, couldn't change anything in a day. You're going to Rocky as you are.'

'Has anyone gotten out of here?' asks Mick, taking a breath, inflating his bull-like features, his animal grace. 'By means fair or foul?'

It's a challenge to Ron. The two of them are going to work this out. Murray and Drew, the geek chorus.

'No,' says Ron flatly.

'It's impossible?'

'It's not that. It's just that we're too old to try. And compare this' – he jerks his thumb towards a scrum of scraggy men washing cake down with tea; Father Ahern, glancing over, a benevolent nod, as if blessing the mischief being discussed – 'to what's waiting for us outside. Which is fuck all. We'd be dying on park benches.'

'Also,' says Murray, 'we've done what we've done.'

He and Ron snicker. 'It's a fact,' says Ron, delighting in his friend's wit. 'Most prisoners are doing time on a fraction of the crimes and felonies they've committed. Forty per cent?'

'Thirty,' says Murray. 'With me, it would be twenty. I did some terrible things.'

'You boys are clean.'

'What do you mean too old?' asks Drew.

'The nearest road west, which is the direction anyone leaving here would want to go, is the Warrego Highway. It's sixty k's. Thirty to the rim, thirty to the road. You'd have to do it at night, right? And the ground is rough and rocky and there's gullies and scrub to hack through. Oh thanks, this is Max.'

Max is carrying four mugs of tea.

'Could you keep things going over there, mate,' says Ron. 'Another round of tea. Did you bake anymore? We're talking here.'

'And if we got caught,' he eyes the songwriters sternly, 'they wouldn't drag us back here. It would be a proper fucking nick with arsehole guards and shotguns.'

Song title, thinks Drew. *Hi, everyone, great to be at the Tivoli Theatre. This is a new song called 'Arsehole Guards and Shotguns'.*

'And you're sure Knowles isn't back till Tuesday?' asks Mick.

'That's the one piece of information we can rely on.'

'If you *were* thirty years younger, how would you do it?'

'One of the . . . consequences of being incarcerated, confined to a small space, is that you observe things. Even if it is just a game. And we've got some of the best criminal minds in Australia in here. Sneaky and clever. Very impressive.'

'Okay, and what do they say?'

Ron takes a big sip of tea. It's hot, scalding his smiling lips. 'It's possible, and you've picked the perfect night.'

*

Having dragged chairs out to catch the last of the afternoon sun, cigarettes burning and in need of a drink – it's Stoli and orange juice time – Mick and Drew sit silently. Packed and ready to go:

the Capricorn Correctional Facility, one more departure lounge. The view through the barbed-wire fencing – the thirty k's of dusty ground they could be scrambling over in a few hours' time.

'You nervous?' asks Mick.

'We're putting everything into the hands of someone we've known for twenty-four hours. A bit. And you?'

'I'll be happy to be on the move.'

'This isn't insane, is it?'

Mick laughs. 'If we get Bingo, it's not.'

Drew glances over, knowing there'll be more.

'Ten minutes with him. That's all I'll need.'

*

At dinner, Ron slips them a bag. It's from Max, he says, filled with a few things they'll want. Drew says he'll carry it, his suitcase in his other hand, his guitar slung on his back, Johnny Cash style.

With his arms resting on the table, dirty plates and glasses pushed aside, Ron opens his clenched fist. Sparkling in the palm of his hand under the murky canteen light is a gold key on a silver chain. He waits till the songwriters are on the tip of speaking. 'It opens the front gate.'

He lifts the key like a diamond and delicately holds it before the songwriters' eyes. 'There's an engraving. Can you see it? "CW".' He tilts his head, indicating a riddle. 'Cleveland Walker. Not the best-known locksmith in Rocky, but one who'll cut a key and not ask questions.'

'Who told you that?' asks Drew.

'Someone.'

'He may be a master craftsman, old Cleveland,' says Mick. 'How do we know it works?'

'Does your car start every time? It's all to do with probability, innit?' Ron leans in. 'It was given to me by a bloke who was about to finish his time in here. From memory,' he squints, 'he was in for extortion. He told me he got it from a bloke, one of the first intake of prisoners, a mate of his, who was on his deathbed about to cark it. So this is third hand. You'd be the fourth.'

'Amazing story,' says Drew nervously. 'But I'm not doing whatever you think we're going to do with it.'

'Just wait,' says Mick.

'It's too risky.'

Mick speaks carefully and slowly, each word a bomb. 'How are we going to get to the gates to even put the key into the lock?'

A guard has been clearing the canteen, leaving the three men at their table.

'He'll be back in a while,' says Ron. 'What you're going to do is walk along the southern fence – it's less well lit – to the tower just after seven o'clock. There's one guard sitting up there, Adrian. He's doing Agricultural Science in Rocky. Don't laugh, he's third year – works here on weekends. This joint may look legitimate, but it's a business like everywhere else and students are cheap. He's a clever chap, and between seven and seven-thirty he goes into the guards' room – there's a telly there – to watch the evening news.'

'He mightn't do it tonight?' says Drew, peeking at Mick for support.

'He's done it for the last fifteen nights.' Ron's patience is being tested. 'Probability, it's all we got.'

'Look, I know you guys are old,' says Mick. 'And it's a long way to the highway. But why has no-one ever used the key?'

'It's never been needed. The key is for an emergency. The emergency has *never* come. So it keeps on getting passed down.'

Mick looks at Drew. who is wilting like a flower.

'If you're innocent, it's worth a try,' adds Ron. 'And if it doesn't work – the key's old, there's no click – you walk back.'

Cupping his hands over his brow, and dragging his fingers over his closed eyes, Drew groans. 'What happens when they find out we're gone?'

'Nothing.'

The songwriters are under Ron's spell. His answer is puzzling, but they haven't the brainpower to ask why.

'They'll wait for Knowles to return, won't they? They know he'll want to handle it himself. He won't want Rocky to know that Fort Knox can be breached by two dirty layabouts like you.'

*

At the laundry door they check the room one last time. Drew, with his suitcase and Max's bag in hand, his guitar slung over his back, has placed the empty guitar case lengthwise in his bed under the blanket. 'Does it look like a body?' he'd asked Mick. It was a ridiculous gesture – they both knew it. But it was as good a hiding place as any, and maybe a passing guard would be deceived peeking through the black window at midnight. Every little thing helped.

They reach the southern fence and creep along its perimeter. It is the darker side of the compound, but not as dark as they'd imagined or like. Mick has walked off and is looking through the window of the guards' room.

'What are you doing?' hisses Drew, staggered at his partner's audacity.

He returns to inform Drew there's no-one inside and the television is off.

'*Oh my God.* What are we going to do?'

Mick has no answer. He's spooked. Stumped. His slow deep breaths filled with cold air, in time with Drew's rising and falling chest as they stand face to face.

'I don't know,' he says finally. 'We might have to go back . . .'

A pale stain of colour suddenly comes to Drew's features, and with it the spread of a smile. Bloody Adrian is late. They can hear the faint buzz of the television. There's a glow in the guards' room. No time to bless their luck. They creep on.

The front gates are lit as brightly as a Hollywood premiere. Enough high-beamed wattage to illuminate Julia Roberts and Richard Gere as they walk the red carpet on *Pretty Woman.* Behind the circle of blinding light, the facility is the darkened cinema at its rear. The inmates and guards silent and absorbed.

The songwriters walk into the glare like mountaineers at the start of a climb, loaded with bags and belongings. There was a plan for this moment; no looking over shoulders or furtive glances. If they get caught, they get caught. What was the line from that song, Mick had asked Drew as they packed: *You've got to dance like no-one is watching*. 'We've got to break out of jail like no-one's watching.'

Mick digs the key out from the pocket of his jeans. Holding it to Drew's eyes like Ron had held it to theirs. *Here goes.* It fits – there's the first thing. It turns – there's the second. A gentle one-finger push and a wall of barbed wire and steel on hinges, topped with the word 'Capricorn', swings open.

Now they play it ultra-cool. Through the gate, closing it softly. *Lock it*, Ron had commanded. *Don't leave clues.*

They walk quickly to their freedom – to the moment they shed the bright rim of light for the night's cape of darkness. Then stumbling and scrambling blindly over rocks and shrubs, swearing as they tumble, the musicians stop just once. 'Look,' says Drew, turning.

It's Murray. His legs straddling the roof of a dormitory block. A lit torch in one hand. The other, windmilling generous sweeps of farewell.

*

After five hours tramping hurriedly over dark ground, scratched and pelted by bush and branch, above them a slice of cheesecake moon and a field of stars, the songwriters, clearing the cratered rim, choose a clearing behind an outcrop of rocks to spend the last hours of the winter night.

Mick heads off to collect scraps of wood, while Drew pulls a lighter and a tin of beans from the bag.

The fire lights their faces, the smoke disappearing into the overwhelming dark. Dinner now done, the fire on its embers, Mick breaks the silence and, it seems, the quiet of fifty square kilometres.

'Been working on a tune. Want to hear it?'

Although they write their songs separately, they're credited to Woods/Lovelock. Each writer has his strengths. Mick's is melody;

a gift for enticing tunes from a guitar like a snake-handler coaxing cobras from a cane basket. Drew's metier is lyrics. Melodies are harder for him, but once he gets one, a song is made in a day.

Mick starts strumming. He hums a melody over a three-chord sequence, and then, over the same chords, by starting on a different beat, teases a second tune. It's a neat trick. Already a verse and chorus are being outlined.

'That's pretty,' says Drew.

'Thanks,' whispers Mick, lost in his music.

Drew reaches for his guitar. There are no words to the song yet; the tune, though, is compelling. Listening to its melodic turns, Drew begins to receive the telegraphed messages to the brain that cultural theorists refer to as 'inspiration'. Is this a story song? If so, about what? A love song? For whom? Or could it be a travel song? To do with trains? Too cliched. He doesn't know, switching off his brain to fall in with his partner on their lonesome desert guitars.

They wake at dim-lit dawn, grumbling as they pack and nibble from Max's Tupperware box of nuts and raisins – knowing the biting cold will ease the strain of their long morning trek.

By midday, they are standing exhausted by the side of the Warrego Highway. Thumbs out and vulnerable; two daubs of paint on a euchre-tinged Fred Williams landscape. Over the next three hours, the sun falling slowly through the sky, four trucks and seven cars pass by.

'We're fucked,' cries Drew deliriously, as the last vehicle, a 1982 Land Rover, camping gear packed on top, pig-shooting headlights up front, zooms off into the red-dust distance. His philosophy of life – a belief he has never shared with anyone – is to always assume the worst and slowly work your way back from there. It has come in handy, like when enthusiastic friends and fans of The Shells predicted a Top 40 hit for every single. 'Top 400, *maybe*,' he would reply, and mostly be proved right.

But he can't see a way back from this. A sense of panic, stalled courageously through the agonising afternoon, sets in and makes itself at home by the fire in the recesses of his fevered mind. *Knowles knows! The lizard-faced Rocky copper too! Helicopters will, at any second, rise above the horizon and fill the sky like a swarm of bees.*

Mick, trying to ignore his friend's hysteria, checks his watch: 3.22pm. That's late. Then another vehicle, so soon after the last – is that a sign? – dots the horizon.

Thundering down from the north, the car's shape and model are unclear against the slanted and enchanted rays of the sun. The tell-tale signs of braking not happening until the vehicle has reached the exhausted songwriters. The pull so fierce the 1985 Holden Rodeo swerves to a skidded stop in the middle of the highway, smoke pouring from the red-hot wheels of the ute. The engine is a nasty growl. The songwriters' relief salted with a sudden concern about the person or persons sitting in the front of the car.

'Youse been waiting long?'

He's a boy. A grinning, chubby-cheeked, country boy, high on life, with a ring of black curls poking out from under a black cowboy hat. The car is filled with the glorious stink of gasoline and the dead smoke of a freshly extinguished Marlboro; the pack and a pair of sunglasses on the dashboard. The volume of Paul Kelly and The Coloured Girls' 'Under The Sun' has been lowered – Mick and Drew will have to tell Paul one day – as they buckle in and roar off.

The mood is jubilant. It's as if they've met in a bar, not a car. Mick and Drew are smoking – their own ciggies greedily puffed away through the afternoon – and the music is back up at good volume.

'I'm Dan.'

'Bill.'

'Sylvester.'

Dan works on a cattle property two hours up the road. He's on his way to visit his girlfriend, Stacey, 'a stunner', who he met at a Bachelors' Ball at Charters Towers last summer and hasn't seen in a month. He's itchy for her. He also wants to get there for dinner. It's steak and chips.

'Where does she live?' asks Drew, his window half down, his hair billowing around his neck.

'On a sorghum farm near Lipton. Where are you guys headin'?'

'As far as you can take us, I guess,' reasons Drew. 'Thamalgah?'

'I go past that. Turn off half an hour later.'

'Drop us there,' says Mick casually.

'Alright then.' Dan steals a look at his passengers. 'You're musos, aren't ya?'

'We travel and play a bit,' admits Drew with an easy grin.

'I knew it. Professionally?'

'Nah,' they chorus.

'I got an aunt that plays. She writes her own songs, though.'

He checks his passengers again, flashing a smile that would melt any heart west of Rocky. And with his eyes on the road, pulling a cigarette from between his teeth, he sings in a yodelling twang.

His manner was so sweet
I got jitters to my feet
And I really did think my heart would break
But as the days flew by
Those jitters went away
And I landed back on my feet.

Drew slow claps in appreciation. Mick says, 'Sounds like a Hank Williams song.'

'It's as good as a Hank song, Bill. It's called "Jitters". Some of her songs are a bit out there.' He giggles. 'She's got this one that my dad reckons is crazy, It's called "Waiting On Scientists". It's a country tune with science-fiction words. She's a favourite, Aunt Betty.'

There's an idea, thinks Mick. An otherworldly lyric grafted to a folky tune. He's thinking of his new song. Perhaps it's time for a swing away from the observational rootsy stuff. Something to shake people up, including Drew.

The next question has to come.

'We were dumped there,' says Mick gravely, as if still shaken from the experience. 'The truckie that picked us up was mad. Drifting all over the road, talking bullshit. Indonesia is going to attack Australia – that kind of stuff. They'll come down through New Guinea. We tried to talk him down. He said, "If you don't like it, you can get out."' Mick clicks his tongue. 'We thought he was joking.'

'I was glad to get away,' chips in Drew.

'Where did he pick you up?'

'Ah . . . where was it?' Drew looks to Mick.

'Drugs,' announces Dan. Not taking his eyes off the road. 'They buy them at truck stops.'

'Right,' nods Drew.

'You can get pills – not like aspirin or anything. They make you do things you wouldn't believe.' He makes goggle eyes. 'Insane things.'

'Really?' asks Mick.

'That's probably what your guy was on.'

'He must be clear through Brisbane by now,' jokes Drew.

'He's not stopping, hey,' laughs Dan, giving the ute a playful spurt with the accelerator.

Approaching Thamalgah, Dan says he needs petrol and there's a station on the other side of town.

'I don't need anything, thanks,' shrugs Mick.

'How about you, Sylvester?'

'Ah . . . actually,' says Drew, 'a couple of cans of ginger beer and a packet of chips, and *maybe* . . . two packs of Camel filters would be fantastic.'

While Dan fills up the ute, the songwriters know it must seem odd they don't get out and help. Drew lowers his window, shouting back, 'Pretty thirsty engine, eh?'

'Yeah.'

'I got the money for the drinks and stuff,' Drew says, waving a twenty-dollar note. 'Thanks, mate.'

After filling the tank, Dan takes the cash and walks off to pay.

A car pulls up. Four teenagers – two girls, two guys. They snicker as they pass the two long-haired blokes sitting shoulder to shoulder in the front seat of a ute.

'They'd laugh less if they'd seen me in Splinters Of Blood,' drawls Mick.

'I thought we fitted in,' says Drew, inching away from Mick, while tapping his pearl-buttoned shirt.

'Apparently not.'

They watch the kids jump and joke into the service station. Drew winds up his window. Without the motion of the road, the real world sneaks in.

'Let's hope they're not missing us yet,' says Drew.

'We're alright.'

'Yeah?'

'It was pretty low-key back there. And it's not as if we're murderers, or bank robbers with guns and shit.'

'I know we're not everyday criminals, but they'll still come looking for us. You can't think that's not going to happen.'

'It'll happen, but we'll either have Bingo by then or be far away.' The frightened vibe and silence from Drew unnerves him. 'Don't freak, man.'

'I'm not freaking.'

'You are. I know you. Look, as Ron said . . . even if they find out we're gone, they'll wait for Knowles to come back. He'll be the one in trouble. Maybe more than us. Here comes Dan with your goodies.'

Out on the highway, five minutes out of town, Dan's eyes flick and stay on the rear-view mirror. Mick and Drew spin around.

Fifty metres back and already perched to pounce in the overtaking lane are the hotrod teenagers from the service station. In an instant, they're 'parked' at a hundred and thirty k's by Dan's door. With their windows down, they hoot and holler, holding beer bottles aloft. A girl in the back seat, tongue out, lifts her top. The boy beside her does the same. Their car dips in dangerously, the driver looking over for what seems like minutes, mad-eyed and grinning.

Dan and the songwriters know there's nothing to do but grin back like fools, hoping a car is coming at not too quick a speed from the opposite direction. Everything is sudden; fun had, the teenagers zoom off, arms and legs waving from windows.

Dan riffles through his cassettes. 'I need music after that.'

The musicians, drowsy in the hot chamber of the front seat, smoke and watch the countryside change. The desert landscape taking on a sparse cover of gum trees and bush. In this mood the Lipton turn-off comes up quickly.

Mick and Drew clinch Dan's hand through the window. His cowboy hat is off – he looks younger with his head of thick dark curls.

'You take care of yourselves,' he says. 'It's a wild world out there.'

The songwriters tell him he's a hero and to say hello to Stacey. They watch the ute drive off, down a dip to cross a narrow bridge, a parachute of dust blooming from the back bumper.

In the last minutes of the day, the departing sun leaving a golden bowl of light filtering across the land, the songwriters detect a broken line of houses leading to a congestion of dwellings in the distance. Walking off with bags and guitars, they reach a crooked sign tilted into the dry earth. Flats Crossing.

'I don't think we've been here before,' Mick notes wryly.

Passing the first house, he stops in front of the second, 200 metres ahead and on the opposite side of the road. Two large mango trees shield a weatherbeaten Queenslander. Few of the homes they've seen that day, near or far from the Warrego, have been in the best repair – this one looks ghostly.

No lights shine in the house and no cars are in sight as they amble down the dirt driveway, to jump the front fence, the last specks of white paint breaking off in their hands. Moving on, they creep past a garden bed the length of a cricket pitch – home to a gallant pair of red roses, fighting for life in a world of weeds and tall grass. An old wire chicken coop appears, and the wrecked frame of an aviary housing thick lantana. The songwriters reach the back of the dwelling with the grass at their waists. An animal scoots from under their feet.

'Jesus,' says Drew in a wavering, horror-movie voice.

They can see little in the backyard shadows, but enough to notice the open door.

'We're going in, aren't we?' says Drew.

Mick's yeah is a breath. He's liking this. It reminds him of boyhood pranks in the old Webster house.

The first room is the kitchen, the bulk of a gas stove squatting toad-like in a corner. Mick, reaching for where a light switch might be, finds one. 'Bugger,' he says, flicking it for the darkness to stay.

Feeling for walls and trusting the floorboards won't splinter, they edge through a doorway into another room. It feels less enclosed and, bending to place their possessions on the floor, they straighten slowly – alert to sounds and their vision yet to adjust.

'There could be anything living in here,' says Drew.

'Get the matches.'

Drew's hand snakes through a jumble of shapes and objects in the bag, coming to grip on a metallic tube. Dear Max had thought of a torch. Under its glare a large bare room is revealed. The shell of the house is a wreck, but the guts are in good condition; it could have been the other way round, to the songwriters' cost.

Drew holds the torch outstretched, wanting to keep whatever the light finds as far from himself as possible. Manoeuvring the beam slowly, it suddenly flares – catching a pair of windows edged with amber-and-green stained glass. *Nice.* Moving it on, a brick fireplace is picked out; above it, on a mantelpiece, an oval-shaped plaque leans against the wall.

'Hold this,' says Drew, walking at the light's edge. His right hand brushing the grooves of the plaque's letters, feeling for history. 'Cranfield.'

'Why would they leave that here?'

'They might have been in a hurry.'

The rest of the house is the same: swept and clean, not unlike a series of theatre stages. Mick and Drew settle in the dining-room, believing the fire they've lit can't be seen from the road. The bag provides a meal of dry white rolls and tinned sardines, and they drink the last of their water. They are seated on the floor. They have survived one day on the run.

'Interesting that that boy at the radio station knew Toy Crime.'

Drew has to be careful. His early band got mentioned, while Mick's were gathered in a clump.

'It's the single. Younger people have discovered it. They go for 130 bucks now.'

'Gee,' says Mick flatly. 'You got one stashed away in a sock drawer?'

'No, unfortunately. My family have got copies. There were only 500 made. We thought we'd struggle to sell them.'

'It's Roz and Greg, right? And they were a couple?'

'Yeah, I knew Greg from school and we both went to uni. He was doing engineering and I was studying town planning.'

'I always find that funny.' A light has returned to Mick's eyes. '"Town" and "planning" aren't you.'

It was the course he'd chosen at seventeen for Queensland University. Failing subjects from the start, overawed by the freedoms and size of the campus, it had kept him out of the workforce and the grasp of the suburbs. Places where teenage dreams – shaky as his were – can get lost or trampled on.

Drew closes the top button of his shirt, taking a smouldering stick from the fire to light a Camel. 'Greg played drums and he and I were jamming on some of the first things I wrote. I was listening to Wire, The Cure, Talking Heads – that kind of stuff, twenty-four hours day. Roz was there at a rehearsal, if you can call it that. She played a little bit of guitar, had piano lessons, and she bought a bass. People liked us from our first shows.'

Mick makes a grunting *Ha* sound. 'How long did it last? Two years?'

'Almost three. Perfect for a cult band.' Drew enjoys this, entertaining Mick, to open those Easter Island features and suddenly see the boy. A toothy smile taking ten years off his face. 'We broke up at the end of 1980. Greg wanted to stick with studying and Roz was nursing. The band was fun and a distraction for them, while I was serious.'

'The bright lights.'

'And the pop phase was coming on. So I moved to Sydney and started The Shells, met Jill, and there you are. You know she's married with a kid.'

'You've told me that.'

'So what's the plan for tomorrow? Get up early, walk into town and take it from there?'

Actually, that sounded like their everyday.

'Yeah,' says Mick, distracted. He leans back on his elbows, his thin body a mile long. 'You remember that club we played up in the Border Ranges?'

'Broken Pieces. No, that's not it.'

Mick points at Drew proudly. 'Bakers Dozen! I'm beginning to sound like you. Patting myself on the back when I get something right. What would be the last place the cops would think we'd go?'

'Another show,' says Drew.

'Not Brisbane.'

'It's over the border. A place to get a car, maybe. An old Volvo from a hippie.'

'Yeah, and we can't hitch anymore. Word will be out tomorrow, and we have to contact Swifty. Do that as soon as we can.'

Mick stands up and stretches. 'Want to play some guitar? We'll have to play low.'

They tinker till the fire dies. Mick's new melody and a sketchy 'Don't Ask Me How', for old times' sake.

Early the next morning the songwriters are walking through cold black air. Down the middle of the road, daylight not yet picking out the centre of Flats Crossing. Tall and menacing, Mick and Drew may look like avengers coming to threaten a small community, but they are at its mercy and their under-slept minds are ticking. Maybe they are walking into a trap.

A sign, biro etched into a strip of cardboard, is stuck to the fly-screened front door of the town's general store. Opening hours are between seven and five. Disappointed and aware of the unusual nature of their appearance and business, the songwriters walk off with purpose, not knowing where they are walking to.

Beyond the shop is a park, and finding a bench nestled near a row of wattle trees, Mick and Drew watch a country town wake up. It's like one of those movie camera tricks, where a flower is shown to open, bloom and die in thirty seconds. Light floods the streets, cars appear, birds sing, an elderly couple in dressing-gowns water their front garden as the first trucks roll through, and suddenly, as part of this unfolding magic, it's 7am and Mick and Drew are pushing through the fly-screened door to gather groceries and a newspaper from the store's dusty shelves.

Having paid for their supplies, Drew tries to open a conversation with a watchful ten-year-old girl behind the counter, who had coolly counted their money and put it in the till.

'You're a bit young to be owning a shop, aren't you?'

This earns a smile.

'Is there a public telephone around here?'

'Don't think so.'

'That's a shame.'

With a slow deliberate turning of his head, Drew checks for other customers. He's got a secret to share. 'You see . . . we've got a very important phone call to make.'

The girl's face betrays not a hint of care.

'You're off to school?'

She nods.

'In town? No, it's too small.'

'In Childers.'

'*In Childers*. How far away is that?'

'An hour.'

'By car?'

'Bus.'

'When does it leave?'

She looks at her watch. A gift from Grandma Boone. 'Eleven minutes.'

*

There is an order to the main street queue. A straight line. Shoe to shoe. Kiralee first; behind her is her best friend, Lucy, fresh from the shop. Next are the Watson brothers, Lister and Craig, aged eight and eleven. Then come the taller boys.

They have scanned the local newspaper and found no mention of their escape. Still, the sight of a school bus is a relief, puttering into town to stop at their feet.

The driver is in her fifties. She has a worn, caramel-coloured face that creases into a thin smile as she greets each child by name with a smoker's rasp.

Stepping onto the bus, Mick asks, 'Do you go any further than Childers?'

'Just the school, darling.'

'You can take us?' He squares his handsome jaw.

Her eyes travel up and down the songwriters. The kids are seated; she is five minutes late.

'Three bucks for both of ya.'

The children, sitting alone and in groups, watch the two men wrestle their way down the tight centre aisle, their heads scraping the roof, to plop with bags and guitars onto the bank of rear seats. The *put-put* of the engine as the bus pulls out of town, one of the most beautiful sounds the songwriters have ever heard.

They haven't gone far when the first heads turn. Friends leaning into Lucy, whispering and glancing back. The songwriters admire the countryside – a barn, some guy in a tatty straw hat on a tractor – when the first kids scoot back, hunched as if under gunfire; two boys and a gap-toothed Indigenous girl with brown hair in her eyes.

They perch on seats, peering at the men in the manner naturalists examine exotic animals. The animals, as they often do in the wild, reacting with disinterest.

'Are you musicians?' asks the girl, cheeky and bold.

'Yeah,' says Mick offhandedly.

'Are you rock stars?' asks a boy.

Mick jerks his thumb at Drew. 'He is.'

Drew sharpens his cheekbones to a pout. 'I'm a rock star.'

'What are you doing on our school bus then?' asks the other boy, adjusting his glasses.

'Have you been on TV?' interrupts the girl.

'Once,' says Drew. 'And do you know who else was on the show?' Drew's eyes widen. 'Mental As Anything.'

The boy and the girl look at each other, their mouths falling open in a silent scream.

'Are you friends with them?' enquires Glasses.

'A little – it was before they got their big hit.'

'"Live It Up",' he mumbles.

'Lucy says you wanted to make a secret phone call.'

'Who were you calling?' asks the girl. 'Your mums?'

Mick whispers side of mouth to Drew, 'This is worse than the cops.'

'What's the name of your band now?'

'We haven't got one,' says Mick. 'What grades are you kids in?'

More children have joined their mates. They circle the songwriters, firing questions. Mick catches the driver's glance in the front mirror. The smoke from her cigarette billowing back down the aisles.

The bold girl says loudly, 'Julie plays the guitar.'

'She's good,' everyone choruses.

'Is she?' remarks Drew.

'Play for them. Go on. Show them.' The young voices push and plead.

'Look,' says Mick, 'if she doesn't . . .'

A splayed hand emerges from a tangle of bodies squeezed into a seat. Drew, glancing at Mick in resignation, lifts his guitar and watches it being passed to a milk-skinned, red-haired Renaissance child of twelve.

She crosses her legs and lays the instrument on her knee; the wooden body competing with the size of her own. Steadied, she fingers a D chord at the bottom of the fretboard and plucks a rhythm. It's a pleasant sound, a beginner's mastering of a basic skill.

Then a zing of the fingers and she is flicking trills and arpeggios at the top of the neck, making the guitar sound like an Appalachian banjo at a jamboree – to just as quickly return to her low steady rhythm. Introduction done, she lifts her head, her face content and passive; Mick and Drew recognise the blissful state of mind.

She begins to sing 'Morning Has Broken' in a voice as pure and high as mountain water. Mick and Drew, who have recently admitted Cat Stevens, 'The Cat', to their pantheon of great singer-songwriters, to the derision of a few hipster musician friends in Darlinghurst, approve.

It's enchantment to Childers.

After the children are deposited at school, the songwriters are dropped at one end of the town's main street. Walking around a corner, along a line of shops and businesses housed in turn-of-the-century brick, they spot a telephone booth across the street.

The phone is ringing long, Mick's eyes flickering with concern, when a voice croaks hello.

'Swifty?'

'Mick! Finally! Gee, it's great to hear your voice.'

'Yours too, mate. You got back okay?'

'On Saturday night. I flew into Brisbane and then got the last plane out to Melbourne. How are you guys?'

'It's a bit of a story. I gotta be quick.'

'Man, that was crazy up there. I went to the police station the next morning and they were *not* helpful. They told me to come back Tuesday. I thought I'd get more done down here. Where are ya? Can you talk?'

'I think so.' Mick lifts his gaze from the phone cupped at his chin to the street. 'We've broken out of jail.' Despite the disaster of their situation, he can't keep a nick of pride from his voice.

'Wow. For dope? Is that a good idea?'

'It's more than that. Have you heard from the cops?'

'No.'

'Good. And Bingo? What's he saying?'

'That's the frustrating thing. I can't get onto him. I've phoned his place and been around a few times. Phoned the office, nothing. I don't get it . . . are you there?'

'The car we bought in Sydney was stolen. The credit card is in our names and owing eighteen grand.'

Swifty blows a gush of air.

'That's why the cops told you to come back on Tuesday.'

'I never trusted him. You remember that time, where was it . . .?'

'You've got to find him.'

'I'm *trying*. I'll ask around.'

'They'll hang us in Rocky. Put us in a real jail this time, not some joint you can walk out of. What we need is a place to hide and a car.'

'Where are ya?'

'Childers, it's –'

'I know it.'

There's a pause. Mick sliding coins down the slot to keep the connection – and any hope he and Drew have – alive.

'I had an idea,' Mick adds. 'That club up in the Border Ranges . . .'

'Bakers Dozen. Nice room.'

'We thought if we could get there. Get a car. Drive down to Melbourne. Ten minutes with Bingo and it's sorted out.'

'This is heavy. The club is a good idea. Let me think. Call me back in five, okay.'

'What's the great man saying?' Drew is lounging on the grass with a paper cup in his hand and an opened packet of Scotch Finger biscuits balanced on his chest. He'd crossed the street and bought two cups of coffee; a heaped teaspoon of International Roast in each.

Mick winces on his first mouthful.

'The first person to bring a cappuccino machine to this town,' opines Drew, 'is going to make a fortune.'

'Or be run out of town.' Mick's face lightens. 'Not everyone is open to new ideas.'

'Very true, my friend.' He holds up the biscuits. 'Have one . . . it helps.'

Mick shakes his head. Here they are again – out in the open, looking like the drifters every country town hates, and every country-town cop finds. He takes another sip of coffee, throwing the remaining liquid onto the grass in disgust.

'He'll come up with something,' reassures Drew. 'That's what we pay him for.'

Mick phones back. Swifty talks first.

'This has to be handled properly. Someone is coming to pick you up in a couple of hours.'

Mick fires off a hoot of relief. 'You're a hero.'

'Is there a place where you can stay until they get there?'

'Let me see . . . There's a coffee shop across the street. A bakery.' Mick relaxes. 'A pub on the next corner.'

'The first place the police will look for ya.'

'On our side of the street, there's a building. Hey, Drew, can you check out that big place up there? He's going – it's not far. You said you've been here before. When was that?'

'Must have been '86, with The Johnnys. We were just passing through. I remember we stopped at a pub with a beer garden. It could be the one you're talking about.'

'Could be. He's back. Oh . . . it's a library.'

'Perfect.'

'Alright. Who's coming?'

'No questions,' says Swifty. 'And don't talk to them in the car either. If this goes wrong, I don't want them involved or hurt. Got it?'

'The Secret Network of Roadies, eh. Who is he?'

'Stay in the library.'

And for the first time ever, Swifty hangs up on Mick.

'Bastard,' he mutters, coming out of the booth. 'We're fixed.'

Squeezed between a row of businesses – light industrial and an accountant offering budget tax returns – is an op shop. The songwriters seldom turn down thrift shops, especially ones in the country unpicked by city hands.

'Good morning, boys,' trills a tall, elderly woman behind the counter. Her reading glasses hang on a beaded chain, her hair a blue-rinsed afro.

'Good morning,' replies Drew cheerfully. 'How are you?'

'Enjoying my morning cup of tea and a biscuit, thank you very much. Do you need help?'

'Men's clothing?'

'Up the back on the left, past women's blouses.'

Spotting a milk crate filled with albums on the low shelf of a bookcase heavy with airport novels and bibles, Drew kneels down and starts flicking.

'What do you think?'

Mick has ditched his denim and is standing stiffly in a brown suit. Getting up, Drew lifts the shoulders of his partner's jacket in an attempt to shake a better fit into the suit. Then leaning back, his right arm cocked at the elbow, two fingers over his mouth in contemplation, he says with deliberation, 'Not bad. But I don't think brown is your colour.'

Finding Drew's touch uncomfortable, Mick remarks, 'Well, I think it is.'

'Try a white shirt,' says Drew. Mick is walking off. 'That could work. Are you doing this because you think we should look different? Like a disguise?'

'Yeah, maybe. It's time for a shake-up, anyway? You should do it too.'

'I will. Hey, check this out.'

Cradling two albums while glancing smugly at Mick, Drew points to a price tag in the corner of the top record. To slip away the austere black-and-white front cover of Patti Smith's *Horses*, revealing in a flourish the rich psychedelic reds and purples of Chain's *Toward The Blues*. Mick doesn't have to be guided to the price. Four dollars for both. 'You've scored, man.'

While flicking though the records in the box, a thought had hit Drew. He was getting a picture of the town, like if you did a door-to-door survey. Instead of walking the streets with questions, his fingers were telling him the story. Lots of John Denver, stacks of Slim Dusty, and some weird Scottish shit – guys in kilts on castle turrets blowing bagpipes – the two-dollar surprises coming at the back of the shuffle. Someone at some time must have been hip around here.

Maybe it was just one person, but they had a wire out to the world, receiving the signals both records sent. That person could still be here, he thought. Working in a bank. Teaching primary-school kids. Now that was who they needed to find when reaching Childers. The owner of *Horses* and *Toward The Blues* would have driven them straight to Melbourne.

In the changing room, a tight space with a rag curtain, Drew unbuttons his cowboy shirt. Button by button, they click apart. On the floor is a high-collared, blue-and-white-striped business shirt from Pierre Cardin he'd plucked from a rack. At his elbow on a hanger are a pair of dark slacks with a thin leather belt.

Slipping out of his boots, he peels his grimy tight Levi's down his legs – it feels like the shedding of a skin. Stepping out of the changing room in socked feet, he admires himself, an angle at a time in a mirror. The new gear isn't going to fool anyone into thinking he isn't Drew Lovelock; but *he* can imagine himself as someone else. As a cult rock star, that was all you needed to do to bloom into a fresh persona.

Looking again at himself, his thin face attractive when held at the appropriate tilt, he needs a haircut and the boots have to go. He's seen a pair of pointed black shoes, Bata Scouts, on a rack beside the bookshelf. They'll be part of his new look; the stylish schoolboy moving elegantly into his thirties.

*

Nez had left the shower tap dripping. It was a West End house so you could hear everything – the neighbours could too. A Greek family who brought over a plate of sugar-dusted almond cakes each week, while having to endure bands practising in the collapsing timber and corrugated-iron worker's cottage next door; guitar amps and a drum kit permanently installed in the lounge-room. Kate had been too lazy to get up in the night to check the shower. She'd woken early, and, soon after, Swifty had called.

It wasn't the normal Swifty, gregarious and kind. He was serious – a bit rude even. She was being sworn to secrecy before she'd said 'Hello'. At least, that's how it felt. And without telling her exactly what he wanted her to do, he was outlining in black marker pen the dangers involved if she did. *And don't tell anyone anything*, he added.

She hadn't had the chance to slow him down when he blurted out the reason for the early morning call: she then understood why he'd been so abrupt and breathless. He was asking a lot, but her gut told her to do it. The roadie was relieved, thankful – teary, it sounded like – and then he had to go. His last words to her? *Don't talk to Mick Woods.*

Kate called her mum, telling her she couldn't do lunch in Milton with her and the Stevensons; a childless couple in their mid-fifties, fond of Kate since childhood. Her mother wasn't happy, although she didn't say it. With mums, you sometimes have to read between the lines: disappointing old friends and making new ones was something Kate was doing lately.

Grabbing the keys to her green Corolla E30, she cuts herself a line of speed on the laminated kitchen table. She thinks of washing it down with a calming tipple of cask wine, but decides against it, not wishing to drive under the influence of alcohol.

On the four-hour trip to Childers, she considers her decision. To leave Brisbane super-quick and pick up two singer-songwriters she doesn't know, who are on the run from the law. Surely, that makes her an accessory or something, to whatever bad things they've done. What they've done exactly, Swifty hadn't the time to tell.

He's been a good friend, getting her on crews when he comes to town on big tours. She lugs gear, does lights, having to be twice as good at her job in the boys' world of rock and roll. She's making her way, determined to find a place in music – the passion of her life.

Fortunately, the local scene is blossoming. Just last week she caught Custard: four young guys with a confident, funny lead singer, playing a cut-up kind of pop that blew the Brisbane doldrums away. They'd heard The Pixies, Jonathan Richman – she loved The Modern Lovers – and they weren't mired in heavy guitar fuzz; a downer vibe that was wrapping itself like a vine around a slew of bands in awe of what was coming out of Seattle. There was room for everyone – that's what was good about the Brisbane scene. Not as cutthroat as Sydney and Melbourne, and her rent was thirty bucks a week. Swifty had urged her to come south. In the eighties someone like her would have run, but not now. Life was good.

At first she can't find them in the library; attracting astonished glances from readers as she buzzes past History. Has she got there too late, she wonders as she paces along Modern Fiction. She pauses by Philosophy to get her bearings, which is when a concerned librarian approaches her, pointing to an alcove in a corner with sofa chairs.

Their heads are down, barely breathing, lost in books. The guy in the brown suit is reading a Raymond Chandler novel. The pretty boy wearing the type of shoes the guys at her high school used to wear is bent over an oldy-worldy poetry book opened on his lap. She's so close, she can almost read the print. She waits. She could walk away. Tiptoe out of the library and slip back to Brisbane. It would be like nothing ever happened. But then, what kind of adventurer would she be?

'Hi.'

*

They jump. Their eyes and mouths springing open to appraise, in a blitz of first impressions, the young woman standing before them.

Short. Tight black jeans and Converse sneakers. Sonic Youth T-shirt. *Sonic Grandad*, Drew calls them. Hacked, dyed-black hair. Tiny nose tipped at its end. Green eyes, cat's eyes, missing nothing.

'Hey ho, let's go,' she says, picking up a guitar in each hand.

Closing their books and lifting themselves stiffly from their chairs, the songwriters glance at each other. They aren't on the run anymore. They're back on the road.

Her car is parked at the rear of the library. Gear in, Drew in the front seat, Mick in the back, Kate drives cautiously out of town, all a bluff, to hit a hundred and ten and stay on it for the next two hours.

Mick and Drew suspect she's on speed, and the first words they exchange with their driver as she tops her car up at a highway service station is whether she has drugs: a conversation opener not unknown to the musicians. And if she does, would it at all be possible – *if* she has sufficient quantity – to spare a line for them, *please*. Pulling her wallet from her back pocket, she hands them a small rectangular envelope. The songwriters cut and snort two fat lines in the back seat, leaving one line as requested for the driver.

Back on the highway with the clumpy white powder sliding snail-like down their throats, Mick is intent on breaking the no-talking rule. Swifty will be pissed off, but he's 2000 kilometres away and who gives a fuck what he thinks, anyway. Leaning forward, he asks if it is at all possible to get some beer. With her eyes drilled to the road behind a pair of sixties Raybans, the kind Debbie Harry wore in early Blondie, Kate informs him the next pub is at the edge of a small town, twenty minutes away. She asked at the gas station. Waves of gratitude engulf the songwriters.

She emerges from the sun-beaten, shed-shaped pub, carrying two bulging plastic bags. Drew knows the guy in the back seat is mighty impressed with this behaviour. Soon they're sorted. Sipping beer, chain-smoking, teeth grinding, hearts pumping. The scenery – dry bush and clusters of gum trees – of no interest to anyone in the car.

It's time to talk and Mick has a theory he wants to share.

It started in Sydney a few months back. He'd been to an album launch in Newtown, and went on with friends, including a few members of the Beasts Of Bourbon, to a bar in Kings Cross. Around the table, there was talk of the inner-city scene and the current state of rock music in general; people throwing in band names and trashing them, mostly.

And somehow it came up, how strange it was that mediocre or crap bands can have good songs, and good bands can have just average songs. INXS and a few hip Melbourne groups were used as examples.

Mick, who'd once considered band image and distorted noise as *everything*, said, to some surprise, 'So what we're saying is . . . is that rock and roll is essentially a songwriting contest.'

Spencer from The Beasts agreed. 'I think you've nailed it, Mick.'

Since then, Mick has tweaked his theory, adding a coda.

'Are you ready?' he burps, clearing his throat with a deep drag of a fag and the remains of beer two. 'It's an idea. Tell me what you think. Here it is . . .' He clears his throat. 'Rock and roll is a songwriting contest, and whoever has the best songs wins.'

Drew thinks it's a good line. Kate nods in appreciation, amazed at how at odds the musicians are proving to be with their public image. Mick is less intimidating, a gentle bear behind the public growl, and Drew, when sliced away from the album covers and pouting publicity shots, is playful and a little camp.

She shouldn't have been surprised, her time around the scene revealing to her that, despite the eccentricities musicians presented to their audiences, away from the lights most of them were like their audiences – same complaints, same joys. It was just the hour on stage when they crossed into another world.

'Take any music festival,' continues Mick, lighting a cigarette off the tip of the last, opening beer three, a plastic bag wedged between him and Drew's guitar in the back seat. 'The bands on the main stage are there, because they have the most songs people know, right? If you're playing some shitty tent at midday, *maybe* you have one song people recognise, and it's the reason a hundred people are looking at you, waiting for that song.'

'It doesn't matter how hip or groovy you are,' throws in Drew. Enjoying the road, the car, the driver's company, the ecstatic sense of motion.

'It's the songs. And this is where the competition side of it comes in. Because your good-song count layers everything in the business. Who gets on the radio – there's the first thing. Radio programmers don't play mediocre songs from hip bands, they play good songs from crap bands. That's how The Police got a career. And it filters down through everything. Who gets to play on what stage at the festival. What size venues bands play in towns. Is it the busy pub on the corner or is it the art space to eight people, leaning against a wall waiting for a decent tune? Who gets the money and who gets the fame. Who's doing it hard and who has the glory. Single of the week. Song of the week and all that shit. The press love it. It's all one big *fat* song contest.'

'So you could say, and I know I'm simplifying,' says Kate, catching Mick's gaze in the rear-view mirror, 'The Beatles won the sixties, because they had the best songs.'

'You got it, baby!'

'And why ABBA won the seventies,' adds Drew. 'There's one flaw, though, with your theory.' He turns around to Mick. 'If . . . *if* the artist with the best songs wins, why aren't we winning?'

'The American Dream.'

Drew screws his face up, confused and annoyed. Even if Mick is on speed and booze and running his mouth off, it's hitting a bum note.

'We're special,' confides Mick. 'No-one is doing what we're doing. Imitators will come, but for the moment it's just us doing this. Looking the way we do. Sounding like us. Which is why we have to clutch at big straws.' He drops another decibel, a whisper, aimed at Drew's ear. 'That's why we've got to find Bingo, to sort this out and have our shot. We can still do it. It's not gone.' A twitch of the head. Is it the speed or resolute conviction? 'It's not gone at all.'

'Good,' says Drew. 'Sometimes you scare me.' He looks at Kate. 'Sorry.'

Bingo? Sort this out? American Dream?

'It's okay,' she says. 'I'm getting an insight into your band dynamic.'

'What's it like?' asks Drew.

'Just like any other group,' she says, knowing that will disappoint him. 'Arguing amidst yourselves.'

'It's not like that,' says Mick, chuckling. 'He just prefers to look at the dark side of things. I'm Mr Sunshine.'

Drew asks Kate if she's in a band.

'I do sound.'

'Oh.'

'Mainly friends' bands, at the moment. Ultimately, I'd like to work in a studio and make records with musicians I feel I have a connection to. That's *my* dream.'

She peeks at Drew, aware the songwriters have tuned out a little. Strange, how some musicians weren't interested in sound. 'And I play a little guitar.'

'Electric?' asks Mick.

'Just jamming around. People that drop by my house.'

'You've got to find someone on your wavelength,' says Drew.

Mick starts humming.

'It doesn't matter how well they play, or even if they play at all. It's what they're like as a person that counts.'

Waaayve . . . length.

'Maybe,' she says, half-hearted.

'People laughed when he and I got together,' says Drew. 'They couldn't believe it. Have you heard of a band called A Terror Decides or Long Gone Train?'

'Goth was before my time.'

'He was in them while I was in The Shells, a wanna-be pop group. People thought we could be pop stars and we went along with it, basically. It was stupid but we kept on trying. The crazy thing was, we weren't even top-forty people!' The speed has got his tongue and it's jabbering of its own accord. He takes a monster guzzle of beer, hoping to slow himself down. The beer loosening the last clump of speed, forcing a spluttering sneeze. Rubbing mucus with his shirt sleeve, he adds, 'But it worked. I could see what he had and he was intrigued by what I had. And we could talk to each other. *That's* important. Most bands can't do that and it's their downfall. So it can happen like that.'

'Uh-huh.'

'Sorry to carry on. What's Brisbane like these days?'

'Good. More venues are opening up and they're better than the ones before.'

'I'm from there.' He pauses. 'Has that been forgotten in the city's rock history? Oh dear. I guess every generation forgets the one before. It's only natural.'

Waaaayvelength.

'You're paranoid,' she grins. 'You had a sold-out show last week. I would have gone, but I had a gig doing lights.'

'You're from Brisbane?'

'Bardon.'

'I used to play soccer against Bardon Latrobe at Bowman Park.'

'We're past that, up towards Mount Coot-tha.'

'That must be nice.'

'It was. I'm in West End now.'

Waaaaay . . . ve . . . length.

From the back seat comes the Van Morrison chorus again, sung in a bluesy croon, a touch of Dean Martin too.

'Sounds good,' says Drew.

'I think we should cover it.'

'You think so?'

'Why not?'

'A lot of people cover Van.'

'Not "Wavelength".'

'But there's so many songs of his that people cover.'

'You know what, Mr Smartypants? That's why Van's headlining on the main stage.'

*

They are quiet in the car. The gum trees and bush are thickening; vertigo-inducing ravines dropping off from both sides of the road. On the first slow turn of the climb – a giant arch of bitumen girded with metal fencing and traffic signs – the songwriters look back in awe at the flat brown plain they'd crossed that day. The Warrego Highway swinging off to the golden cities of the coast, the turnoff they'd taken splitting – one road heading west to desert; the other, curling through green farm country to the foot of the Border Ranges.

Mick and Drew are digging the ascension. Like cats running from dogs, they're happier on higher ground. An accompanying pleasure is the popping of their ears; the world is falling away.

Twenty minutes later, rainforest. A deeper green enclosing the car, making it matchbox size as it passes rows of roadside trees as tall and straight as telegraph poles down a suburban street. For the landscape to change once more, the car bursting into the last sunlight of the day, when reaching a flattened ridge. Suddenly, there are weatherboard houses and driveways fronted by letterboxes – tantalising for Drew: what lives are lived at the end of those winding tracks? Blissful seclusion or paranoid loneliness? Gardens or guns?

A 'Produce For Sale' stand before the last house of the settlement is spotted as they speed by. The songwriters are wont to stop at produce stalls – to load up with farm fruit, homemade jam and herbs, coins dutifully dropped into the honour box – but not this time.

The journey is not all one climb, the road dipping into a gorge to rise and offer another sweeping view – a purple line of distant mountains topped by a diamond peak. Drew swivels to Mick, knowing there will be an appropriate line. *Our Shangri-La*. The beer is gone, the rush of the speed too; the landscape is delivering the kicks now.

They are nearing the far mountain summit, its approach a snaking twist of tight corners, when the car is swallowed by fog. The stretch of bitumen before them ripped away and replaced by a blurred ghostly sheet. Kate brakes, the songwriters tense; Mount Drake is throwing up its last challenge to those crazy or persistent enough to reach its top.

The Corolla inches on, bend to bend, when a pair of beams bursts out of the mist; a car at speed shaving past them on its charge downhill. No respect for life or fear of death for them.

'Idiots,' spits Kate.

For the fog to lift as it descended, without warning. Fog, another thing Drew can't explain. The car crests a gentle rise, to hit the long welcoming avenue into town – handcrafted signs for food-by-the-fire restaurants and health retreats at its side.

Mick and Drew aren't sure which end of the main street Bakers Dozen is located. It was past the shops – left or right, they don't know. It's now dark and no-one is walking about to ask. They find it second go, Kate parking a short distance from the club's entrance.

After a day boxed in a car, the goodbye is awkward. But then being in a rock band is full of goodbyes. That's all it seems to be sometimes. This one is tougher than most.

'You saved us,' says Mick.

'You did,' insists Drew. 'It was all over back there.'

'Just helping a friend help friends. I'm glad I did it.'

'The next time we come to Brisbane, which may be sometime in the distant future, you could do our sound if you want?'

'Great, but I'd better get going.'

'You're not driving back to Brisbane, are you?' calls Mick.

'No, I have friends in Lismore. I can stay with them.' She opens the car door. 'I know my way.'

'Be careful.'

'I will.'

'And start that band,' says Drew. 'Find that friend. Oh . . . and one other thing.'

He takes a step towards her.

'In about forty years, our biographer is going to track you down. If you could please tell them two things.' His arm is out. Fingers splayed. 'We never took drugs. And we were always on time. If you could relay that, it would be much appreciated.'

She is able to smile. But if you didn't know Drew and Mick, spend at least half a day with them in a car, you'd think they were both a little crazy.

*

Tuesday at Bakers Dozen is open mic night. A blackboard balanced on a rocking chair by the front door has the time slots, most of them filled. The prized ten o'clock spot they can see has been written in and then smudged out.

'That's lucky,' says Drew, picking up the chalk.

'We can't use our real names.'

'Oh, you're right.'

The chief source of friction to their friendship is generated by artistic decisions. Who can come up with the better ideas. Album titles. Album cover designs. Both men want the last word, but don't want to injure the partnership in securing it. It's tricky.

They take their positions; nervous glances and foot shuffling between them.

Mick goes first.

'I know, A Tankard Of Beer.' For him to swiftly pivot, '*Or* The Tankards.'

'Fox,' Drew cunningly counters.

'Time Of The Owl.'

'Fantastic Stump . . . and the . . .'

'Devils.'

'Angels.'

'Fish.'

'Fantastic Stump and the Fish?' formulates Drew. 'That makes no sense.

'Gee,' pouts Mick in mock surprise.

'The John Keats Band?'

'We're saving that . . . remember?'

It's starting to get heated. 'How about this,' says Mick, a smirk signalling confidence. 'Pancho and Lefty.'

That's good. That's really good, thinks Drew. A cool Townes Van Zandt song title. He puts the chalk into his mouth, pretending to smoke it. 'I *know*.'

He leans into the board, blocking his partner's view. Then standing back, he reveals the one-night-only band name. Mick recognises it. Near the end of a long night's drinking – a twilight time when all kinds of admissions are voiced; when you're drunk enough to say something in the mixed-up hope that the other person is too drunk to recall it the next day – Drew let slip a name for some crazy new adventure he envisaged the two of them undertaking. Mick had shot a look of horror, the idea killed and buried, he thought.

'What do you think?'

'*G-r-e-a-t.*'

The venue, built a year ago into the bones of an old bakery, is home to a thriving local music scene, and has become a beloved outpost for bands on national tours, up for an offbeat low-paying gig. It's a hippie place serving vegetarian food and booze, with a stage and a ring of tables that get pushed back when people wish to dance – which is often, sometimes to the sound of one person plucking a banjo. The room is low lit, tea candles spaced along the bar. Lounge lamps are dotted between tables. The worn wooden interior not unlike a saloon in an old Western movie.

The songwriters order food and drinks at the bar and take a table in a corner away from the stage. They're drinking red wine, and have just lit after-dinner cigarettes, when a high-pitched squeal from the PA system alerts them and the audience to the first performer of the night. At the microphone to introduce him is a curly-haired woman wearing baggy Chaplin trousers and a tattered tuxedo jacket over a t-shirt – she's the resident MC.

Mick and Drew are critical of music and other musicians; particularly those with a similar style to their own, upon whom they are brutal. In general, what they dislike they dismiss, and what they love they laud to the heavens. Middle ground doesn't exist.

During the first months of their partnership, the glory days of four-day-a-week practice sessions at Mick's place, he and Drew would rifle through a record collection they'd combined, playing key records to each other and praising a select few they'd deemed as 'classics'. All the while, album sleeves in hand, bantering on the fashion choices and cultural clues they got off each artist or band.

Listening to *Astral Weeks*, they heard Van putting an entire city, his home town Belfast, into song. *Blood On The Tracks* was a movie; ten views of love, written and directed by Bob Dylan. And later, when their first album, *Introducing Mick Woods and Drew Lovelock*, was released and journalists herded a fairly accurate set of influences around their songs, the songwriters would delight in springing calculated odd choices of reference – their love for the cheese of Seals & Crofts, the genius of Brill-Building-period Neil Diamond – the second Neil to Neil Young. Mick and Drew bubble on music; not for them the mumbled recognition of an odd influence or two, or the highhanded wish of some singer-songwriters to retain mystery around their craft. That usually meant one thing – they had shit songs.

The first performer appears promising; a mop of curls, sensitive face, a twelve-string guitar. He looks like Tim Buckley, but it's third-division Billy Bragg. Next up are a husband-and-wife team in their late sixties on guitars called Stonewall Junction. What they lack in slick professionalism, they make up for in country charm and three-chord originals – their hokey presentation skipping the last thirty years of the music business. Mick and Drew toast them with raised glasses.

They aren't so impressed with an earnest – he sings with his eyes closed; a mortal sin to the songwriters – folk singer. He's ripping into traditional ballads.

'Why is it,' asks Mick mid-song, 'when certain people pick up an acoustic guitar, they immediately think they've just landed in Botany Bay on a convict ship?'

Following him is a harpist, her long straight hair to the floor, glistening in the spotlight, and at nine-twenty comes a hippie four piece – two women, two men, with guitars and congas – who wander competently through Santana and Bob Marley covers, to end on Jimmy Cliff's 'Many Rivers To Cross'. By then, Mick and Drew are tuned up, side of stage.

Waiting for them is the smallest audience they've faced since Greece: a mix-up had them performing to three tables of old men, pushing dominoes at a beachside taverna outside of Patros. Tonight, eighty people are positioned around the room – at tables, at the bar, a line of young folk sit crosslegged before the stage.

Mick thanks them in his introduction, acknowledges the club for letting them perform, and then for the next forty minutes they stun the crowd, who bring them back for an encore. A rare thing at an open-mic night. If there was any intention of disguising or fudging their identity, Mick and Drew's competitiveness, and love of what they do, holds them true to themselves. At their peril.

A few beaming faces recognise the two men; most, though, content themselves with the notion that two very talented singer-songwriters have just wandered in off the street. It can happen in New York, London, Dublin – and Mount Drake.

Back at their table, Mick is grumpy. 'What's the matter?'

Drew looks rebuked. 'Nothing.'

'You missed the harmony on the second chorus of "Easy Come, Easy Go". You forgot a verse to one of your own songs, and your solo on "Tamworth Massacre" – hate to say it, man – was pretty poor.'

'I know . . . *sorry.* Do you want a drink?'

Mick lifts his empty glass, 'I'll stay on the wine.'

Drew sets off.

'Oh, and remember,' calls out Mick, 'we're in desperate need of a place to stay. Ask around.'

Drew nods obediently.

Mick's eyes are on him when a voice asks, 'Do you mind if I join you?'

He had noticed the guy in the audience. He was leaning forward in his chair, drinking in each word he and Drew sang. Sitting opposite him now, Mick takes in his appearance, beginning with the full head of grey-flecked brown hair, swept back from his forehead to end in outlaw mode over the collar.

He isn't dressed like the others at the club either; smart jeans offset with a black suit jacket, crisp white shirt unbuttoned low, and cowboy boots. The one fashion faux pas: a coral necklace. If Mick had to guess . . . author? Scholar? Funky lawyer? A closer look shows some unaccounted-for-by-age wear and tear of the handsome face. Some hard living has evidently been done.

'That was fantastic,' the stranger says. 'Where are you from?'

'Sydney.'

'Great to hear "Fleetwood Plain". The last person I heard sing that was the guy who wrote it. Greg Quill and Country Radio at a tiny festival outside of Bellingen *in* . . . 1975, I believe. Their last tour.'

'Great band.'

'Oh yeah, I knew Greg. Hey, do you mind if I pinch one of your cigarettes.' He smiles ruefully. 'Whenever I'm near music, I have to smoke.' Mick watches him slide a Stuyvesant out of the packet, light it, and take a satisfying draw in one stylish sweep. 'He used to run a folk club on the North Shore in the early sixties. Lots of guitars and good times there. He's in Canada now, I hear, working as a journalist.'

'I didn't know that.'

'He gave it up here. I don't know why. They went out of fashion, I guess. It's all cycles, isn't it.'

'Drew and I think he looks like Rasputin. The thick black hair. The full beard.'

'I hadn't thought of that.' He draws on the cigarette. 'But good songwriting never fades. You guys are proof of that.'

'Thanks, man,' says Mick, in need of a drink, glancing at the bar – no sign of Drew. 'You live around here?'

'A property out of town. That was so good. I thought it was all gone.'

'It's not.'

'So they're listening to Greg Quill in Sydney?'

'A few of us more enlightened types are. How did you know him?'

'Long story.' But intent on keeping it short, he speaks in clipped cadences; the cigarette in his silver-ringed fingers, a prop to stab out each turn of his life. 'I started as a folkie and then went electric. I'm assuming you haven't heard of The Electric Train Set? We did one single, supported The Easybeats and then broke up. Did psychedelia. More for the clothes than the drugs, although I got my hands on some of them. I'd loved The Byrds through it all – "Eight Miles High" and all that stuff. And then in '68 . . .'

'*Sweetheart Of The Rodeo*.'

'Exactly. And then the singer-songwriters started coming through. James Taylor, Joni, Carole King. Some people formed groups like Greg. I wrote songs. Still do, actually.'

'You recorded them?'

'One album in '72. It sold 800 copies.' He chuckles. 'My mother bought fifty.' Another laugh. These are practised lines. 'I've got a box of them at home. I'll give you one if you want.'

'I'd like that.'

'It's overproduced, of course. Strings, a choir, the whole box and dice.' Recalling magic times, he's relieved to be telling them to someone who knows what he's talking about. 'I was a good-looking boy. But the record company and my management didn't know what to do with me. Was I a pop star or was I a singer-songwriter? You couldn't be both back *then*.

'I liked a Canadian guy called Gordon Lightfoot. Just me and my guitar and a bit of backing is what I needed. *But* . . . it was *Jesus Christ Superstar* time. Everything was a big, loud, never-ending hymn.'

'What's your name? I'm Mick.' He extends his hand across the table.

'Russell Duggan. Can I get you a drink?'

*

Drew had choked on stage. When he first saw her, she was standing behind the bar. Then she brought food to a table. Then she stood in the shadows watching him and Mick play. To leave and return with a camera around her neck and click a few shots – which is when he stuffed up, doing the things that had got Mick angry.

He had tried not to play to her. Yet on certain lines of his songs that seemed to have a relevance to his current situation – singing to an attentive woman with her appraising eye upon him – he did redirect his gaze from the audience to fall on her.

Saw her at the crossroads
Tell you what we did
We threw kisses off bridges on country roads
Mmm, that's what we did.

The chorus was a shift of gears. His voice had urgency.

Heart out to tender
I came along with my bid.

There's a scrum of people at the bar, Drew at ease, accepting their compliments with good cheer. A wild-eyed guy in flannel shirt and string hair has a copy of *Vestiges* to sign, having raced home to collect it. All the while, Drew's attention – when it can be diverted – falls on the bar, where the woman, aided by a tall jangling boy with acne and a prominent Adam's apple, is serving drinks.

'Two glasses of red wine, please.'

She reaches for a bottle on the shelf. 'Good set.'

'Thank you, it's a lovely room.'

'It works' – she smiles – 'when the music's good.'

'We've played here before.'

'Someone told me that. My name's Heather, by the way, and you're . . . I'm sorry.'

'I'm Drew.'

'I manage the place and book the acts.' She pours the wine, generous amounts in both glasses. 'With a little bar work thrown in.'

With her finger and thumb, she drags long strands of her side-parted honey-blonde hair back from her face. She'd done that when raising the camera to her eye. Her prominent feature is a long straight nose, dividing her face into two attractive sides. Her eyes hold his with ease.

'You like working here?'

'I've never done anything like it before. Actually, it was the only thing going. But I get to meet lots of musicians and interesting people, which I like. The hours are demanding. Normally I have Tuesdays off, minding the twins . . . oh, excuse me.'

As he tries to place her accent, he watches her talk to the harpist at the end of the bar, and is caught staring at them as they look back at him. He swings away to spot Mick chatting to an older guy at their table. That reminds him. He has their drinks in his hand and is about to walk off.

'Can I ask a favour, Drew?'

The harp is bloody heavy. He and the harpist haul it through the carpark; a bulb above the club's back door lighting their way.

'Over there.' She puffs, indicating, with a nod, a late-seventies green Volvo station wagon.

'Nice car. You get it up here?' he asks under the strain.

'Kingscliff,' she grunts.

They stand the harp, and, while she unwraps a thick blanket from the boot, a wind as cold as moving ice whistles through the strings. Drew feels them sing. The soundtrack to his night.

He returns her last wave, watching the Volvo clear a hump of stony ground and disappear. Jamming his hands into his pockets, his shoulders hunched, he looks to a jagged, distant line of purple mountains. The moon dropping silver over a vast pool of darkness before him. In supplication to this view and the moment's reprieve from people and noise, he extends his arms Christ-like, tilting his head back with closed eyes to further brick off the world.

He'd forgotten this. The power of being alone. No Mick, if only for a second. He should do it more often; step out of life. *His* has been a rush, spinning for years, spun over the last days to the point of madness.

Back arched, arms stretched wide, he's twice dreamt of flying. A psychologist friend told him it was an expression of inner peace. In his dreams, he was standing on a high cliff, to jump off, and discover his body could be supported by the flap of his extended arms.

It was an extraordinary sensation slicing through the sky.

To glide and descend, then propel his arms and be lifted up once more. *Eek, eek, eek*, he squeaks softly to himself. He's a bird twittering. *Eek, eek, eek.* He's an eagle, spotting food when soaring over a gorge. *Eek, eek, eek.* He's one of the hungry babies in the nest, waiting for mama's food.

A cough.

He knows it's her.

He scrambles for something to say. 'You're probably wondering what I'm doing.'

'You're communing with the night.'

'And it doesn't seem strange to you?' His shoulders are tiring.

'People often do it when they first get up here.'

Smiling to himself, he drops his arms.

Heather is standing by the back door, the overhead light bleaching her features. She's wearing a green corduroy skirt, black stockings and a pair of ankle-high, lace-up leather boots.

'They're from Italy.' She lifts a heel, turning one leg in front of the other. 'Nice, aren't they? Have you been?'

'Bologna. We just did one show.'

'That's a start. Rimini is nearby at the coast. And behind Rimini, up in the hills, is a beautiful stone village called Mondiano.' She gives the name the full Italian twist. Normally, Drew hates that; people showing off their language skills in the pronunciation of one word. 'I bought them in a tiny shop there for 75,000 lira.'

'Oh, what's that in Aussie dollars?'

'Ah . . . about seventy-five.'

'You were there on holidays?' he asks hesitantly.

'I was on assignment. I'm a travel writer and photographer. I was based in London at the time. I moved about doing stories for newspapers and magazines. Corporate stuff too.'

'So that's what you do, or you did before what you do now?'

She grins at his tangles.

'So how did you end up in Mount Drake?'

'Umm . . . it was my daughter Jazzy's choice. She's a wilful five-year-old who wanted to be with her new cousins and Aunty Emma.'

He's taking that in. They must be the twins.

'I have to close up. Nice talking to you, and thank you for helping Miranda. She's very fussy about who gets to carry the *sacred* harp.'

He walks to her. 'Anytime.'

'Why did you play under another name, by the way? No-one would have minded your own.'

'We're just . . . travelling around doing low-key shows. Breaking in new songs. So we thought, why not try something different?' He shrugs. 'I don't know.'

He's by her now. She's standing aside to let him pass. He can feel a wattage coming off her body. An electric current silently ticking as he passes. God knows what she's feeling. He can't guess.

'Puffy and The Lizard Tonks,' she says, a question in her voice.

Coming out of her mouth, it sounds very him. Flashy and attention seeking. Not enough gravity or gravitas, or whatever that term is. The stuff he needs more of.

'It's not that good, is it?'

'It's funny,' she offers.

He's tempted to say it was Mick's idea. He's told her one fib – he doesn't want to risk another.

*

He's in trouble *again,* he realises, passing the dark bare stage. The guitars are packed and set side by side, the suitcase and bag too. Also neat and ready to go are Mick and the older guy he'd seen from the bar. Mick makes the introduction, telling Drew with a sting of rebuke that Russell is putting them up for the night.

Passing a table, a ring of the night's performers, united by the glory of a gig, sit over last drinks. There are good-hearted shouts inviting the songwriters back for next week's show. Mick gives them a 'Who knows?' chuckle and a wave. Drew glances back at the empty room.

Russell's backyard shed is a granny flat, if granny was a bohemian artist with a guitar collection. He and his wife, Susan, share the room. She paints watercolours of the rainforest – leaves the size and shape of elephant ears and whizzing parakeets in flight; painted at pointblank range, to blur the greenery into abstraction. He writes songs and listens to music, sitting on a treasured wooden chair with woven cane seating.

Pinned samples of her work cover the walls. Spaced between them are posters chronicling his gig career, petering out – the songwriters notice as they explore the room – in the mid-eighties. A torn and frayed Brett Whiteley print of Sydney Harbour is taped behind the front door. *To Russ & Susan, May Your Art Set You Free, Love Brett*, splashed in ink in a corner. The couch against the wall folds out into a double bed, and a large red-and-gold

Moroccan rug covers the floor. The songwriters are settling in, the heater on, when their host returns with a bottle of Scotch and an apology for having no hash.

Snatching a guitar off a stand, Russell plays them a few of his songs. Mick and Drew have heard this kind of material before; well put together, treading tried melodic lines and lyrical intent, lacking ingredient X. After he's performed three or four of his most recent numbers, the songwriters, tired and further dragged by the pull of the sipped Scotch, are sliding to sleep. Russell, sensing the impending loss of his audience, says he'll play a song he wrote in Glebe in the mid-seventies.

There's magic in the first strum; a tingling, original melody encoded in the song's four circular chords. And instead of the grumpy-older-man musings of the previous numbers, this song nails emotional drama. The singer pleading for a woman's love as she ponders her choices between lovers and cities.

'That's good, man,' says Mick, awakening.

'Wow,' drawls Drew, an appreciative, hey-did-he-just-do-that grin to his face.

The songwriters unpack their guitars: Drew capo-ing at the fifth fret to give his guitar a mandolin ring; Mick, to lean on a heavy rhythm. And as they perform 'Three Way Tie', the musicians, although deep in concentration, are trying to hide smiles as the song builds. They play it three times, on each pass promising it will be the last – till satisfied and exhausted they down guitars.

Mick and Drew are jolly over last drinks, promising to add the number to their repertoire, maybe even their next album. In return,

Russell, buoyant, offers Drew a case for his guitar, to then tumble out the door and trip over a guinea-pig cage in the dark.

Earlier at the club, Mick had quizzed him about cars: they need one quickly. Russell had said he'd think about it, and when the songwriters come in the next morning for a late breakfast, he tells them he's phoned around and found two options. One is for 800 dollars. The other, with some bargaining, could be got for two grand. It depends on how far you want to go? Melbourne, they reply. Russell thinks both cars are worth a shot.

In daylight, the charms of Mount Drake are revealed; cute, single lanes cutting through dairy land and old timber farmhouses, to join a road that runs into the town's shopping village. It's a fine day, last night's wind gone, when a police car comes towards them appearing to slow and then pass. To the songwriters, it feels like a shark circling in the surf.

'You see police up here much?' Drew asks Russell casually.

'Nah,' he says, from behind aviator shades. 'It's one of the reasons people move up here.' He glances at the disappearing car in the rear-view window. 'A bit of a surprise, actually.'

They split up in the village, Russell striding off to the organic-produce store for fruit and veg, Drew sneaking into the newsagent to buy a paper and ciggies. Mick finds a phone booth at the end of the street.

'It's me.'

'The police were here this morning,' intones Swifty. 'They asked if I'd heard from you or knew your whereabouts.'

'What did you say?'

'That I haven't heard from you, and they seemed okay with that.'

'Find Bingo.'

'I'm trying, Mick. I've checked his apartment and the office twice. Phoned around, still nothing. You know . . . he could have left town. That's a possibility.'

'It's a possibility, but we've got to keep believing he's still there.'

Mick slides another run of coins into the phone-box slot.

'I hear Childers went well. The driver picked you up and got you to where you wanted to go.'

'She sure did. Thanks for that and we missed you at the gig last night.'

'You *played*?'

'Yeah, why not?' deadpans Mick. 'And we picked up a new song.'

'What?'

'I'll tell you later. It was a funny show.'

'How's Drew?'

'In love. He became acquainted with a woman. He was playing to her. It completely threw him.'

'Did you see her?'

'From a distance. I've gotta go – we're off to see cars. Wish us luck.'

'What's she like?'

'How should I know? Hopefully we'll get something and be on the road tonight.'

Jiggling and extracting more coins from his suit pocket, Mick makes a second call.

Drew is waiting outside the newsagent. Quite the cosmopolitan gent: paper tucked under his arm, scanning the street while puffing on a smoke. He watches Mick's loping approach, tossing him a packet of cigarettes, caught low down with one hand. Mick relates Swifty's news, and then, eyeing the newspaper, 'Anything about us?'

'We're at the bottom of page 7.'

'That all?'

'A small story. The bad things we're supposed to have done and the jailbreak.'

'Any photo?'

'No, but a headline.' He waits, sure he's got Mick's eye. '"Songwriters On The Run".'

They break grins. Sometimes life and art are just too beautifully entwined.

*

'So where are we headed, driver?' Mick in the back seat has been patient for fifteen minutes.

Russell is navigating his 1984 Nissan Pathfinder down a dirt track. Walls of green vegetation thick with sticks and Tarzan-swinging vines scrape against the sides of the car. High above, a strip of sky as wide as the road is all that can be seen of the outside world. Wherever they're going, it's deeper into the mysteries of the mountain.

'We're almost there,' he says, above the crunch of tyres spitting rocks.

'Where's there?' asks Drew, remembering Russell's cagey smile when he had suggested viewing the cheaper car first.

'You'll see.'

Eight minutes later, the car bursts into a large oval clearance, reminding Drew of a golf course he once played with his family, cut into the edges of a pine forest. Striding towards the Nissan as if anticipating its arrival is a stocky man in his late fifties, wearing a white linen shirt and a jewel-encrusted waistcoat over black corduroy pants – his bald crown shooting off a fizz of black and grey hair – a wooden staff clasped in his hand.

Russell, stopping the car, winds down his window.

'Greetings,' says the man in a rich, bell-toned voice. 'How can I be of help?'

'I'm Russell Duggan. I've been here a few times before. These are friends of mine, Mick and Drew.'

'I'm Winston.' He bends down, spreading his legs for leverage to peer further into the car. 'And you're Mick Woods and Drew Lovelock. I very much like your last album. And would I be amiss,' he grips his staff for support, 'if I said I can hear the influence – I hope that is not too strong a word – of the minstrel poet Bob Dylan?'

Looking past an amused Russell, Drew says, 'It wouldn't be amiss at all. We particularly like the albums he made in the mid-sixties.'

'So you're not admirers of the pastoral Dylan,' twinkles Winston. 'By that I mean his early folk albums or his post-motorcycle-crash work up until *Blood On The Tracks*, which, I presume from your songwriting, you like a great deal.'

'And *John Wesley Harding*,' pipes up Mick.

'This is an important record.' Winston straightens and gestures to the bent bodies in the fields, harvesting and planting rows of vegetables and flowers. 'Those simple songs of wisdom and great mystery. Bob once said in an interview, and I'm not quoting directly, *I didn't have to make it, but I'm glad I did* . . . and we're very grateful for that.'

'I remember when it came out,' says Russell. 'People didn't know what to make of it and then it really caught on.'

The fate of a lot of great art, notes Winston.

'Sorry to get to business,' grimaces Russell. 'We're in a bit of a hurry. I phoned Allen this morning. We've come to inspect a car he has.'

'Ah, I've been told about this.' He points with his stick to a building below the slope of the fields. 'Drive down and park. I will follow.'

Russell and the songwriters are appraising a wooden two-storey building – the windows cut in hexagonal shapes, the front door heavy with ornamental hinges – when Winston approaches a little breathless. 'Come in,' he exhorts good-naturedly, 'I think you will appreciate what I am about to show you.'

The parting of heavy brocade curtains reveals a rectangular hall, not unlike the interior of a country town school of arts. Spaced evenly along opposing walls, hanging six to a side, are a series of large glass-framed photographs. Winston's smile, and a flourish of his hand, an invitation to the visitors to inspect the treasures on display.

Passing the first photographs, each containing an image from a period of Bob Dylan's career, it's a reminder to the three musicians of the mercurial swiftness of Dylan's changes, and his ability to conjure up an appropriate face and costume for each new set of songs. Having stopped to inspect many of the photographs, muttering appreciation, picking over detail, they are before the last photograph: Dylan at dawn, wearing a flower-garlanded, broad-brimmed hat, a trumpet in his hands, a ragged troop of friends at his heels, when they are startled from their reverie.

'Bang and Olufsen.'

The names, ringing in the hall, sound like characters in a Restoration comedy. Winston has been shadowing the musicians. He gestures to a stack of stereo gear mounted on a stage at the end of the hall.

'It's very impressive,' says Russell, recovering.

'We purchased it two years ago and the sound is amazing. Features in the mixes we'd never heard before. The speakers are early-seventies, 15-inch speaker Tannoys – from Abbey Road, at least that's what we were told.' A glint in his eyes. Suddenly, the musicians can see his role. He's a teacher. 'Let me play you something.'

Springing onto the platform with an awkward leap, he takes a toothed iron key from his waistcoat to open a wooden cabinet near the stereo. Flicking through shelves of albums, Winston says, 'Dylan's entire catalogue is here, and we have multiple pressings, originals and reissued editions. Mono and stereo. And an extensive bootleg collection of material he has, for whatever reasons, impossible to second guess Bob, failed to release. Some live '66 stuff that would blow your minds. Let me see . . . it's here, somewhere . . . here.'

'Winston,' says Russell gently, 'the guys are a little pressed for time . . .'

'Of course. We could do this later. Let's go and see Allen.'

The mechanic's workshop is a tin shed on a concrete slab, tucked behind the Listening House. It also serves as an informal meeting place for the less industrious members of the Dylan community: those who prefer to come and gather around a weatherbeaten table over coffee and rolled cigarettes; to chat, or pick from a shelf of esoteric books, heavy on history, philosophy and mysticism, that Allen collects and keeps above his tool bench.

'Hell-o,' calls Winston, over a hum of Chicago blues coming from a brown, leather-cased cassette player. 'Russell and his friends are here to look at the car.'

He slides out on a trolley from under a 1981 Ford Escort. Mick and Drew look down on a wispy bearded man in his late twenties, waves of curly dark hair, offering a shy grin as welcome.

'Fixing up our car?' asks Drew cheekily. It would be an 800 dollar bargain.

'No,' says the mechanic, getting up, apologetic, 'this is not what . . . this isn't . . . it's around the corner.'

Standing together in a paddock behind the workshop, no-one knows what to say at first. Winston, presumably, had known the state of the vehicle. Russell should have guessed when hearing the price. The songwriters are undecided. To laugh or to cry?

'Ummm,' says Drew slowly, searching, searching, searching for a word. 'It's a . . . beauty.'

'Uh-huh,' says Allen, rocking on his heels. He extracts a pair of round silver spectacles from the pocket of his overalls, better to feast with absorbed affection upon the bubbles of rust running along the door frames, a mural of breaking waves on a sun-drenched beach, painted Van Gogh style in swirling shades of yellow and blue, covering the length of one of the side panels.

'You'll want to test-drive it,' says Winston without a blink.

Drew is surprised when Mick takes the keys.

'I've always wanted to drive a Kombi,' he yells above the engine's roar.

'Right,' says Drew, surprised again. They are looping a ring of unsealed roads, passing a lake where naked children swim, watched by a couple on a blanket.

'Kim's boyfriend had one.' Kim is Mick's elder sister. 'Probably as old as this.

'They were surfers, and on weekends they'd take me on trips to Lennox Heads. I would have been ah . . . ten. I'd sit on the rocks eating bowls of Sultana Bran and watch them get waves.'

It's an evocative picture. Drew mulls it over. He ate Sultana Bran too. It was one of life's early mysteries: the dark sultanas from the cardboard box, chewed slowly, doused in cold milk, tasted better than any other sultanas you could buy in the supermarket.

'Don't worry, the fantasy ends here.' He crunches the gears, hitting the accelerator to little response. 'Just give me a bit more time, then we drive back and tell Allen we'll think it over.'

Drew pops the glovebox. Pulling out a cassette. J.J. Cale's *Naturally*.

Getting out of the van and not wishing to immediately confront the question of purchase, he enquires about a cluster of houses they'd seen on a far field.

Winston winces.

'They're followers of *Slow Train Coming* and *Saved*, you know,

Bob's Christian albums. Sometimes they try and convert us . . . not only to the faith, but to the musical worth of the records.'

His eyes darken.

'So far we've resisted.'

*

They are reaching the end of the dirt road, the rainforest thinning; the real world – if Mount Drake can be called that – about to return with crushing force.

'That was a beautiful scene back there. What's next?'

'Well, it's the other car, Mick. It'll be better, but we're not going to get that welcome,' answers Russell, braking on gravel to make a turn onto the bitumen glide. 'This guy lives by himself and is a bit of a wheeler and dealer. Sells pot while holding down a government job. Don't know how he does it.'

Mount Drake has two settlements. Grouped around the main street is a cluster of timber houses built early in the century that thin out to dotted farmhouses and farmland. In the early seventies, a flush of new arrivals fleeing from the cities, 'the blocks' were constructed. A modern grid of homes, some of quirky design, A-frame dwellings popular – a square slice of suburbia surrounded by bush. It's to a brick house in 'the blocks' that Russell pulls over and parks.

On the front lawn is a blue 1983 Toyota Corolla parked at the angle they are in big city car yards – a residue of suds, indicating a fresh wash, pooled at the wheels. Mick and Drew won't have to kick tyres to know this sedan will get them to where they want to go.

The front door of the home is opened by a small young man

with thinning brown hair and glasses, not groovy black-rimmed specs, but sensible silver frames that someone in their forties would wear. Behind them are parked a set of alert eyes. 'I'm Andrew,' he says, sizing up his prospective buyers from the top of the stairs.

The engine is looked at and the four of them do a kind of inspection dance around the vehicle. Mick and Drew know little about cars, relying on a nod from Russell, who says, 'You said two thousand, right?'

'I'm looking at two two.'

The songwriters have a thousand dollars – a wad of notes Tom at the Durango Bar had slipped to Swifty as they were being bundled out of the club by the cops. There is another two hundred they'd found rolled in a sock in Max's bag: they're holding that for petrol money.

Two two, mutters Mick. 'We'll offer you twelve hundred in cash.'

Andrew looks at Russell. *What kind of jokers are these?*

'I can put in another three hundred,' says Russell.

'No deal.'

It's awkward. Andrew goes first. 'Unless you've got something to sell?'

'I've got a guitar,' says Mick.

'Don't,' says Drew.

'What kind?'

'A Martin.'

'A Martin what?'

'D18.'

'In what condition?'

'I could get it.' Mick looks at Russell.

'You can bring mine too,' says Drew.

Another stand-off. Anger in check, each playing his hand as carefully as he can.

'How about this?' reasons Mick. 'You guys go and get the guitars and I'll stay here with Andy.'

*

Drew waits until they are almost at Russell's. 'Do you know Heather?'

'At the club? She runs it well – everyone says that. It's better than it was.'

'What else?'

'She brought in vegetarian food and someone that can cook it. That's gone down well.' He glances over. 'The chickpea samosas are amazing.'

'Uh-huh.'

'They come with a tangy relish.'

'She has a daughter, Jazzy.'

'And she lives with her sister – I don't know her name. She has a couple of kids. Susan would know more. Her and Heather are putting on an art show at Bakers.'

'Really? That's a good idea.'

Russell grins. A tip of his tongue poking through his lips.

'What?' asks Drew.

'When she was watching you play, you got *very* distracted. You were messing up, my friend.'

'Was it obvious, was it?'

'To the trained eye.'

'Fuck.'

'Don't worry. No-one else got it.'

'I talked to her after the show. She asked me to carry out the harp with Miranda and we got chatting in the car park.'

Drew can relax. He's said it. Spreading his legs, he continues to talk to the driver with the Western-movie-hero profile. 'She used to work as a travel writer and photographer. She lived in London and travelled around Europe with her job. Did you know that?'

'I don't go to the club often enough. It was a fluke I saw you guys.'

'You know how you can talk with someone and it's kind of like you're talking in shorthand, or you've met the person before.' Drew turns away, scanning the scenery. A treehouse in a front yard, big enough for a family to live in. 'It was something like that.'

'And she's an attractive lady.'

'Yeah, I've got that.'

The house is coming up. A dog jumping circles at the sight of Russell and the car.

'I didn't sense anything from her. Musicians and people would be passing through all the time. She kept looking at me and I couldn't figure it out. Normally I can.' He's not in control of where this conversation is going. 'I don't know. There was a click, and when I sang to her, which you probably saw . . . the way she stood and looked at me . . .'

'It was touching. You can't hang around to find out?'

'Nah, and someone like her would have someone somewhere. The father of the child, perhaps.'

'And if she doesn't?'

'I can't. We should drop it.'

They're in the driveway. Russell pulls the keys from the ignition and looks at Drew.

'Mick and I have to move on.'

'More gigs. That's good.'

'Yeah,' says Drew softly, clicking his door handle, swivelling to get out.

'What was it again?' Russell's lips are making shapes, trying to form the words, his eyes begging for assistance. 'Puffy and . . .'

Drew sighs. 'The Lizard Tonks.'

'That can't be your real band name?'

'It's not.'

'Thank goodness for that.'

'Let me tell you something,' says Russell, his eyes sharp, yet giving. 'I'm not a great songwriter, not like you guys. But sometimes you fluke one and "Three Way Tie" is as good a song as I'm ever going to write. Listen, let me finish. I was in love with Susan and so was another guy . . . my best friend. It was tense and confusing while we pretended it was all free and easy – I know, the seventies. But it wasn't.

'One day, I told her how I *really* felt, that I couldn't stand the situation any longer, and that she was free to choose. If it wasn't me, I'd go away and that would be it. And at that moment I wrote the song. Willing what I was hoping to happen to happen. And maybe' – he raises a hand – 'it made no difference. But I told the person I had feelings for how I felt and I wrote the song. *Now*, let's go and get those guitars.'

*

One look at Mick, he's stoned immaculate.

'Andy has been quite hospitable,' he slurs, beer bottle in hand, a sag to his legs, 'but I haven't been able to budge him from his exorbitant price.'

Drew gives the car door a slam. *Why can't he say no for once?*

He and Russell unload the guitar cases; side by side on the grass, they look like tiny coffins. Asleep inside, cradled and nestled by ruffles of soft felt, are the most precious possessions the songwriters have in the world.

Mick opens his case first. The nutty brown body may be scratched and weathered, yet there are the magic words stamped on the headstock thirty years ago in a Tennessee guitar factory: Martin & Co. Mick was cock-a-hoop, knowing he was getting a once-in-a-lifetime deal, when he spotted it in a side street Newcastle music shop for nine hundred dollars back in '88.

'Five hundred bucks,' says Andy crisply.

The Woods jaw sets. Andy isn't budging; his open-palmed hands raised in supplication to the Trading Gods. He knows he's got these pretty-boy musos strapped over a barrel. They need to sell. Mick has told him as much. A withering 'Fuck you' is the songwriter's reply.

'What's in the other?' asks Andy, backing away.

It's a sunburst sixties Gibson Dove that Drew bought off the ex-girlfriend of a playboy Brisbane songwriter, eager to sell her partner's guitar at a giveaway price. A week later, Drew had driven to Sydney with a suitcase and the Dove, wanting them to be his essential baggage for the next decade.

'Beautiful guitars,' says Russell; not the salesman pitch, but the songwriter's awe.

'This is what I'll do,' says Andy, a smack to his lips – he's enjoying this. 'Give me your thousand and the guitars and you can drive the car away now.'

Drew takes his turn. 'We're selling you almost three thousand dollars' worth of guitars and you're giving us a little over a grand? Oh, man.'

'Come on,' pleads Russell. 'The guys are in a jam.'

'We're *all* in a jam, man,' says Andy, heated.

The songwriters stagger as if hit by a punch. The smug puny bastard before them, the latest in a long line of people who've screwed them over money. It's the root of all their evils. Every time it looks like they're winning, money brings them back to the pack.

Russell has kept his stare on Andy. The old lion not wanting the young scavenger to take every scrap of food.

'I'll do this,' concedes Andy. 'You come back in a week with fifteen hundred and you can have them back.' He bends down, flicking Mick's guitar case shut. 'Otherwise I sell.'

*

The sun is behind the trees, the air is cold on the back verandah. Fairy lights run along the railings. Flowering pot plants hang on hooks. Susan's touch is felt throughout the house.

She surprised the songwriters when they arrived back from Andy's. Expecting a statuesque hippie queen, they were greeted by a short woman with clipped grey hair, and a manner that exuded practicality and good humour. She'd just returned home from teaching Art at Capricorn University in Lismore.

Mick comes out and sits with Drew on a bench.

'Russell let me have the call with Swifty. I told him we have a car and we're heading off tonight. So he knows.'

'Did he say anything about Bingo?'

'Susan walked in. I had to stop.'

'Okay,' says Drew softly, miles away. 'Good to know, I guess.'

'How are you feeling?'

Mick's concern is surprising and welcome.

'We *had* to trade the guitars, but Jesus, it's hard without them.'

'Yeah, it is. I'll take the first shift.'

'I'll do it – you can sleep. We've got a long night.' He can feel Mick's eyes on him as he looks to the forest, alive with birds and fruit bats, spilling over the back fence. The chill in the air carrying a sweet scent. 'It's nice up here.'

'It would be quiet,' says Mick gently. 'I always wonder how much time you can spend in places like this.'

'In paradise?'

'You know what I mean. You're a long way from the action. The places we love.'

'It would be a trade-off. If you had money, you'd have your seclusion.'

'I never knew you were into seclusion. When did that begin?'

'I don't know. I'll do the first shift.'

'Give me your cup.' Mick rests his hand on Drew's knee as he rises. A playful groan pushing himself up. 'I'll tell them we're leaving.'

It was dark on the verandah – more noise inside the house than out. Drew can hear the children in the kitchen laughing as they prepare food, Mick and Russell chatting, a goodbye drink probably. Susan has gone off to the shed to paint.

Mick is ready to go. Mount Drake for him was one more gig in a life of gigs; Drew knows that feeling. Standing on stage entertaining the crowd while your mind is already at the next show; calculating the miles to get there, and what you'll have for breakfast before setting off. The crowd's applause pulling you out of your trance, back to the job of introducing the night's next song.

Thank you kindly. This is a recent composition of mine called 'Thyme In The Garden'.

If it wasn't for Knowles and the cops, he'd be hesitating. Willing to hang around town a day or two and drop by Bakers Dozen. It's most likely nothing. He'd walk in, they'd talk, and there'd be less spark. Things can be magical on gig night and flat the next day.

He remembers her eyes on him as he sang. That was really it. 'Heart Out To Tender'. *I came along with my bid.* The delicious moment she spoke to him as his back was turned. The swing of the leg as she modelled her boots. The pain and pleasure increases as he tries to reason her feelings; what clock ticks behind those fearless eyes. To scold himself for pumping up a fantasy.

What to do?

Expect the worst, a boyfriend or girlfriend around town, a husband in London waiting for her and Jazzy to return to his family's two-storey Hampstead mansion, and slowly work your way back from there.

DAYS BEFORE

The light blue 1986 Chrysler LeBaron coupe pulls a left off Sunset Boulevard and begins the wind up La Brea Avenue to the Hollywood Hills. In the spring evening the traffic has thinned, and Ruth O'Connor, peering over the steering wheel, her bony arms strong, swings through the oncoming curves confidently. 'Let them talk.'

'Oh, definitely,' replies Ira Isherwood, snapping out of his passenger-window daydream. An REM gig in Austin on the Document tour. Hanging out with Peter Buck after the show. His insane love of music.

'And then we strike.'

'You make it sound like we're the Manson family.'

'Don't joke. I was here when that happened.'

'No way.'

'We'd just moved.'

'What a welcome.' He checks her taut, bird-like face. 'Scary time.'

'There's a book you oughta read called *The Family* by Ed Sanders. He's a hippie poet, a Beat Generation guy. It's very good. It came out not long after the murders, with a really witchy photo of Manson on the cover.' She shakes. 'Ugh.'

'I'll get it. I know a good second-hand book place.'

'A sort of fluorescent purple glow to the photo. My brother got the book and he later told me he slept with a knife under his pillow for months.'

'It's hard to believe it happened just over twenty years ago. 1969 is not that long ago.'

'What do you mean?'

'It's close, but in another way so far away. How people dressed and what they believed in. The music is so different.'

'The San Francisco sound,' she says to herself softly, checking the numbers of passing houses.

Ira is on a roll. 'Imagine going into Warners or Sony today, and telling the person at reception you believe in a free society and you play acid rock.'

'Wouldn't get far. Security would lead you out. A few of the older musicians have Manson stories, and it's funny, they're all the same. They didn't like his vibe and backed off.'

'Manson was pitching songs.'

'He was, and by the sound of it, not good ones.' Her eyes, raisin-black in her attentive face, flicker to Ira. 'Nothing we could sell.'

Returning her smile, he turns to the window, the hills and canyons are nearing dark. The car's beams picking out driveways and metal gates like a swinging spotlight on a movie set.

'We're coming with the best of intentions,' she says with a chirp. 'We're bringing bad news, though.'

Not as bad as Charlie's, he could add.

At the intercom, Ruth takes a slip of paper from her purse and checks the address. She'd imagined something more ostentatious and secluded; a castle guarded by pillars and marble, perhaps, or a terracotta-tiled Spanish villa with twenty bedrooms. She pushes the button and, before she can begin her introduction, there's a buzz at the gate.

Leaning against the front door frame, a welcoming expression on her tanned pretty face, is a young woman wearing an oversized blue and black checked flannel shirt over a pair of frayed cut-off jeans. Her mess of long brown hair, dyed with red streaks, is topped by a white bow. She's barefoot.

'Hi, I'm Ariel, Lex's sister,' she calls to the odd couple. He's tall, a bit goofy, cute face, with a tight mop of black curls. She's significantly shorter – her hand reaching out in welcome as she crunches the pebble stone path with her heels.

'I'm Ruth and this is Ira.' Her voice, throaty and warm, rises a notch. 'We're from Warner Brothers Publishing.'

'I know,' she laughs. 'I can't believe it.'

They follow their host across a large sunken living-room with a fireplace cut into a feature stone wall. Kitchen staff are glimpsed through a side door, preparing food – Japanese, hopes Ruth. She'd had her first sushi and saki a week ago with Hank Wilson, an arty New York record producer, scouting for work on the West Coast. Opening a set of floor-to-ceiling glass doors, Ariel ushers the publishers out onto a long verandah and a million-dollar view.

Ruth has met the woman and man rising from a circle of couches before: Irene Lambetti is Lex's manager. Ben Robbins is a big-time producer from Palm Pictures. She introduces Ira, and while he charms with a stuttered appreciation of the outlook – a twinkling grid of lights stretching off to the horizon – she spots two young men at the dark end of the verandah. Dressed in downbeat jeans, one guy with his back to her, they are huddled over intimate talk.

The two groups remain apart until the serving of food at the couches. 'That's Jessie,' says Ariel, as the two men depart, one offering a shy wave. 'He's an actor. They're rehearsing a scene.'

Ruth's mind ticks – the other guy is Lex Garland. The reason she and Ira sped through peak hour after work.

'For a movie?' asks Ira.

'A TV thing.'

'*The Young And The Restless*,' drawls Irene.

It's dark; a lone star in the sky pushing its shine through the smog. Ira, at a table loaded with sushi and sashimi and steaming bowls of broth – kitchen staff on hand with drinks, pleased to be in the company of a legendary actor's agent – asks her with a gallant formality how she met Lex.

Ariel and Ben have heard the story before. Irene, patting down her strands of wiry, grey-streaked, black hair, licks sticky rice from one of her fingers to free her waving hands – she had been an actress in a few early seventies experimental films – in preparation of telling the story one more time.

'In the summer of 1960 at Hollywood High, I met a girl called Yolanda Heath. She was a beatnik chick and I was the new girl, and she took me under her wing. The early sixties go by – I won't go into that.' She swats a number of joyous, adventurous years away like flies. 'And one night on Santa Monica, outside the Whisky A Go Go – Jim Morrison was a friend of ours, by the way, from film-school days – Yolanda and her boyfriend, Harrison, who was, still *is*, a gorgeous hippie carpenter, drove off to a commune in New Mexico.'

'Fascinating,' whispers Ira, catching Ariel with a smile.

'It was,' says Irene, with a dip of her eyelids. 'She was pregnant with Lex.'

'Two years later came the child of myth, Ariel, born on a leaky yacht circumnavigating South America. I'd get the most wonderful letters and cards from her mother. Then came the Oregon farm where they settled, and our letters almost tapered off. I was in the same apartment I'd been in forever, doing what I was doing, managing people.

'It was the mid-eighties' – a dismissive sniff – 'I got a call. She was back in LA, the city completely changed, and with her was her teenage son who had acting dreams.'

Creeping in, in comic tiptoe-style, Lex has slipped down beside his sister on a couch. And as his manager continues to narrate their first meeting, Ruth appraises the famous actor sitting opposite her.

It is as if a camera is trained on him and he gives as little as possible, knowing it will expand and explode on the screen. The delicate twist of a smile in recognition of a truth, the slow turn of his eyes in wonder. He is offscreen what he is on. She is formulating this, and his cute teenage-boy face that hadn't undergone the disaster of late puberty, the centre-parted dyed black hair touching the base of his swan neck, when he catches her with a look, and instead of a gotcha grin, he responds with a silly smile, as Irene reaches his breakthrough performance in *8 Monkeys On Mars*.

'Just ten minutes' screen time. It's all the boy needed.'

'It wasn't a first-rate movie,' adds Ben. A stick of a man with side patches of black hair on a bald head. Wearing a dark suit and a white open-collared shirt, he has the appearance and smooth assurance of a hip Christian minister. 'In the future I think the film will only be remembered for being Lex's first role.'

'We've come a long way.' She gazes at her star client affectionately. He strokes the tufts of his goatee. 'So tell us, Ben, what's Carlos saying?'

'Casting is done. You know we had options on Rachel.'

'Who have they got? Please don't tell me . . .'

'Laura Dern.'

'Oh, she's cool,' says Ariel. 'We know her.'

'The script is finished. Shooting starts in Baltimore in six weeks. Locations are being scoped as we sit here enjoying your hospitality. Finance good. We're very solid at Palm Pictures. A premiere at Cannes?' An eyebrow lifts. 'I guess that leaves the soundtrack.'

'And what's Carlos saying about that?'

Ben lets the movie star have his moment.

'He liked the songs I played him.'

'What did he say?' teases Ariel. 'Oh, come on, shy boy, tell them.'

A flash transformation. Lex's face muscles rearrange and settle on a new mask. '*It's az if de script and de songs were written by ze same person, no?'* To as quickly vanish back inside himself. A breezy shrug. 'Somethin' like that.'

'What did you play him?' asks Ruth, above the dying laughter.

'I've got them here.' He fumbles to extract a cassette from his shirt pocket. He hands it to her. 'We've made copies. But that's the original.'

Turning the clear plastic case in her fingers, Ruth could be examining an excavated vase fragment from an Egyptian crypt. Removing the tape carefully from its case, the words 'The Hoodoo Gurus' are visible in faint pencil on a thin strip of paper between the two spooling reels.

'They're very good,' says Irene. 'I like them a lot.'

'A touch of the sixties to them, but heavier,' nods Lex.

'That's not the music, though,' says Ariel, leaning into her brother.

'No, another film, perhaps.' He grins. 'One with more action and speed. Some go-go girls too.'

Noticing Ruth's confusion, Irene says, 'It's on the other side, babe.'

Ruth has been carrying an odd feeling since meeting Ben. She had not been told he'd be present. Since then, the night has been moving in a strange way; nothing she can put a finger on, an unease she's learnt to detect. Warners were wont to send her and Ira into meetings where people who shouldn't know more than they did, *did*. Leaving her and him to follow a trail of assumptions that the others weren't on. The lights of the city, the food and wine, a gentle nudge to let go and surrender. She turns the cassette over. It's blank.

Ariel starts to speak. Irene comes in over her. 'We don't know who the artist is.'

'But Carlos is still wanting these songs to be in the film.' She allows a hint of incredulity to shade her voice.

'Yes, he is,' says Ben.

'So how did you find it?' Ruth asks Lex, cheerful and patient. Indulging a movie star whim.

'I found it,' says Ariel, pointing to herself.

'Oh, sorry, I didn't know.'

She waves it off.

'Lex and I had Australian friends when we were growing up.'

'Fiona and Scott,' giggles the actor. 'Their parents were crazy.'

'I always wanted to go and so did he.' She looks at her brother, imagining the shared adventure. 'And earlier this year I went, and after seeing some of the places in the tourist books, I found this really sweet little beach community that no-one's heard of called Byron Bay.'

'I know it,' says Ira, proudly. 'A surfing buddy of mine went there. He said incredible waves?'

'Incredible everything! Have you ever been to Hawaii?'

'Once, to Honolulu with my folks when I was ten. I know it doesn't count. You mean somewhere . . . untouched and exotic.'

'I said to Lex it was like a farm village by the sea. Here,' she pouts, 'there'd be fucking malls and highways running through it. Anyway, I was there for two weeks and towards the end I meet these two New Zealand girls. Sticks and Stones,' she smirks, 'I know. And they invited me to a party. There was a fire and guitars and everyone's smoking dope . . . and I was talking about the LA music scene to someone, or a group of people, when this guy stepped around the fire and handed me a cassette. He had long dirty blond hair and a beard and he didn't say a word and walked off. I must have put it in my coat and forgotten about it, and it was at the bottom of my suitcase when I got home.'

'Such a lucky thing,' says Lex. 'It was only later . . .'

'We were driving up to visit our folks at the farm. We do it every May if Lex is free. I'd packed some tapes and CDs for the trip. We'd listened to just about everything and then put on the Hoodoo Gurus and liked them, bopping along.' She bounces, swinging her arms in time. 'And then I flipped it over and . . . here we are, folks.'

'We were just out of Anaheim on Interstate 5 when it came on.'

'We'd both read the script,' says the sister.

'And it was about the fourth song . . .'

'Third for me.'

'Really?'

Yeah, she smiles.

'Okay, and I said, "You know what . . . we're listening to the soundtrack of our goddam movie."'

'It must have been quite an experience,' says Ruth dryly.

'I could hear how certain songs connected to certain scenes, like they were pieces in a puzzle.' He looks down despondently. 'I've never been happy with the music in any of my films. They've messed it up.'

'It is a delicate process,' admits Ruth. 'The soundtrack can't overwhelm the action, while still needing to help the narrative move along.'

Ben chimes in. 'The number of times I've seen the right song save a director's ass.'

'So what's the sound of the music on the tape?' asks Ira.

'Oh,' says Ariel, caught off guard. 'There's two of them singing and they alternate songs.'

'Kind of weird,' cuts in Lex. 'The guy singing the drifty, poetic lyrics has the straight tunes. While the one with the more straightforward lyrics has the stranger tunes.'

'And their sound?'

'Soft compared to a lot of other things,' says Ariel. 'It's not Jane's Addiction.'

'Who is?' chuckles Ira.

'It's its own thing,' says Lex. 'A kind of seventies folk-rock sound. Acoustic guitars. Some pedal steel. Some light drums and bass. It's pretty sparse and so the lyrics and the melodies cut through, shine through like diamonds,' he whispers intently, 'or some poetic thing like that.'

'Sounds like classic singer-songwriter to me,' mulls Ruth. 'I'm just wondering . . . at Warners we've got a lot of this in our catalogue. It may be the originals of what these guys are going for. Let me explain.' She's quick enough to catch Ben's smirk. 'If a client comes to us and asks for something like Joni Mitchell. We've *got* Joni's publishing. Crosby, Stills, Nash and Young? You want "Teach Your Children", we can license it to you. I'm just saying this so you know, *and* it may be cheaper. Who knows what *these* guys want for their songs? They, and their manager, may think' – she adopts a deep, lunkheaded voice – '"*Hey, big Hollywood movie*," and ask a fortune.'

'They wouldn't be like that,' says Ariel, tenderly.

'I'm not saying they are,' concedes Ruth. 'But when they hear that . . . you know, what's at stake. Well . . .'

Ben clinks the ice in his soda and lime. He'd thought the same – soundtrack the movie with classic songs. But with film director and leading man seeing eye to eye, he'd learnt: don't rock that boat.

It's colder on the porch; the nights can still hold a chill in early June. Lex has drawn his legs up to his chest. Irene is pissed off. She asked for someone young to be sent over from Warners, open to exploring, not closing down, Lex's and Ariel's ideas.

'You're doing your job and I appreciate that,' says Lex. 'We're all cogs in the machine. I get it. It's a shame you haven't read the script. Can we get them one, Ben?'

'Not yet. When shooting's underway.'

'Let me tell you this.' In the soft evening light, candles burning, tiger-striped shadows flickering across his face, Lex is shifting again. The role he is preparing, with the publishers pinned to their seats, is the narrator. A newsreader type, able to entwine storytelling with the pearl thread of confession.

'The film's called *Hearing Voices*. It's about an author in his late twenties, who wrote a bestseller when he was young. His second book bombed and he's now living in a house just outside of Baltimore, writing short stories. His agent is pushing him to write a big novel like his debut. There's a love story, some family trouble, and all the while there are ghosts in the house, people you see on the screen who he knew or knows, who sit down and talk to him about his past.

'You've got to understand, this is a different kind of role for me – that's why the music is so important. I'm like Jules King, this author. There's a lot of pressure on me to do what I've done before. The songs have my back. The lyrics are like messages I'm getting that feel true and meaningful to the character. They can't be famous songs, because that would ruin it. "Teach Your Children" – cool song, but it doesn't fit the movie. They have to be floating in . . . like the ghosts and the stories forming in Jules's head.'

His face relaxes, giving way; he brings his glass to his mouth. 'And . . . we haven't told you this yet.' He looks gorgeous, the candlelight sharpening his hollow cheekbones. 'We were listening to the tape for the first time, both minds blown when the last song came on.' His face tingles with excitement, trying not to say what he has to say too quickly. 'It's called "Hearing Voices".

'We were screaming. Holy fuck! How weird and beautiful is that.' He turns to his sister, petals of tears rimming her flower-like eyes. 'When *that* came on . . .'

Lex or Jules? Ruth doesn't know if he knows who he is or is becoming. Perhaps this is where great actors go before taking on a role. It doesn't matter, anyway – eyes like heat lamps are on her. She's gripping the cassette so hard it could crack.

'And you can't guess who they are? Australian, probably.'

'They're not American,' says Lex.

'Their voices are kind of like what I heard when I was there.'

'Unknown voices from a far-off land,' says Ruth to Ariel to Lex to Irene to Ben to Ira and to herself. 'We've some got work to do.'

*

Ruth is snug in a booth by the window when the taxi pulls up. Ira gives her a quick wave as the driver inches into a parking spot before a line of businesses on an El Segundo backstreet. He muses as he gets out of the cab that if Jonathan Richman was to write a song about this place, it would be called something like 'Lonely Forgotten Little Suburban Shopping Centre'.

La Paz is a family-owned Mexican restaurant that Ruth frequents and where she enjoys bringing friends or business associates. On first appearance, it's a bit rough and tumble, no airs and graces, but as soon as the food arrives, any quibbles about 'atmosphere' melt away as easily as the cheese on the chicken and pinto bean quenelles – one of the house specialties.

'Thanks for coming over,' she says, as Ira slides in opposite her.

He's showered and happy to be out of work clothes and into black jeans, a seventies Hawaiian shirt and denim jacket. This is his second visit to the restaurant; the first was nine months ago, with Ruth and a bunch of people from work soon after he began at the company. He picks up the floppy plastic menu, noticing hers is to her side. Turning the pages he says softly to himself, 'What did I have last time?'

'The guacamole with nachos. And two pork quesadillas with beans and rice.' She pauses. 'But that's only a guess.'

He returns to the menu, knowing he must be quick.

A waiter in a worn t-shirt and jeans appears. He takes their order and asks about drinks.

'Another margarita, please,' she says sweetly.

Ira scrambles. 'Ah . . . iced water, thanks.'

'He'll have a Dos Equis with that.'

The waiter gone, he asks, 'What are we celebrating?'

'Dead-end street. Nothing so far.'

'I've spent the day listening to the tape,' says Ira, 'and you know what? We should be thankful – it could have been shit. An actor's idea of something cool. When, actually, it's very good.' He shrugs, grinning, 'Whoever they are.'

'*Wherever* they are.'

'"Easy Come, Easy Go" is a potential hit single. Tom Petty would kill for it. And "Thyme In The Garden", well . . . what can you say? Six minutes of bliss.'

'My favourite's "Born Again Eyes", the big ballad.'

'I think they were in rock bands. The way they play, they're not virtuosos. And they're not traditionalists either. There's an edge and a pop character to what they do.'

'The sound indicates a recording budget. It's not slick, but it's not cheap. So they must be established at some level.'

'Let's hope not *too* high a level.'

'I've been wondering,' says Ruth slyly. 'These songwriters – and I guess they'll have a manager, or maybe not; depends on what kind of profile they've got – are a little bit like a lost tribe. Whoever contacts them first gets them when they don't know anything.'

'That's true.' There's a bowl of purple corn chips on the table. He takes one; the salty crunch will set up the taste of his beer.

'And I want to be the person who gets to them first.'

'You'd go there?'

'To Melbourne. I've faxed the Warners publishing arm. I could work out of their office. They may know the songwriters, the band, if it is a band, and if they don't, they can ask around *discreetly*.'

'And Barry?'

'He'll be assuming the company songs are in the movie. That it's business as usual. Which gives us a couple of weeks to land the songs that are actually going to be *in* the movie.'

'Okay, earning Warners what?'

'Half a million. At least triple what they'd get from catalogue songs. The rock classics Lex doesn't want. And there would be a soundtrack album too. His last two films each grossed a hundred million dollars plus.'

'How much would you offer?'

The drinks arrive. Both gulp. The Dos Equis giving a delicious wash and clean to Ira's mouth. Ruth's margarita, her third, hitting the spot.

'Something fair, but low. Seventy grand?' Noting Ira's wince. 'The band might just be a hobby. They could have day jobs, wives, kids, mortgages . . .'

'Or . . . they may already have a publishing deal.'

'We'd buy them out.'

'Before they know what their songs are really worth,' notes Ira. 'I've been trying to picture what these guys are like. They don't seem mousy types to me. There's plenty of defiance and wit. They're not anthem writers either – it's more subtle, which could be why they're in obscurity.'

'They'll get a big career bump, if they want it. A major-label record deal on the back of the film, if it was handled properly.'

'Hmm.'

'And let's not only think of them. How about us? Where are we going? If we get this and present it to Barry, and Maggie and

Simon in catalogue acquisition, we *might* be where we should be. On the eighth floor, not sharing an office the size of this booth. And not being flung into meetings where we haven't been briefed. I'm tired of it. You still want to do A&R?'

'Yeah, sure. You can only get excited about Toto's "Africa" so many times.' She smiles at him, her eyes gentle and encouraging. 'Of course I'd like to sign bands.'

'Like who?'

'Howling Bell Tower. Strong songs. Great energy from DC *and* they're under thirty – let's not forget that. And you know, I really like Peggy Symonds. Again, songs, and I do believe she's got mainstream potential, and Warners should at least give her studio time for some demos, but . . .'

'Anita Jay?'

'They tell me old-school soul will never come back.'

'I love her!'

Ira opens his hands. A wistful sucking of his teeth.

'You should do it.'

His face burns. 'Let's change the subject. I'll hold the fort.'

'You'll have to keep Ariel and Irene happy.' She can't resist. 'I'm sure you can do that on your own.'

He mouths it, while rattling his beer for its last drop. *Fuck you.*

*

At lunch, Ruth had met Nathanael McPherson. Her side of the family had not been close to his; a pair of feuding uncles meant she only saw her second cousin at birthdays and Christmases in the years when the uncles declared peace and were talking. Nathanael had moved to LA from Tucson in the mid-eighties, eager to find a successful rock band and become their guitarist. A year ago, and rechristened Charlie Zero, he'd joined a hardcore group who did international tours, called High Risk.

Tall and square-jawed good looking – his side of the family contrasting with the tiny, intense O'Connors – he could have been groomed to fit any kind of rock group. He'd arrived at the Rainbow Room on Sunset in a leather jacket and a short hacked haircut – the bar, his idea of a gag.

Ruth knew its reputation. Trading on its early-seventies glory days, it was now a home to saggy-eyed major label A&R dudes, convinced the next big thing in rawk'n'roll would be playing two blocks away from their trashy apartments. Ira would have puked if he'd known she was there.

They had swapped stories over drinks, burgers and fries – their domestic situations: she's dating a nurse, he's hanging loose like Iggy. Then moved onto around-town music gossip, Ruth delivering the corporate view about large amounts of money to be made in movie soundtracks, telling him his band should consider such work – low-budget films, admittedly, but there is cash and exposure. Charlie covers the street, the cool indie label he's on and his adventures out on the road.

They *have* toured Australia, actually; just a few months back. It was a blitz, twelve shows in eight days. He told her she's lucky to be going to Melbourne – a good place to check out acts and more of a music town than Sydney – although all of Australia is, he drawled, a blast.

Contacts? He doesn't know anyone in publicity or management. But he can recommend one person. A hardworking guy they worked with, and would have loved to bring back to the States. A cool guy. A roadie with a heart of gold.

CHAPTER 3

'Imagine you could be in one sixties Australian band . . .?'

'The Masters Apprentices. I'd be Jim Keays. And they're from Adelaide. I love that.'

'Good choice.'

'You?'

Drew is tempted to say The Seekers. Very him: some truth, some fun. 'The Easybeats, I suppose.'

'Who would you be?'

'It would have to be Stevie.' He begins to tap a frantic two-beat rhythm on the steering wheel. 'Imagine George Young and Harry Vanda coming to me with "Friday On My Mind". *Tap. Tap.* He carries a fragment of the 1966 London conversation in his head. *Here, Stevie, sing your heart out on this.*'

'Do you think we should go to London?'

'Umm . . . it's not the sixties anymore.'

'We could make it work.'

'We'd have to stay, though. Not flitter in for a week, see Soho and then piss off. It's not really our scene. It's Manchester now with The Stone Roses.'

'We bring the scene with us. We make the scene. Get a residency in a pub and word gets out, just like it did in Sydney. Stars start dropping in to check us out . . .'

'Jagger, Julie Christie . . .'

'And we're earning a thousand pounds a week, cash in hand.'

'We could do that.'

They've navigated the tight turns down the mountain and, with a flat ribbon of road ahead, the Corolla is getting its first test of speed as the songwriters settle in for a night of highway driving. The car feels good. Good old Andy.

After Lismore, it's Casino; no time to find Mick's old home, just his jutting finger pointing out a succession of historically significant landmarks along the town's dark main street. The department store where he'd bought his first single, Freda Payne's 'Band Of Gold'. The milk bar Kim had worked at on weekends, slipping him delicious, tummy-expanding milkshakes. And at the edge of town on a sharp corner, a sign on a squat, two-storey, red-brick building reads 'J.C. Hovis & Co'.

'My mum worked there.'

Mick can't bring himself to say more. It was 2 August 1971. A lorry at highway speed collecting his mother's tin-can Suzuki as she pulled out from a day's work to drive home.

He was in grade seven. Somehow Drew knows that. Not the location or the details of the crash. What he remembers is a melancholy and a hard-to-put-your-finger-on sense of loss he heard when Mick played him his first songs in a one-bedroom flat in Surry Hills.

It was 1987, Mick and Delilah were back from their Berlin honeymoon, and the songwriters had just hooked up. It was *there*, buried in the lyrics, a distress code, and it surprised Drew. He was expecting something new from Mick, but rooted in his past style; horror tales of knives and blood and the Bible, not the switch to a heartbreaking personal touch.

And as they etched their backgrounds to each other over the proceeding months – a process always involving heavy editing – Mick spoke of a father, rarely of a mother. Since then, Drew had made the link, helped by the penny drop of each piece of the past Mick let slip, intentionally or not. Perhaps that was why Drew occasionally offered to write lyrics to Mick's tunes. To part the curtains and invite the light.

If Mick was ever going to talk, this would have been the moment. A highway moment. Drew's eyes on the road, not searching his partner's face for pain or tears.

But Mick resolutely stays on the lighter stuff as they pull away from the first eleven years of his life; Drew able to prod the childhood reminiscing, whenever the story pond threatens to run dry. Mick's baritone drawl is a storyteller's dream, and puffing cigarettes with a foot up on the glovebox, he takes some pleasure in entertaining his friend. Mick, also recognising prods, tailoring the tales to those he knows will elicit the most laughter or interest from his songwriting partner: the quaint-sounding family names – his uncle 'King' Ledbridge – and small-town hijinks at bush dances.

He's been sneaking more of this into his songs; it's good subject matter and a point of difference from the quirky urban anxieties and relationship dramas of his bandmate's material. Mick's other kick – one that he can't quite explain, but which underpins much of what he says to Drew – is recalling those summer afternoons with neighbourhood kids that seemed like they'd never end – that darkness would never come and engulf their running games. His mother's voice ringing over the fences and yards like a siren, calling him in for dinner. The four of them bunched around the table. For him to stagger off to bed, a kiss and hug from Mum and Dad, and surrender to a sleep deeper than he would know for the rest of his life.

Eventually, the stories peter out and the songwriters feel the chill of the vast darkness around them. This would *not* be a place to break down. No streetlights, and no idea of what creeps, crawls or breathes, animal, human or alien, metres from the single-lane road.

Drew, fighting tiredness, lets his mind drift to 'Songwriters On The Run'; that's what he'll call Mick's new tune. He'd considered starting the song's three verses – for that's how many there will be, he reckons – at the Durango Bar, even name-checking Tom, but now thinks better of it. To start at the jailbreak is punchier.

They both broke out of jail, and walked quickly to the nearest hill. That's the truth. Where they . . . saw . . . remembered . . . stumbled over . . . *Where they looked back upon the scale, of what they'd done to get to the hill.* He's getting tingles; it's like a quirky newspaper report.

Now a change of tone is needed to fit the melody change of the coming chorus. If the song is about songwriters, he has to bring in songs – to emphasise that they were the one thing in their possession as they fled – the uncut diamonds bouncing in their pockets. It could be the song's theme. They had their songs to play or packed away? Both. *And they had their songs packed away, no time to waste or lose / And they had their songs to play.*

Second verse? He has to jump the action and he's beginning to wonder if he can store all these lines in his head. He needs pen and paper. What happened next? *A ute picked them up*, no . . . *A hero answering to Dan said*, no . . . *The police*, no . . . *They made it to the nearest town, and found an empty house there to hide.* That's good. And then they . . .?

'Lights ahead,' grunts Mick.

*

They order the bucket. With a long night of driving ahead, they'd decided to eat in store and keep the crispy chicken leftovers to dip into when out on the road. They'd considered the family-box deal and nixed it. Drew calling to Mick, as he went to the counter, not to forget the large tub of mashed potato with pepper gravy.

'This is good KFC,' says Mick, elbows on the table, licking his greasy lips. His bull nose over the bucket. 'We've got a good batch.'

'It can vary,' admits Drew, elegantly spooning the mash into his mouth, the zap and tang of the gravy sending him straight back to Brisbane, September 1978.

'There was a Kentucky Fried, probably one of the first in Brisbane, just near Indooroopilly Shopping Town. It's how I got into it.' Drew's aware he's sounding like a recovering drug addict. 'Toy Crime used to have band meetings there.' He drifts off, his spoon, a time-bending wand, dangling in his fingers. 'It's hard to explain how good and different the chicken tasted to what was on offer. The eleven herbs and spices really went over well.' He bows his head, sucking the last Coke from the dice-sized ice cubes at the bottom of his cup. 'It revolutionised Brisbane cuisine.'

'What was the town like during punk?'

'It was fantastic. A golden two years. We always say it, don't we? The first two years of a band's life are always the best. And they were.'

They're alone in the dining-room. Mick is listening.

'Maybe 500 people going to gigs. Brisbane was share-house paradise. Most bands rehearsed at home – practice rooms were for the straight bands. Gigs were in houses too. There weren't that many places to play, not like Sydney or Melbourne.'

'Do you mind?' Mick points to the last drumstick. 'You can have the rest.'

'We did lounge-room gigs . . . until the cops arrived and broke them up. But it couldn't last. That's why it was so beautiful.'

'I've never got Brisbane.'

'It's in the suburbs. Forget the city.'

Mick snorts.

'That's why tourists walk around baffled. *Where is everything?* The girl that picked us up is from Bardon. It's gorgeous, a green jungle with houses. You'd never want to leave; I mean, there are some suburbs that are so ugly, I can only go through them blindfolded.' Mick is laughing. 'Which is difficult, because I'm driving.'

'And the chicken's taking you back. I can see it in your eyes and around your mouth.'

'You can't go back,' says Drew, full and satisfied, 'but the herbs and spices remain.'

The next run of towns, with their high-set churches and castle-like pubs, dot a favoured stretch of the New England Highway that the songwriters have covered often. The last time a week ago in Gary's car, on their way to Brisbane to pick up Swifty. He'd just finished a Cruel Sea tour; to start with them and head north. Everyone was on the merry-go-round.

With Mick at the wheel, they roll through Glen Innes and Armidale, turning west two hours later at Tamworth. The songwriters begin to reminisce. A disastrous early show at the Tamworth Music Festival in '88, the country-and-western fans not taking to two dusty rock and rollers in cowboy shirts and gritty jeans, playing songs that didn't fit the strict three-chord formula. A John Prine cover falling flat. And they were surly – too few homespun stories and smiles between songs.

Back at the motor inn after the show, spread out on twin beds, with Bingo and pizza boxes and beers and two grams of Kings Cross cocaine, there were jokes and the manager's bug-eyed conviction that an audience was waiting for them in inner-city pubs.

Heading west to avoid Sydney, there's little traffic past midnight. Trucks mostly – eight-eyed monsters barrelling down the pencil-thin, two-lane highway, giving the Corolla a violent shake as they pass. And having driven through Dubbo near dawn, the sun is coming up as they approach Parkes.

'We'll park in Parkes,' Drew had announced, looking up from a scrum of maps on Russell's kitchen table.

They spot two long transport trucks stacked end to end at a roadside rest stop lined with trees. Squeezing and parking their car behind the monsters, the musicians sleep soundly in their seats through the day, shielded as they always need to be from the passing daytime world.

*

Ruth had wheeled her suitcase into her hotel room, kicked off her shoes, come out of the bathroom, to fall in a fainting motion onto her back on the bed. A heavy blow of breath, she closes her eyes to open them again, afraid she will doze off to sleep. With a determined grunt, she swings herself to the telephone and dials the number.

'What do ya want?'

It's not a question – it's a slap to the face. And people thought Americans were rude.

'My name is Ruth O' Connor and I'm looking for a friend of mine called Swifty.' She stays polite. 'This is the number I've been given.'

Her reward is a thud of the telephone being dropped onto a table. Then footsteps. The terrifying sound of dead air. Sitting on the edge of the bed, she distracts herself by nervously studying the pattern of the carpet. Fluff the cleaner missed. Specks of lint. The fibres in the grooves.

'Hello?'

'Swifty?'

'It's Carl.'

'Who . . .?'

'He's not here.'

'What?'

'I took his room.'

'Oh.'

'He'd been gone a month when I moved my stuff in.'

'Do you know where's he's gone to, Carl?'

'It's just Bones and me here and we don't get out much.'

'I understand. Is there anyone who might know where he is? A friend or . . . an acquaintance? Anyone, really.'

'Don't think so.'

'It's important, I've just arrived from Los Angeles this morning and he's the only person I know in the city. He's the one who was going to show me around.'

'I could try and trace a girl who's a friend of a guy called Jack . . . no, Jake. He might know.'

'Can I give you my number, and if you find out anything from the girl or Jake, give me a call. I'll be here in my room.'

'Sounds reasonable. Tell me your number and I'll memorise it.'

'I'm happy for you to get a pen and paper. Take your time.' Even if she'd wanted to, she can't keep the desperation from her voice. 'I'd really like you to have my phone number.'

'Hang on, Ruth.'

The phone is placed down gently.

*

At a truck stop an hour past Parkes, a flyscreen door opens onto long glass display cases containing the leftovers of the day's bakery goods. Mick considers the last lamington. He's known to wolf six in a sitting. They order breakfast as the sun is going down, a few of the other customers, beefy blokes in singlets or stained jumpers, munching bacon, eggs, fried tomato and wedges of toast – fuel for a night's driving.

Spotting a spare table by the front window, the musicians amble over, Drew picking up a worn copy of a local newspaper: *Post Office Painted*, the front-page headline. They have come to appreciate these kinds of places. Swifty can recite a list of them from Adelaide to Cairns. They are vibing on the room's soft yellow light and the still beauty of the petrol pumps outside, waiting for their meals, when Mick says he'll call their roadie.

With Mick in the phone booth, Drew approaches the young waitress. A country girl used to dealing with blokes passing through, she's not fazed by the pouty, scruffy-haired, skinny guy asking daintily if she has a pen he can borrow.

She hands over a biro from the till.

'And . . .' his hand on hip, 'do you happen to have a scrap of paper or a spare napkin I could use?'

'By the salt and pepper and tomato sauce, darl.'

Back at the table, Drew scribbles down the three verses to 'Songwriters On The Run'. Folding the napkins in half, he slides them into his jacket pocket with satisfaction. Songwriting on the run.

'Is that you?'

'Mick, where are ya?'

'Nearby. Drew reckons we'll be there by nine tomorrow morning.'

'Hey, sorry, but you can't stay here. I should have told you. The cops have been around again and everyone in the house is pretty edgy.'

'No problem, baby, it's already been taken care of. You know us, Swifty, *always* thinking of the future.' The roadie cackles. 'Any news?'

'I went around again today. His office and apartment were locked. No word around town, although I did hear that Simone is in Adelaide. What do you think of that?'

'He's gotten her out of the way. The thing is, have the cops got onto him? We don't know.'

'You got a car up the mountain?'

'We did.' Mick coughs a dry laugh. 'Had to sell the guitars for it.'

'Aw no. The Martin and the Gibson.'

'That's us. Got peanuts for them too.'

'You've got to get them back.'

'Oh yeah, I'll just turn around and drive back to Mount Drake, won't I? We're *here* – that's what matters.'

'Yeah, but how are you going to write songs in the future?'

'We'll phone you when we get there. Can't wait for Melbourne, man.'

*

Drew called it 'The Dark Lady' in his younger, joking days. He was a sunshine boy ripe for corruption when Toy Crime made their first trips south in 1980. It was a glittering tram grid, often under cloud or rain, glimpsed on the way to sound-checks and gigs. A hint of what Vienna or Budapest would be like, he fancifully thought.

He'd played some of his best shows in Collingwood clubs and city pubs. You had to. The sharp-tongued denizens of the post-punk scene, some of his new flamboyant friends, would pull you down if you did anything less. It wasn't Brisbane, where you played in the clothes you put on in the morning, and any kind of showmanship outside of pulling an agonised face on a difficult guitar chord was regarded as a sell-out. Drew, moving through the eighties with his new band The Shells, ever more outlandish in his op-shop finery and fey hetero manner, had grown to love Melbourne.

For Mick, the city wasn't the jump it was for Drew. While The Shells chased pop dreams, assessing every gig for its career exposure, Mick and his underground groups conducted guerrilla raids down from Surry Hills, content to play graffiti-infested clubs and pubs. For a time, virtually every musician he knew in the city had a gorgeous girlfriend and a heroin habit – some cutting to the chase, acquiring druggy girlfriends.

From this scene, a few climbed out of the muddy trenches and made a dash for freedom. Sophie Chabowski, dropping out of uni at nineteen, had cleaned up and re-enrolled. She was now a lawyer at Sutcliffe and Howard; one of the city's oldest law firms, with grand offices in Collins Street. She'd seemed to welcome Mick's call at work, while wondering what 'in trouble' meant. He and Drew could bunk a few nights at her apartment. The key was under the mat. The cat answered to Nico.

*

Propped up on three plush pillows, Ruth stares at her hotel telephone, daring it to ring. Ira would be waking in his Santa Monica apartment; she is staggering through the mind and body contortions of jet lag to reach midnight in her dark tenth-floor room. Her entertainment is the television at the end of the bed, and even though she's at the Hilton, incredibly it only has five stations. In LA, they have eighty, and by the time you flick through them in search of something to watch, a solid ten minutes has ticked by.

'How are you? What's Melbourne like?' Ira bursts down the line.

'Ah . . . good.' She smiles, feasting on his energy. 'It's freezing outside.'

'But you're in Australia,' a tickle of laughter, 'a land Down Under.'

'I'm *way* down under. Think of New York in November. Windy too.'

'You arrived this morning and you've just been in the hotel?'

'That would have been sensible. No, I went into Warners this afternoon.'

'Cool. I didn't want to ask.'

'Nice offices. I played them the tape; first, to two people in publishing. Three songs in was all it took.'

'Hey!'

'For them to say they didn't know the band or the artist.'

'Uh.'

'I then managed to grab the head guy of A&R. His name is Jeremy Crowther. He's English. From Virgin Records in London and been in Melbourne six months. He doesn't know the local scene too well. He listened to the first two songs, "Lorraine It's Me" and "Born Again Eyes", and then he played me a few demo songs from a Sydney band he's thinking of signing, wondering if we had a match. It wasn't them. They were too slick and rocky. Not our guys.'

'Damn. What was the band's name?'

'Circle Boxx.'

'That has to be one of the worst band names I have ever heard.'

'Two xx's on box.'

'Of course. What did Jeremy and the people in publishing make of you?'

'Umm, what did they make of me? An intense, attractive woman unafraid to ask questions.'

'What I mean is . . .'

'I'd phoned them from LA. Fine. I told them a client was interested in the music. And I had other business too.'

'This isn't good. I thought someone in there would know. The Australian scene can't be *that* big.'

'I'll go back in tomorrow. I'll be brighter and feel it out more. How are things with you?'

'I'm hanging in there. Howling Bell Tower are in town and I went and saw them play last night. Oh, man, they were great – a couple new songs – and it really got me thinking what we were talking about the other night. We were chatting after the show and they're starting to get fazed – no-one's made them an offer. I'd love to sign them.'

'I'd love you to sign them too.'

'Otherwise, Irene hasn't called, so I'm assuming her and Palm Pictures are happy. They're like Warners – the bigger the corporation, the bigger the belief that everything will take care of itself.

They live in a *golden* haze. I'm glad you're down there. This would *not* have taken care of itself.'

'Oh thanks, I wasn't sure.'

'It's the right thing.'

'It was spontaneous.'

'Anything you want, let me know.'

'I will.'

'I'll let you go. You sound tired.'

'I am.' She yawns. 'Living the day that hasn't yet happened in LA is exhausting.'

*

After the songwriters' long, first-night sprint to Parkes, the second night is a leisurely roll down the Hume Highway into Melbourne. Arriving on the tail-end of rush hour, the pulse and vastness of the city is comforting. Bingo is somewhere here, they can feel it. Although that wasn't so clear in Childers or Flats Crossing; inching down Smith Street under a dark hang of clouds, passing one side street after another packed with brick-box houses, a person, scared, and with something to hide, would feel a sense of protection in the crowded maze.

Drew suggests a stop for coffee and cake in Lygon Street, a sugar hit of the city – to relax in a dark cafe with pastries in the window and Italian spoken at the counter. But Mick wants to push on to the wide tree-lined streets of East Melbourne, where Sophie lives in a third-floor apartment within walking distance to her office in the centre of town.

She's left breakfast – toast, Vegemite and peanut butter – and instructions for the stovetop coffee machine. Mick and Drew are aware their dirty appearance and criminal status are at odds with the neat array of kitchen appliances on hooks and racks, and the fifties formica table and four-chair set that Sophie had 'rescued' from her parents' Sorrento beach house.

'He may be staying with his mum and dad,' suggests Drew. 'They wouldn't know anything. He's hardly going to say, "I've lobbed Mick and Drew in jail and they're out and after me."'

Mick's face – gaunt handsome with stubble after four nights on the run – is impassive. Drew pushes on, needing a reaction, 'We can't door-knock Toorak.'

'He won't want them to know,' agrees Mick, crunching his fifth slice of toast. 'His mum would kill him.'

Occasionally, at one of their classier shows, a sit-down venue with a decent bar, Bingo would bring his parents backstage. The boys would flick to best behaviour, amusing and serious to their manager's delight. The father is in his mid-fifties, possessing the vitality and tan of someone who's cracked the balance between the demands of his architecture company and the tennis court. The mother is taller than her husband, a brittle beauty, her blonde hair worn high in a French bun, imperious as she walks the wards of the city's hospitals where she works as a surgeon.

They would enjoy a drink and a jokey chat before the gig, comfortable in the company of the musicians and their son's show-business ambitions. At the door she'd turn for a final glance, a coat of ice to her farewell; she'd figured Mick and Drew. *Moochers.*

Strolling into the Tote hotel, a fifteen-minute drive from Sophie's apartment, the smell of booze and booze-stained carpet reaching their nostrils, it occurs to the songwriters: a week ago they were chatting with Tom at the Durango Bar in Rocky, Swifty loading in their equipment. *And there he is*, tucked into a corduroy coat two sizes too big, ginger hair, sundial face, two vacant stools at his side, laughing with the barman – no doubt a muso – a Stoli and orange and a beer waiting on the bar.

There are hugs, an appreciation of Mick's brown suit, and a quick round-up of the town's rock gossip.

'The Big Day Out is coming,' chirps Swifty, rubbing his hands in child-like glee.

'What's that – a picnic?' asks Drew.

'That's funny. Can I tell people you said that?'

'Go ahead.'

'Vivian and Ken are organising a new festival with an insane line-up. The Beasts are playing. The Cosmic Psychos. Clouds. I'm roadie-ing for my old friends the Violent Femmes. They're headlining.'

'When is it?'

'Probably January.'

The songwriters nod. That's a long way away.

'Does anyone know about us?' asks Drew, glancing at the pub door. 'Has anyone said anything?'

'If it had been Sydney or Brisbane.' The roadie smiles, a sip of beer. 'But it's Rocky – you're lucky.'

'What did your friends say when you got back?' asks Mick.

'"Hi, Swifty,"' he grins, touching Mick's knee. 'I've come back from tours early before. It's the police you've got to worry about. The jailbreak has pushed it up a couple of notches.'

'Correctional facility,' corrects Mick. 'But you're right.'

'And Bingo?' asks Drew.

'I've been telling Mick, not a squeak.'

Mick and Drew look at each other. It's time for one of them to be brilliant.

'I was talking to Jason from Honeycrunch yesterday,' announces Swifty.

Groans.

'I know you think they're a shit band with no songs. You can be a bit tough on other musicians, you know.'

Mick bites his tongue.

'I think their next EP is really going to change things for them.'

'Jason's a sweet guy,' says Drew. 'We like him. Please go on.'

Eyeing them both, a rare victory had. 'Jason says his girlfriend, Tilda, was at a party in Prahran and some people were talking about your bust. They thought it happened in Cairns and that the cops beat the shit out of you.' He giggles, the songwriters not so much. 'Anyway, Bingo's name came up, and someone said they think he's staying at Bob Burtell's place or was seen there.'

Blank looks.

'He's promoted some of your shows. A round-shaped guy. From Sydney. Does coke.' Still nothing. 'You'd know him if you saw him.'

'Oh yeah,' says Drew airily.

Mick is more direct. 'Where does he live?'

*

He orders a XXXX. A sip of the sour, bitter beer shaking any fogginess out of the mind of Detective Brian Bishop. His overnight bag checked in, boarding pass on the counter, he is standing at a bar at Brisbane domestic airport.

Another sip, and he remembers six months in a workers' cottage in Milton, not far from the high brick walls and pumping chimneys of the brewery. The tangy smell of hops coming through the open window of the bedroom he shared with the woman he was going out with at the time.

Abigail, who worked in Driving Licence Renewal at the Department of Main Roads in Spring Hill. They met through a group of young people, pretty fresh out of high school, working in government and the police force. In early-eighties Brisbane, that was a tight circle.

A person who passed through the house that summer was Harry Coote. Harry was lean and handsome, a TV star's face shaped to a pointy chin, waves of sandy hair coming back from a broad forehead. He and Harry were a double act in Special Branch. The odd couple up for promotion, with other cops gravitating to their spirit and games. Harry was smooth and funny and a devil with the women.

Brian was the short sidekick: laconic and calculating, the silent savour of Harry's arse on a number of occasions. Affairs with officers' wives, dumb stuff with the drug squad. Favours flew back and forward between them, even when they were stationed apart. There'd been chatter over the last days.

Bishop had heard the songwriters had made it to Childers. A kid on a school bus had told his mum of two strange men with bags and guitars. And when Harry called late yesterday afternoon to say a speed dealer they'd busted – speed dealers *always* talk – spoke of a Brisbane girl who'd driven to Childers to pick up two musicians and take them across the border, he knew where Woods and Lovelock were heading. He'd booked the first flight out of Rocky, to make his connection.

Meeting at a coffee shop outside the airport, Harry told him they were zeroing in on the girl. She's part of the Brisbane music scene. Maybe she knows Drew Lovelock – he's a local boy. Harry promised to pass on the girl's name in the next days.

Would all passengers on Qantas Flight 932 to Melbourne please make your way to Gate 23.

He picks up his boarding pass, leaving half a glass of beer.

*

They are driving down Punt Road in the rain. Listening to RRR. Swifty at the wheel; if they get pulled over, he'll produce the licence.

A familiar sound and melody drifts through the car. The intro to 'Dark Room Moon' – a deep cut off *Vestiges*. Mick wrote it in the months after he and Delilah split up. He'd said yes to another tour without consulting her, and there was more. Suspicions he'd been fooling around on the road. Mysterious postcards arriving from Spain.

She was wanting stability in their Sydney lives; to push her career in fashion design and start the discussion on having kids. He was fine with the first, unenthusiastic about the second. She'd told him by phone. He and Drew were in Linz, Austria, a country they toured often. Her decision hit him hard – he hadn't seen it coming. He thought they were soulmates. She did too. That's why she'd left.

And so it comes to this
Me chewing on an old kiss
Every day is dawning too soon
As I sit in my dark room moon

'I met an American woman yesterday,' says Swifty. The rain easing, a thin line of blue sky under a deck of threatening cloud on the horizon.

'Uh-huh,' grunts Drew, knowing this is not the moment to talk.

'She knows High Risk.'

Drew has no idea what he's talking about. His impulse is to crack, 'Don't we all, mate?' Better, though, to say nothing, hoping Swifty picks up the hint.

'She's the second cousin of Charlie, the lead guitarist. And she said – and you're going to love this – she thinks . . .'

'Swifty.'

'Ah, yeah, Mick?'

In a quiet voice, hinting at great hurt, menace and bewilderment, Mick points at the dashboard. 'We're *on* . . . the radio.'

'Oh, okay.'

It's a strange pleasure hearing yourself come over the airwaves, knowing people dotted around the city are picking up on your song and your pain. He really was laying himself bare with this one. He may have to wind some of the misery back from a few of the new numbers. Be universal, not personal. Do sneaky things like bring in characters, male or female, living in the present or past, to say and emote things you want to get across.

He's recasting a few lines in his head as the music fades, hearing Drew tell Swifty, as they zoom down Fitzroy Street past the old Seaview Ballroom, 'The Shells once did a crazy gig there with The Wreckery. A full house and full-on backstage debauchery that I unfortunately . . . whoa, slow down!' The car, then, makes a jolting left turn into the heart of St Kilda.

It's as if the city – proud and business-like along its long tree-lined boulevards – spits out a last suburb to reach the harbour. It wasn't always like this. At the turn of the century, crowds flocked to the beachfront and pier on weekends: women swung parasols, men tipped boaters to passing promenaders, whilst wide-eyed families stopped for lemonade and cake to count pennies and talk the dare of a carousel ride at the amusement park.

By the early 1980s, when Mick and Drew first visited friends living in the dilapidated grand houses and Deco apartments back from the water, the promenaders were whippet-thin, track-suited desperadoes, hunting for heroin, avoiding eye contact with hipsters who strolled by in op-shop threads. The few families that remained rarely ventured out at night. What was once opulent, colourful and gay was now in a delicious state of ruin; appreciated by those with the eye to dig it and those too desperate to escape.

A minute later, parked in Robe Street, Swifty is put under instructions. He is to ascertain whether Bingo is inside Bob's apartment, and if he is, to excuse himself and come and tell Mick and Drew. They watch him cross the street, worried, given his accommodating nature, that their wait could be long. But five minutes haven't passed when the front door of the Art Deco block of flats springs open; the songwriters' affectionate mirth at the roadie's arm-swinging, splayed-footed waddle souring on the dismissive shake of his head.

Mick has another plan.

Tracey Hoffs, kindergarten teacher and lead guitarist for The Highway Killers, lives around the corner. 'She's good friends with Troy Keenan,' says Mick. 'Maybe he knows something. We need to tap into the scene.'

Tracey also smokes 'boo' – St Kilda for marijuana – and she and Mick, Drew suspects, once had a fling. Drew says he'll stay in the Corolla. Maybe Bob was fibbing and he'll catch Bingo sauntering down the street.

Left alone, hunched low in the car, Drew thinks of Heather; evincing with all his creative and imaginative powers her face and presence, whilst chastising himself for not impressing upon her more the extent of his affections. That was his problem: he could write love songs, but he wasn't a fearless lover. Someone who could move confidently around women. *Confidence* – women picked up on that. They sensed his hesitancy, even though his looks attracted their eye.

Or is he utterly deluded?

Falling prey to a swirling smoke of false first impressions? Was the touch of her hand on his shoulder a sign of her affection, or was she just guiding him across uneven ground as they walked back into the club? For God's sake, they met for a night. Conversation time, twenty-seven minutes, tops.

The tap on the window startles him. He winds it down to hear Swifty babbling and check Mick's sleepy grin. They have a lead.

*

Ruth had held back one piece of information from Ira on the phone yesterday. Telling him of her meeting with Swifty would have meant explaining her meeting with cousin Nathanael from High Risk, and she didn't want to pump Ira up before she had something special to reveal. The cards were in her hands – she liked that – and they had to be played delicately.

She'd enjoyed the roadie's company in the busy coffee shop he'd suggested in one of the city's arcades. As she apologised for the urgent tone of her call to him, he'd laughed. *She* was the one who'd spoken with Bones and Carl. 'Odd guys,' he'd said. And upon her noting that Carl had discovered his number, the roadie adjusted his shy fluttering gaze, to hold her stare. Odd guys, he'd repeated.

She'd been careful to mask the significance of the moment. She was on a scouting mission of Australian acts interested in being promoted in the US. She worked for a touring company out of LA. The band on the cassette she took from her shoulder bag, she found interesting, but didn't know who they were. Did he?

Taking her Walkman, and stretching the headphones to breaking point to cover his large head covered with ginger curls, he'd pressed 'play'. She'd watched him close his eyes and lift his chin like a contestant on a television quiz show.

'It's Mick and Drew,' he'd grinned, seconds into the song. His voice carrying through the room, startling a table of elderly ladies taking high tea.

'Very interesting to hear the album version,' he continued at a lower volume, nodding to the beat. 'They play it slower now and I think it works better. Suits the song.'

Ruth watched him listen, not wishing to interrupt.

'I've found that often. Bands will change their material when they're on tour. I think they get more comfortable with it and tempos will slow down. They get a groove.'

'I agree,' she said. 'And sometimes bands do it the other way round, and trial songs on the road and find the groove, before going into the studio to record. So you said Mick and Drew. Who are they?'

'Mick Woods and Drew Lovelock.' He took a messy bite of a custard tart. Added a slurp of hot chocolate. 'Do you have any more cassettes in the bag?'

'No more – they're the only band I didn't know about.'

'I work for them on tours. That's "Tender Tender Kisses" off their first album.'

'How many have they made?'

'Two so far. You can get the other one in town. Gaslight Records is just around the corner. It won't be in the big stores like Virgin. Mick and Drew are on a small indie label. I'll take you there, but we'll have to go soon.'

'And they're singer-songwriters, right? I'd assumed that. They're not a full band.'

'They *used* to be in bands. Mick in lots. But not anymore.'

'Do you know where they live? Here, or in Sydney . . . or . . .?' She shot him a pleading smile. 'I'm just guessing. It's my first trip here.'

He said they spent a lot of time on the road, promoting their records. Australia and Europe mostly. Japan and New Zealand too. Never the US and Canada, so they'd be interested in anything she had to say about gigs. He didn't know where they were now.

Maybe on holidays. He couldn't help with that and he was in a hurry – he had to go.

She had pushed. She really liked their songs, and the roadie had said they were his favourite act to work with. He took a pen from his shirt pocket, and paper from his wallet. On the flipside of a musical-equipment-hire business card he scribbled a name, a number and address.

'That's the manager. If you can reach him, he might help.'

She'd been in her hotel calling since this morning. Nothing. Frustrated, coat on, bag swung over her shoulder, walking out of her room down the carpeted corridor, she had one last option.

*

'So it's settled,' confirms Sophie, licking a wooden spoon coated with sauce from a casserole pot cooking on the stove. Tucking a strand of her luxurious curly black hair behind her ear, the spill of her breasts at the top of her tight blue velvet dress, she reaches for a bottle of wine, adding a generous splash to the food.

'It's not bad,' says Drew. Mick, taking another mouthful, agrees. 'What is it?' asks Drew. 'A burgundy?'

She reaches for the bottle. 'I got it from a box at Dad's.'

Slipping on a pair of glasses resting on an opened recipe book. 'Penfolds.'

'Classic Aussie brand,' says Mick.

'Grange Hermitage.' Looking for a reaction across the kitchen and getting none. 'There's a year . . . 1968.'

'*Music From Big Pink* came out,' notes Drew. 'I don't know what it was like for wine . . . a great year for music. How are Naj and Paul?'

'Good. You know they've moved to Daylesford.'

'No, I didn't. Where's that?'

'About an hour and a half away in the country. A cute town. I'm surprised Bingo hasn't got you a gig up there.'

'Maybe we have,' says Drew, glancing at Mick, who doesn't look up from the delicate business of unpacking tobacco from a cigarette and replacing it with thin strands of marijuana.

'They sold their tiny apartment in Collingwood and got a house with a garden *and* she's pregnant.'

'Lovely.'

'Twins.'

'Oh wow,' swoons Drew.

'They're fucked!'

Drew, slack mouthed, glares at his partner. 'You can't say that.'

'God, Mick!'

'Hold on, you two. It's true. You won't see 'em for ten years.'

'They're happy,' insists Sophie, taking a sip of wine. 'By the way, food's almost ready.'

'After dinner, we're going to see Troy and his band,' says Drew. 'Maybe they can help us.'

'Handsome Troy.'

'It's all we've got, really.'

She pouts a smile. 'Still breaking hearts?'

'Probably.'

'I met him through Bingo,' remembers Sophie. 'He'd give me door jobs at Infusion and paid me even when I didn't turn up. Troy would come with the in-crowd.' Her voice shakes. 'Bingo was good to me when I wasn't being good to myself.'

Mick lights his cigarette and takes a deep draw.

They're eating, Mick and Drew trying not to consume the first good food they've had in weeks too quickly. Sophie more measured, and willing to talk to heads bent over plates.

'With the credit card, if you make an offer to settle, it may help with the other charges. Do you have much savings?'

The songwriters are too ashamed to answer.

'But you guys tour overseas. I hear you on the radio when I'm driving to work.'

'It makes no difference,' says Drew, looking up, knife and fork in hand. 'Marcel Duchamp once said, and I don't know if I've got this exactly right. He said, "Life is more a question of what one spends than what one earns." It's the costs. Swifty, transport, hotels. And when you account for them and Bingo's commission, there ain't much left.'

'I find that hard to believe.'

'It's true,' says Mick, chewing.

'Look, you're right, we should have checked the credit-card bills and found that they were in our names. But Bingo's in the office, we're on the road, it looked like the system was working great.'

'You're going to need money.' She has the songwriters' attention. 'Because you need legal representation . . . and I'm not cheap.'

She'd only ever seen them fly. Drew super-sweet in The Shells. Mick crawling around on stage, once naked, with Long Gone Train. Their first gigs as a duo. Their swagger and ludicrous amount of self-belief. To the faces across the table softened by gratitude. They'd aged too. Boys no more.

She doesn't want to say it, adding more pain. 'You can stay one night. It's all I can do. You're dangerous.'

*

Ruth has taken a cab, sitting in the back seat, the driver mercifully quiet – the one from the airport early yesterday morning, a yakkity-yak merchant pulverising her after her sixteen-hour flight. She observes the passing city. The swift change from the columns of high-rise to the dark cottages ringed by bare winter trees. She has never left the USA, and is trying to place the cold, old-world feel of the houses in the context of her own country – *Boston?* – when the driver says hesitantly, 'It should be here.'

She looks out, wishing she could say, 'Ah, there it is.'

He stops at the mouth of a thin shadowy lane. 'This is the number. It's offices, by the looks of it. That right?'

'I guess so.'

She's standing before an alley of rain-stained cobblestones; access to a row of offices carved into the bones of old work sheds. A large window fronts the street, but no lights shine inside and the small car park is empty.

She passes a smart sign advertising an architectural firm; a photography company is next, a light flaring from an upstairs window. She walks on. A dog barking over a high wooden fence is quickly silenced by an old woman's snarl. She walks on. Polygram Records is printed onto the frosted-glass front door of the last business in the lane. Then comes a corner and an alley to the right. No lights here and it's darker, being hidden from the street. Parked beside a rear fence is a car. A red Saab 900 Turbo. The door of the last office opens, and a man walks out, dressed in a tweed suit and a caramel turtle-neck, back arched, carrying a cardboard box.

A folder drops. 'Shit,' he says, bending to pick it up one-handed. Rising with a grunt, he sees her. A slim, short-haired woman in dark slacks and a chic black coat. She walks to him.

'Do you need a hand?'

'No, I'm fine,' he says quickly, opening the car boot, placing the box beside other boxes, shutting the lid. A wipe of his hands, signalling job done.

'I'm sorry to come across you like this. I'm looking for somebody who works around here.'

'They've all gone.'

Her face slackens. 'I've left it too late.'

'It's Friday afternoon.' He notes her distress. Smiles. 'It's an Australian tradition to take it off. We're different to America in that respect.'

It's as if she hasn't heard.

'Who are you looking for?'

'They're in the music business.'

'Ah, Polygram Records. You passed them.' He points. 'Their office is around the corner. There *may* be someone there, if you're lucky.'

'Thanks, but it's not a record company I'm after. It's management.'

'Oh.'

To thaw his frozen expression. 'The people that take care of musicians.'

'Anyone in particular you're after?'

'Alastair Duncan-Smyth.'

'That's me.'

'Ah,' she gasps. A hand to her heart.

'I have to be careful in this business.'

'I'm Ruth O'Connor. I've been calling you over the last day.'

'I've been out, unfortunately.'

'That's fine. Wonderful to meet you at last.'

'So what's it about?'

'Well, I'm out here scouting talent for an American music company. I've been talking to various managers and labels, hoping to see some shows, and I'd very much like to set up a meeting with you, if I can.'

'Ruth, I'd love to, I really would, but I'm very busy at the moment.'

'That's a shame.'

'And I will be for the next week or so. Are you around long?'

'Probably not.'

'Why don't you give me your card and we'll see.'

She reaches inside her coat and pulls out her wallet. She hands him a card.

'You're from LA?'

'Yes, I'm in publishing.'

'My bands write their own songs.'

'Then it would be good to talk. Perhaps I can help.'

He glances at the office door. She can understand his apparent nervousness. Being fronted by someone late on a Friday afternoon as you pile a weekend's work into the back of your car. His car keys are prayer beads turning in his hand.

'How did you know I'd be here?'

'Swifty told me. There's a connection. He gave me your number and address and wished me luck.'

'That sounds like him. It's been nice meeting you.'

He's prepared to leave her here. Like they're meeting in a busy city street or they've bumped into each other over drinks at a local bar.

'I am interested in one of your acts in particular.'

'Oh, which one?'

'Mick Woods and Drew Lovelock.'

She'd expected a swell of managerial pride. Instead, a stern look flashes across his face. He is concentrating on her now.

'I love their songs. "Easy Come, Easy Go" is a hit single.'

*

After Sophie's dinner, the songwriters swing by and pick up Swifty. Drew is driving the Corolla, Mick's beside him, stoned with a glass of wine in his hand, the bottle of Penfolds wedged between his feet. Excited in the back seat, the roadie gives directions as they snake through the backstreets of Northcote to locate a brick building where In The Tropics, Swifty has been told, are practising tonight.

After much banging, the front door is opened by Trevor – drummer, sound engineer, face on the scene – who lives with friends in a spacious, top-floor flat. His welcome in the stairwell is a jerk of the thumb. 'They're in there.' To scuttle barefoot back up the stairs.

Out of sight, Swifty grunts, 'Yeah, hi, Trev, lovely to see you, man.'

The visitors know to enter a practice room gingerly; fortunately, In The Tropics are on a break. Their equipment – a keyboard, electric guitar, an amp, a drum machine and a vocal mic – is set up in a cleared space at the centre of the large, high-ceilinged room. Encircling them are the bulky tools of rock and roll – stacked drum-kit cases and towering bass amps. It looks like twenty bands rehearse here, but it's only five on a tight around-the-clock schedule. Trevor can afford to be sniffy – he has the keys.

The lead singer of the group is Jackie. In her mid-twenties, hip bones holding up her jeans, blonde fringe falling into her pretty eyes, she is an indie-boy heartthrob. Her vocal style a calculated shift away from the belting voices that keyboardist Troy, and his long-time guitarist Gerald, have worked with over the last years; to a cooler, more French-pop approach, which Jackie's breathy voice and appearance plays to.

'Experimental cool pop' is Troy's media-ready description of their music. 'Melbourne's Human League' was the tag he had put to his old band, Theory Of Colour, when Drew first met him on the we-need-our-first-hit circuit of 1984. Back then, Troy was in puffy pirate shirts and a mullet, doing an arms-swinging sideways dance behind a synthesiser, while holding a lemon-sucking pout.

He and Troy were crosstown rivals, both desperate for pop success, each taking his own route to secure it. Drew in thrall to rock history, Troy in league with Kraftwerk and a machine future. Eventually, Troy's band got their hit, 'Passion Is Our Possession', and, as reward, did a tour supporting INXS. Michael Hutchence remains a friend. To Troy's annoyance, when Michael snuck into a Tropics gig recently, Bingo hustled photographers trying to frame a 'romance' between the rock star and Jackie. It isn't only Mick and Drew who have issues with the person guiding their careers.

Not wishing to stay long, Drew introduces his friends, and in a stuttering, convoluted way reaches the reason for their visit.

'We've just got back in town and I know this sounds weird. We can't contact Bingo.'

'Aren't he and Simone in Thailand?' says Jackie.

'No, they're back,' counters Gerald sitting beside her, their legs dangling over an amp case.

'Yeah, that's right,' says Troy. He broadens his glance to include Mick. 'What have you guys been up to?'

'We've been out in the country, songwriting and getting things together, I guess,' says Mick.

'That's something we can't do,' smiles Troy, 'getting *anything* together in the country.'

It's an unintentional snub, thinks Drew. In The Tropics, the urban band. He and Mick, the traditional singer-songwriters. Hopefully, Mick will let it go.

'I'd heard he had some kind of legal problem,' remembers Gerald. 'A financial thing . . .'

'Oh yeah, who did you hear that from?' asks Drew.

Gerald turns to Jackie. She shrugs. 'Who was it?' he asks himself quietly.

'Bingo *is* flaky.' Troy rolls his eyes. 'Two months ago, he booked us into this club in the Cross. He knows we've only got an hour's worth of material and we're very picky where we play. It *has* to be right, right?' Mick and Drew agree. 'So, these two stand-over merchants in boxy suits expected us to start at ten and play through to two in the morning. I mean, what are we?' He splutters, laughing at the absurdity of it all. 'A covers band?'

'The Candy Shack,' nods Swifty sagely.

'Yes!' exclaims Jackie, pointing at him. Happy someone has put a name to a bad memory.

'I know it.' He smiles at her. 'Dodgy people and crap sound.' He turns to Mick. 'A Sambuca and Coke. Eight bucks.'

'Faaack.'

'I don't think we even got a rider,' winces Troy.

Drew is uneasy. When this thing blows up, Troy and the band will know they came fishing for information. He should either tell the truth or go. With a flutter of his hands, he says to Mick and Swifty, 'I think we should head off and leave them to it.'

'Sorry we can't help,' says Troy.

'Bye,' says Jackie.

Drew is cool. 'Worth a shot.'

'Hey, wait.'

It's Troy. Fun and fire in his eyes. Still crazy after all these years. 'Can we play you a new song?' He gives his band a searching look. 'We've got a gig tomorrow night at the Central Club and we want to give this thing a try.'

Jackie, microphone in hand, stands composed: five thousand people could be seated before her, clouds of dry ice swirling at her feet. On either side of her, her bandmates in hip-label casual wear – their short, dark hair cut by cool kids in city salons – bend intently over their instruments.

The emerging song is a two-note droney chug, lacking all the songwriting chops that Mick and Drew stand by. And the lyric is weak – but then, Troy was never a storyteller. Jackie repeats the line, 'The catwalk is her road, up and down, up and down, she goes,' signifying the arrival of what is, despite the dull verse, a very catchy chorus. Melody, as sweet as Grandma's Madeira cake, remains In The Tropics' strength.

The songwriters and Swifty applaud enthusiastically, as the band bows at the end of their performance.

The visitors are walking to the door when Gerald's voice booms over the PA.

'Jack Mitchell told me.'

*

Kebab shop. Saturday morning. Sydney Road, Brunswick. Sophie had apologised as they left her apartment with their bags, but she was right. They'd told her so, when driving off twenty minutes ago.

'I've got to ask you something and answer me truthfully,' says Drew.

He and Mick are sitting on tiny, mushroom-shaped, red plastic stools, baklava and coffees between them.

'Is that Tropics song still in your head?'

Mick, dead-eyed, sings, '*The catwalk is her road / She's in Vogue.*' You mean that one?'

'Not bad.'

'Troy and his fucking dig about not being able to get anything together in the country. Why,' he sneers, 'because the synthesiser won't work on the grass? Fuck him.'

'If you just took the chorus and added a decent verse, it wouldn't be a bad song.' Drew opens his hands, as if presenting the number in its new form.

'I'm not going to sing that,' huffs Mick, ready to repeat the chorus with added drudge.

Drew cuts in, 'We'd rewrite the lyrics.'

Mick relaxes, his partner's intent clear. 'You haven't given up on those top-forty dreams, have you?'

'It's got potential, that's all . . . to be reinvented. Calm down.' He looks at the menu above the rotating grill. 'You gonna eat anything?'

'Where is he? We said eleven. I'm gonna call.'

Mick heads off.

A minute later, standing over Drew. 'Just spoke to Jake at Swifty's house. The cops arrived this morning and took him in.'

*

Bingo is doing maths over a Saturday breakfast of a buttered croissant and strawberry jam – a set of hieroglyphic scrawls on the back of an envelope beside his plate. He looks again at the wobbly lines of columns before him – income streams, his father calls them – wondering if he's forgotten anything.

There's the radio-play money – on the smaller community stations, admittedly. Television income when the videos got a play. And the percentage earned from record sales, which is respectable, but not yet bust-out. He remembers when the songwriters first came to him with the idea of the band – it was all about strategically building the profile.

And he's factored in the expected costs of their current contretemps with the law; the reason he and the songwriters have been playing this dangerous high-stakes game of hide and seek.

Swifty would know if they'd reached Melbourne, and where they'd be if they have. But he's not answering his phone. Bingo has been calling on the hour since waking this morning. It's unusual for the roadie not to be home. Ah . . . perhaps he's finally found himself a girlfriend.

He returns to the figure before him, circling it with a flourish. Including his commission and a ten grand bidding bluff, it comes to fifty thousand dollars.

Chewing the last corner of his pastry, pondering which jacket to wear – the lambswool or the leather; he goes with the lambswool – he can feel the delicious rush of blood in his body. A vigour has returned, changing his posture from cowed animal to avenging rock manager. And one with a plan. A manager needs a plan – he has a beauty.

He shuts the door to Jack's place. The amusing thing is, he has to take a detour around his and Simone's apartment to reach their local pub, the Horseman And Swan. Ten minutes later, striding towards the entrance, he spots Ruth getting out of a cab.

She can see he is more relaxed today. His round smooth face, crowned by golden hair, isn't handsome, but pleasant to look at when hearing him talk. His features reminded her of someone, and as they settle into stools at the bar, ordering coffee, their backs to a television screen shouting Saturday's sport, she recalls a jacket photo of Truman Capote in her copy of *Breakfast At Tiffany's*. He's slimmer and taller than Capote, whom she'd seen scandalise the country with a series of druggy interviews on TV.

Both men had a beaming sense of intelligence and entitlement, and as far as rock managers went, the man scooping the froth off his cappuccino and sucking it into his mouth from a spoon was a refreshing change. A teddy bear, she'd tell Ira.

'How did you get to know their music?' He'd forgotten to ask her that yesterday.

'Someone I met had an album on cassette. They'd been to Australia on holiday.'

'Oh, that's nice, a fan.'

'Then I became one,' she says sweetly. 'Here's the strange thing. I thought they'd only made one album.'

'Which one?'

'The first. I bought *Vestiges And Bridges* when I got here. It's stronger than the first, do you agree, although I love their debut too.'

'They're definitely getting better. They tell me their third is going to be their masterpiece. They talk like that. Particularly Mick – every album is his best.'

'Confidence.'

'Oh yes! Tons of it. It can be difficult, but then again, that's one of the things that attracted me to them. I was tired of managing bands I had to pump up.'

'Had you known them long before you . . .?'

'It depends how far you want to go back.'

Ruth opens her hands: *here we are.* Sitting at a bar, a few old blokes before the TV, not much happening.

He likes her. She's smart and direct. Not the fuzzy, she'll-be-right attitude he constantly faces around town.

'I used to run a club called Infusion in the early eighties around the time of New Romantic. Did you have that in LA? It would be too hot for the clothes, I imagine.'

'Duran Duran. I *loved* "Hungry Like The Wolf".'

'Great song. A favourite of Mick and Drew's, not that they'd admit that in interviews. Actually they would – they enjoy confusing rock journalists. After that, I got into managing DJs and singers. And somewhere there, I met Drew who was in a band called The Shells. Four good-looking boys playing psychedelic pop.

'What sealed it was, a friend of mine's kid sister was having her eighteenth birthday; she was a fan of the band and wanted them to play at the party. Daddy could pay. It was in a big house in South Yarra. It's a bit like Beverly Hills. I put the deal together and the band got their first five-figure fee.' His eyes bulge. 'Drew never forgot that.'

'Well done you.'

'Thank you, and Mick Woods I'd known before they got together as well. He was in this awful Sydney band called Pfud. P-F-U-D. One of them "borrowed" a piece of gear off a band I looked after, and Mick did the honourable thing and returned it the next day. That's how I met him.' His smile brings her further into his confidence. 'Handing over a piece of stolen equipment.'

'He sounds charming.'

'He can be when he wants to. He and Drew have a chemistry. You'd see it.'

'I'd like to. When can we meet?'

'I thought we'd run through the financial side of your offer, if that's alright. So I can go back to them, and when we catch up everyone will know what's on the table.'

'Sounds fair. I'm interested in the publishing for the first two albums and the third,' she notes crisply, relieved to be talking money at last. 'I'd be wanting the worldwide rights for ten years. A fifty-fifty split on royalties after the recouping of an advance I'd pay you. Those are the key points. We can talk promotion of the songs and contacts I have and other things when we all meet up. They'll want to know what I can do for their songs.'

'Okay. That broadly seems in line, but I was thinking seven years for the rights, not ten. And what would the advance be?'

'One hundred thousand US. Which, I think, is about one hundred and fifty thousand Australian dollars.'

'I'd say one hundred and fifty or even sixty. Exchange rates,' he puffs, 'they're funny things, aren't they, up and down like yo-yos. So with an advance like this, you must be working for a large company in LA.' He's confident now. His plan is falling into place. 'You haven't told me who.'

'Green Thumb Publishing.'

'Green Thumb? Don't know it. But I haven't done much in the States yet. Mick and Drew are dying to get there. They have this . . . vision. It's called the American Dream. Tell me about the company.'

'I have a partner, Ira, who has a fantastic ear and loves the Woods Lovelock album too. We're a new independent with major backing. So there's resources to sign and push acts, while offering a smaller, very hands-on approach. Mick and Drew wouldn't be shuffled to the bottom of the pack, under a list of better-known artists. They'd be top priority. And we can help with other things. Getting a recording deal, for instance.'

'Asylum.'

'Pardon?'

'Asylum Records.' Bingo blinks at his own audacity. 'That's what the boys and I would want. It was founded in the early seventies by David Geffen and Elliot Roberts – Neil Young's manager. Tom Waits, Jackson Browne . . .'

'Joni Mitchell. I know. It was a very prestigious label back then. But it's dormant now.'

Bingo's eyes harden, then shine. 'We bring it back to life! You bring it back to life as part of the deal.'

'Warner Bros used to own it, if I remember,' she says carefully. 'Leave this with me.'

The drifting of her eye contact he takes as a winding down of the meeting. He's in need of a break. Time to assess his luck and to calm his exhilaration. He's just made a hundred grand. *His* first six-figure fee. The swift turns of the music business, one of the reasons it had attracted him.

'I'll get in contact with Mick and Drew and tell them all that we've discussed, and get back to you. How does that sound?'

'Wonderful,' she says, standing. Then brightly, 'What do you say to meeting tonight for dinner? An Australian restaurant. What's the local food here?'

'Let me talk to them first. They're cautious with business details.'

'Okay. But I'm leaving soon.'

'I know, I know.'

He reaches for his wallet, but she touches his arm. 'I'll pay.'

Watching her walk to the till at the end of the bar, his nerves calming, contemplating his next move – racing to Swifty's house to trace Mick and Drew – a strong hand grips his shoulder and squeezes. His heart flapping, he turns on his barstool in dread. There's relief and danger. Lance Pierce. Photographer.

'Word's out, mate,' says Lance in a nasal whine. 'Not good, eh?' This is his odd kick: an urban sophisticate playing the outback bloke, rubbing up against the pretensions and delicacies of the inner-city rock and art scenes. Keeping it real. Bingo knows him from Melbourne Grammar; they were in the Air Force cadets together. 'Ooh-ee, they've broken out of the slammer.'

'They have,' says Bingo, intent on keeping the conversation settings on 'low' and 'slow'. 'The police have been involved, of course, and it's rather complicated, happening as it has in central Queensland. So I haven't got all the facts.'

'They've been caught.'

'I don't think so.'

The corners of the photographer's mouth pinch. 'Jennifer at Globe Books, her husband Tim is a lawyer. He said escaping jail is a felony.'

'It was a correctional facility, not a jail. That's a misunderstanding going round.'

'They must be scared?'

'Yes, scared . . . yes.' He can hear Ruth thanking the barman. He's laughing at her offer of a tip. 'I'm trying to contact them, but it's proving difficult.'

'Give them a cheerio from me when talking next.'

'I will, Lance.'

'No more gigs for a while, then?'

'No, unfortunately.'

'It's shocking, mate.'

'Terribly.'

Bingo gestures to Ruth, who is moving to his side. He makes the introductions, taking her arm as he does.

'What was that about?' she asks at the door.

'No idea. My car's parked around the corner. I'll run you back into town.'

*

'Architects,' spits Mick.

After leaving the kebab shop, the songwriters have driven to Jack Mitchell's house. His was the name mentioned by Gerald at the In The Tropics rehearsal: the person who knew of Bingo's 'legal problem'. Stomping through a jungle of overgrowth, the musicians are in search of the front door. Drew, terrified of a tear to a seventies Yves Saint Laurent pink-and-cream silk shirt he'd picked up at a flea market in Lyons.

They find the front door. It is where it last was – at the side of the house – on the occasion Drew visited four years earlier to borrow Jack's copy of John Phillips's *Wolf King Of LA*.

'Important record,' he remarks, as Mick raises himself to peer through a window.

'John was hanging out with Gram Parsons when he made it,' mutters Mick, his neck stretching for signs of life.

'How do you know that?'

Disappointed at the lack of movement inside the house, and realising the muddy rut his and Drew's rock-history bantering can sometimes tip into, he says, lowering himself, 'I just do. We should knock.'

'I feel bad about this.' Drew squints, the face when lighting dynamite.

'You didn't return the album, did you?'

Passing windows as they walk to the rear of the house, Mick notices a plate, knife and an open jar of strawberry jam on a table.

'Hey,' he shouts. 'Do you know what Bingo has for breakfast?'

'No, I don't,' calls Drew, swaying gingerly around prickly bushes. Mick passes a pair of rotting apple trees casting a shadow over the roof, to join his partner in the back garden.

The songwriters have heard nothing during their search, when the quiet is cut by the kicking ignition of a car. There is an engine rev and the sound of wheels on gravel leaving the curb. They freeze, then sprint through an open gate at the end of a moss-upholstered wall, out into the middle of the street, breathless, in time to watch a red Saab 900 elegantly take the far corner.

*

Years later, when he had left rock and roll for the film business, having married a famous actress and fathered three children with her, Swifty learnt that the dying time of day when the light turns purple to fade slowly to black is known as 'the magic hour'. People get filmed or photographed then, because their faces look softer and younger.

It was a time of day he was often working; loading equipment while people walked past to come back at night for the rock show. This time held its own sparkle for him. He'd watch the waiters and waitresses walking through the avenues to work in their dark pants and white shirts, passing club bouncers adjusting cufflinks as they peered out of doorways, assessing the mood of the coming night. The light was purple and Saturday night was definitely coming down, when Swifty, tired and cranky, stepped out of Russell Street Police Station to the rude sounds of the city.

Earlier that morning, having been escorted there by the police from his share house at dawn, he was led away from a crowded front office – cops and robbers doing their morning trading – through a side door, and down a dark flight of twisting stairs. The air below was cold and smelt like it was fifty years old. Through a door of frosted glass, Swifty was following a woman cop along a dim hallway to light and voices at a far room. One voice, a lisping, self-satisfied croak, growing louder as they drew near.

'Ah, it's the roadie.'

Swifty walks the rise of Flinders Lane, changing his mind every few steps; to eat at a cheap Asian in the city, or do toast at home? His decisions clouded by the day. Detective Sergeant Bishop, the sly Rocky copper, had traced Mick and Drew to Childers where they'd been picked up and driven across the border. There'd been a further sighting in Parkes, a truck driver suspicious of a pair of rough-looking blokes sleeping through the day in a car. Bishop assumed they'd reached Melbourne. The detective certain Swifty knew where, and had leant in on him long and hard.

He hails a cab. The sky has now fallen dark. The magic hour is over.

Flicking the light switch by the front door, he strides towards his upstairs room in need of a coat, and stops. He should check the answering machine.

A lamp glows above Jake's chair. Swallowed into its coarse, checked upholstery and wooden armrests, his legs crossed – holding a copy of Raymond Carver's *What We Talk About When We Talk About Love*; Jake, not a reader, had bought it to impress women – sits Bingo.

'How the fuck did you get in?'

'Jake was kind enough . . .'

'You greedy bastard!'

Bingo flinches. The thrust of accusation, even when expected, is always hard to receive, and this is just the opening volley. The first cannon ball whizzing across the bow.

'You screwed them and left them in the lurch. And now, they've jumped jail and they're *really* in the shit, doing what you should be doing, clearing this fucking mess up. You're their manager, for God's sake.' He adopts a whiny, sing-song tone. 'The one who's supposed to make things work, and when they don't' – his eyes narrow in his swelling pink face – 'smooth it out. But you've done nothing except hide. Jeez.'

'You're right, I failed,' gulps Bingo, his admission the cough mixture he has to swallow. 'I haven't protected and helped them as I should have. Obviously, if I could go back and do things differently, I would.' He has uncrossed his legs, his hands cupped in his lap like a begging bowl, straightening himself in his upholstered throne. 'But I've done more than you think.'

'Their careers could be over. This is real jail time they're looking at. They might not recover from this; definitely not Drew.'

The roadie, not a tall man, has menace. This is a guy Bingo has seen put a Fender Twin Reverb amp on his shoulder and walk it up a flight of stairs. He's vexed. His loyalty to the songwriters is real. He stands above the manager, hand on hip, flushed features, waiting.

'Their first phone call last Saturday morning, I missed. I was driving Simone to the airport. Drew sent a fax to the office, not my home. The first I heard of *it* was a phone message from a Rockhampton detective. I called him back, to hear that Mick and Drew have been busted for dealing marijuana. I didn't understand it – they were on tour.'

'A fan gave it to them. It's happened before.'

'Oh, I see. He then told me their car was stolen. I didn't understand that either. Just wait – *please*. Gary Getty, the owner, had been recommended to me by Stan at Top Flight Entertainment, who's been promoting Mick and Drew's shows in Sydney since the start. You know Stan. He vouched for it. This was all news to me.'

'But where have you been? I've been visiting your home and the office for days. Not only are you hiding from the guys, but from me.'

'I was scared. There was the credit card and I knew that would lead to me. But it was still unfolding and it felt far away. *Wait.* I went to Jack's. He's like an elder brother and it meant I was at a safe place to start helping Mick and Drew.'

The roadie, he can see, is ready to detonate again. This time louder.

'Did you do German in school?'

Stunned, Swifty flings his arms in the air, turning to address an imaginary jury of twelve sane people sitting six in a row on wooden benches in judgement. He pleads with them. *Can you see what kind of idiot I'm dealing with here!*

'I'm an *Angsthasse.* Scared rabbit in English. I've hidden from pain my whole life. I've been protected. I went to a private school. Anyway, I contacted lawyers on Monday, mates of mine, to get the ball rolling on bail, engaging a solicitor in Rockhampton, the paperwork, putting things in motion. So that's happening. Then I get a call from the detective two days later. He's angry now. And he tells me they've broken out of a correctional facility in the desert.' Bingo makes a what-the-fuck face. 'He asked me if I'd heard from them and I said I hadn't. I knew they were coming for me.'

'There's the proof,' snaps the roadie, looming above the manager. His enraged face caught in the bright rays of the lamp. 'And because you'd done nothing and they were trapped, they did the thing that they hoped would keep them out of jail. Finding you.'

'I know,' whispers Bingo, collapsing in on himself.

'You've got a web of bullshit going here – some of it may be true. So, the credit card. Laying eighteen grand of debt on them and sending them out on the road one more time.'

'That's another thing.' Bingo twirls an arm over the armrest as if scooping water from a leaky boat, and begins to talk in a way the roadie has never heard before. Not employer to employee. The roles they've been locked into since Mick and Drew's first gigs. But as friends.

'I manage four acts. With Mick and Drew, I make some money on their shows. The records, though – great reviews, people love them – they don't sell in quantities. In The Tropics have been working on their debut album for two years. Troy and Gerald can't make an artistic decision, but they sure know how to spend a recording budget. Debbie G, I thought could be a pop star, but her three singles on Mushroom have bombed. And Zephyr are about to be swamped by grunge.' He eyes Swifty calmly. 'That's my roster.'

'What about the international tours you book?'

'Cult acts. Lots of work and little profit. I'm pedalling hard.'

'You're pedalling enough to live well. I've seen the renovations to your apartment.'

'That's Simone.' Her name, an oyster exploding in his mouth. 'And her parents. That's why she's gone to Adelaide. To beg for more cash.'

'How about *your* folks? They'd have a spare eighteen grand, wouldn't they?'

'My mother would have, you're right, but she's bailed me out before. As for my father . . . asking him for that amount of money would only confirm what he thinks of me and my profession. I'm a failure. I've hung out in record stores, not the halls of power. I can't.' A head shake. 'I just can't.'

'You're still a wanker.'

Bingo clamps his lips in a dumb boy grin. Thankful that despite being a wanker, the roadie seems to have signalled a temporary ceasefire.

Now he can ask his question; the one he's been waiting to pop since dropping Ruth at the Hilton. The possibilities a hundred and sixty thousand dollars can open up, bouncing like a pinball off the bumpers of his brain. His mouth is dry.

'Where are they?'

'At this moment?'

'Yes, okay,' says Bingo, masking frustration. 'At this moment.'

'I don't know. They don't tell me where they are. They're protecting the person they're staying with.'

'Does this person live in Melbourne?'

The roadie hesitates. 'Yeah. And they have a car. They pick me up and we drive around.'

Bingo stands up, adjusting his jacket and straightening the legs of his moleskin jeans. 'Alright.' He takes a slow breath. 'I'm going back to my place.'

The roadie's mouth sags open again.

'You stay here,' says Bingo. 'If they have a car, they'll come to one of us in the next few hours. We contact each other when they do, and we all meet up later tonight. I've got news for them.'

At the door, the manager stops. 'Thank you. I'm very grateful. I messed up, but it's going to be alright. I'll let myself out.'

He pops his head back around the door. 'By the way, where were you all afternoon? I got through quite a lot of those beautiful, but rather brutal Carver stories.'

Then he's gone.

*

The music is so loud Mick has to cup his ears when passing the PA stacks to reach the toilets. Standing at the stall pissing, he wonders if this is still the good idea it seemed when hatched a few hours back at the Horseman And Swan over darts and beers.

After an afternoon stalking Jack and Bingo's abodes, they had retreated to the pub where a sense of fatalism had set in. The high of hitting Melbourne had faded, and, just as a good new song or gig buoyed them, a knock could lower those same spirits. After assessing options – Bingo elusive, maybe he'd left Melbourne; Swifty loyal, but telling the cops what? – they'd decided to hit the Tropics gig, hoping for nothing more than . . . something just might turn up.

Mick looks into the mirror. A blue light above the glass casting a grotesque morgue-like glow over the wash basin and his face, making him look older and haggard. He raises his hair to see small corners creeping back from his hairline. His dad has hair, but two uncles on his mum's side were bald at forty, and Aunt Agatha is wispy.

Beside him, a young guy in ripped jeans and t-shirt, a mane of blond hair, lifts his face from the basin, pearls of water clinging to his shining pink cheekbones. *Sickening*, thinks Mick. Whilst behind him, two brush-cut guys in their early twenties in pastel Lacoste polo shirts are hot-footing it, desperate for mirror time. He needs a drink. A 'stiffie', he'd instruct Swifty to mix him backstage.

The first band has finished and, from the raised platform above the dance floor, Mick judges the crowd at four hundred. He clutches his vodka and orange, the tall glass mercifully cold in a tight room of loud people and louder music.

Suddenly, Drew is at his side with a beer in each hand. He lifts one to Mick in invitation. He takes it, to raise his vodka with a world-weary grin. The juggling of beverages makes the lighting of cigarettes difficult. Lucky Strikes lit, Mick blows a jet of smoke and asks how the vibe is backstage.

'Nervous, but they're happy with the turnout.'

'It's not bad,' admits Mick, eyeing a heavy bank of expectant faces before the stage. He adds casually, 'No sign of our manager?'

'Not yet . . .' Drew lifts his beer to toast, 'but they're expecting him.' Mick clinks in return, breaking out his first smile of the day. 'I think they're starting to wonder why I keep popping up asking about Bingo.'

A new song starts on the sound system.

'Happy Mondays?'

'Aren't they supposed to be funky?'

'This is *kind* of funky,' says Mick.

They listen, holding off their dismissal until the vocal kicks in.

'Where are the toilets?' asks Drew, draining his beer.

The house music fades. The crowd cheers the dimming of the room lights, the stage lights brightening to reveal the arrival of In The Tropics. Troy is on one side of the stage, Gerald the other, Jackie is at the mic, smiling to the fans as the boys sort their gear. Strobe lights flicker and blind the room. *Bang*. First song.

Mick is looking for Tracey Hoffs. It had been fun dropping in on her last night with Swifty and scoring the dope. She isn't tall, so he's up on his toes. Turning around, thinking she's arriving late, he watches Drew torpedo through people like a wild drug addict, clipping people's shoulders, bumping them aside, angry upset faces in his wake, led by a tough bloke yelling and raising a fist at his back.

'Follow me!' he gasps to Mick.

The dressing-room door slammed shut, Drew blurts breathless, 'Bishop's at the bar. I saw him in the mirror.'

'Oh no!' Mick groans.

We're done, thinks Drew. Rats in a cage. The cop and his back-up team to presumably burst through the door any second and haul them off by their tails.

Mick, kicking a chair away, strides to a steel door. He screws the handle violently. Locked.

'The support band were unloading gear out of there.'

'Where's the key?'

Drew shrugs. Looking frantically at the floor, knowing it won't be there.

Moving back across the room, Mick leaps and lands gracefully at the top of a set of stairs. Crouching on his knees, he pulls back a black curtain and crawls forward. Lights hit him. He's on stage. Looking at a show from a new angle; floor level through the guitarist's parted legs.

The song ends. Mick in agony, waiting for the applause to die.

'Gerald,' he hisses. 'Gerald!'

'Mick?'

Trying not to inflect any panic into his voice, while choking on puffs of dry ice billowing from a machine by his leg. 'The key to the dressing-room back door. Where is it?'

Gerald thinks.

On the far side of the stage, Troy, with a theatrical thrust of his head like he'd been slapped, presses a button on his keyboard. A loud metronomic clap fills the room, which Mick recognises as the introduction to 'She's In Vogue'.

A few audience members are wondering why the guitarist has his back to them, in conversation with a long-haired guy crouched at his feet. A roadie?

'Hey, Mick, what are you doing up there?' shouts Tracey from the third row, a bloke in sunglasses squeezing past her.

Troy is puzzled too, as Gerald has missed his cue. *Where's the hooky reverbed guitar lick, you idiot?*

Gerald's eyes pop. 'In Troy's case.'

The songwriters dive into the stacked instrument cases; flipping latches and pulling zippers. Both of them too scared to look at the door. 'Got it!' exclaims Drew, holding their prize aloft.

Outside, Mick grabs Drew's wrist. 'Don't throw it back in.'

In these frenzied first seconds of their escape, Drew looks at his partner, confused. Then understands. Mick raises his boot and kicks the thick silver door shut. Drew drops the key into his pants pocket: Troy will be royally pissed off. Bishop too. Mick and Drew sprint away; still enough schoolboy fitness in their legs to carry them at speed.

*

Loping down Chapel Street through Prahran, the darkness broken up and spotted by the lights of Saturday night, the songwriters blend in. The sidewalks are crowded with pretty young things off to pubs and clubs; the traffic, an occasional police car included, is a cruising molten flow. Mick and Drew aren't freaking. They know their best protection is to be actors in this play. To walk like they're looking for a good time; even when stepping over pools of vomit.

An hour earlier, they'd turned out of the alley, cut around the block to stop on a corner – banging into each other in silent-movie style, when spotting two cops, one with a flash-light, inspecting their car. Retracing their steps, then haring off, they had walked quickly, elbows jutting, long strides, through Collingwood's backstreets. At first, fear had been their guide. Their quick choices, though, were moving them south; a homing instinct, similar to the one guiding migratory birds over vast oceans once a year to land on a familiar rock ledge, was pulling them to nighttime St Kilda.

Fitzroy Street is a scuzzy 2am scene. Fewer people on the sidewalk and the vibe is darker. A squeeze is on – whether it's drugs, drunkenness or sex, or a holy combination of the three, you have to be sorted by this time of night. Those still searching are desperate, darting like fish amidst the last of the night's revellers.

For Drew, the smell of salt air and the sea is one of innocence and sunshine: holidays spent with his mum, dad, brother and sister. Two weeks a year in the pit of summer at timber houses on Bribie Island or at Mooloolaba; driving back to Brisbane with peeling skin and sand in the ears. A magic, water-blinking break from the city's stretch of baking suburbs. There is something odd and discordant for him about beaches in cities; particularly when they sprout a street like this – where all innocence is dead.

They grab kebabs, turn into Acland Street, to sit on a low stone wall skirting a set of three-storey apartments at the first corner. Tahini sauce dripping down their chins and fingers like blood, they hear the distant music, laughter and screams of a party. A drunken dandy, in check suit and rooster hair, stops and asks Drew for a cigarette.

Didn't AC/DC live around here in the mid-seventies, asks Mick. The songwriters are reckoning on the washing-up duties, Bon or Angus, when a police car pulls up and parks before them.

Running away is not an option. They stiffen. Two cops get out, the driver touching the gun on his hip as he comes around the car. They nod to the songwriters and walk to the music.

*

A young girl in a puffy, pink plastic jacket and a knitted blue bonnet, bucket and spade in hand, has gotten ahead of her parents. She walks up a small ridge of sand covered in sea grass. Living a street away from the beach, the night's high tide can bring her treasure. Pieces of driftwood mostly, occasionally a curved line of shells in a necklace shape; once, a green glass globe the size of a football, twined with damp salt-encrusted rope – the words 'Made in Portugal' indented on its base.

This morning she has discovered something equally unusual. Lying motionless, side by side on the sand, are two men. They remind her of a picture in a book her kindergarten teacher, the lovely Miss Hoffs, recently showed her of two baby whales beached after a storm. The local children, living in Riddletown, a fishing village on the Irish coast near Limerick, had gently rolled the whales into a blanket, and, with the help of Fireman Phillip and Ambulance Driver Doris, carried them back to their underwater home in the sea.

'Mummy, Daddy,' she calls, 'see what I found.'

Mick's eyes crack open one at a time to white-light blur and a child's voice. He lifts his head off its hard sand pillow, his vision focusing on the girl, then two adults coming quickly to join her, one of them a woman carrying a baby. He elbows Drew, prodding the sharp bone into his partner's shoulder.

The parents, who are of a similar age to the songwriters, had moved to the seaside suburb seven months ago. A reason for their relocation was the lure of the beach; another, the low price of the apartment they are currently renovating. A new word is going round town. Mick and Drew have heard it. *Gentrification.*

The family stands above the men in silent rebuke; the girl having retreated to the safety of her father's legs, his protective hand resting on her shoulder. Brushing crusted sand off their lips, the songwriters look up with apologetic smiles, to rise painfully and scuttle off to the hustle of people and shops at the far end of Acland Street.

Mick is walking with purpose – Drew has never seen him so resolute. They had stopped for Cokes, sandwiches and an unanswered call to Swifty; to resume their march in the direction of East St Kilda. From the set look on his partner's face, a plan is in place and questions are not in order. Dancing between four lanes of traffic on the Nepean Highway, after the sleep on the beach and every bizarre twist and turn since listening to Ron's whispered instructions in the prison canteen, their escape has been taking on the dimensions of a fevered dream; one that has to crack.

Cars honk as they zoom past, anger and surprise at the two Sunday-morning scarecrow figures, willing to endanger their lives to cross a street.

Another Deco set of flats, dark-wood-panelled entrance hall, up two flights of stairs and knock. Drew is standing behind Mick's right shoulder, dusting the last sand particles from the arse of his pants, when the door opens.

Two years on, Delilah looks the same. Dry straw-blonde hair to the shoulders, her milky skin as if drained of blood. Her hawk-like beauty before him, Mick flashes on their first glance across a crowded room – backstage at the Trade Union Club. She was going out with Scratch from A Terror Decides, he was juggling two women: a music journalist and a singer. A month later they were shacked up, the Sydney scene on its heels in wonder. Her strongest feature she will never lose. A wandering left eye giving her a cross-eyed look that many find adorable. She is tall; it's eye-to-eye stuff. And despite all that has gone down between them, a wisp of a smile came to her lips as she opened the door.

'We're in trouble,' says Mick. 'I need your help.'

She glances at Drew, who offers an old smile. He always liked Delilah.

'Then you'd better come in.'

On hearing the door knock and lounge-room voices, Delilah's boyfriend, Larry, left his books and notepad in the study. Two tall men were talking to his girlfriend. He knows who they are; he and Delilah have raked over each other's pasts. This is the rock-and-roll chapter in the flesh. There's no mistaking Mick Woods – he looks like a werewolf. The other bloke must be Drew Lovelock; a deference to his posture indicating he is more aware than his mate of this gatecrashing into other people's lives. A few nervous pleasantries exchanged, Larry retreats to a new reassurance he finds in Anthropology 104.

Five minutes later, his door opens, Delilah popping her head around the corner. She jiggles the keys to their white 1966 Valiant sedan. 'I'll be gone an hour,' she says. Her expression signalling she is as surprised and bewildered as he is.

'I love you,' she says tenderly.

'Love you too.' He smiles back. 'Be careful.'

Drew is in the back, the hard-on-the-bum seats and spare simplicity of the car's interior buoying spirits already lifted from being driven – not walking or running – to their destiny. Upfront, Delilah and Mick look like film stars – updated versions of Kim Novak and a dishevelled Robert Mitchum.

To think it could have been like this, harmony between them, but then Drew knows it wouldn't have worked. The road he and Mick were on, for better or worse, was only built for two. He watches them chat, the wind from his open window blowing their words around him like the fluttering of birds. He takes another drag of his cigarette. If rock music has taught him one thing – take your pleasures when you can.

It feels like the trip has hardly begun when Delilah pulls up across the street from a modern apartment block. Mick says they'll be minutes and she watches them walk off; ridiculous to her that these guys could ever think they were inconspicuous.

When Mick had begun to tell her of their troubles, she had stopped him, wanting to know as little as possible. There had been a dart to the heart when she'd answered the front door, but she'd learnt that the best-looking guy in town was not the wisest, and definitely not the most reliable.

Mick and Drew's knock opens a neighbour's door. The previous day, they had sneaked up the stairs carrying a crowbar dug out of Max's bag, and been caught trying to wedge Bingo's lock. The elderly gent across the hall – one of those straight-backed blokes in their seventies who still think they have it over younger guys – is glaring at them again. Today he has something to say.

'If you two don't piss off, I'm calling the police.'

They direct Delilah down another street, a left, a right, to park – *there.* The instructions are the same: if someone is in, Mick will come back.

'Boys,' exclaims Jack Mitchell in a dressing-gown and socked feet. A hand patting down bristling strands of salt-and-pepper hair.

'Hi, Jack,' says Drew. 'This is Mick.' The two men eye each other in greeting. 'Sorry to bother you like this on a Sunday morning. You wouldn't happen to know where Bingo is, by any chance?'

'At the airport picking up Simone. She's been in Adelaide for a week, visiting her mother and father.' A knowing look is exchanged. 'You wouldn't want to stay there any longer, would you?'

Like many Melburnians, Jack can't understand why anyone would want to live anywhere else in Australia. And like most of his fellow citizens, he expresses this view to visitors and new arrivals without malice or fear of contradiction.

When Drew had first come to the city, upon learning he was from Brisbane, people had offered him pity. He'd taken it graciously, to be used as fuel if necessary, to prove himself as good a songwriter as any in the nation's cultural capital.

'Do you want to come in?'

Drew looks at Mick.

'I might tell our lift they can go,' he says. 'You don't mind?'

'No, I'll put on coffee.'

'He was here for a week,' calls Jack from the kitchen. 'He came straight from the airport when he dropped her off.' His tone becomes affectionate. 'He's a funny boy. *Always* a scheme and always on the phone. A bit like his father, but you know that.'

'We do,' says Drew without rancour.

'I found this.'

Jack pops his head through a service hatch. 'It's on the traymobile there beside you.'

Drew picks up an envelope. It's Bingo's handwriting. A mad clutter of numbers crossed out and amended. In the bottom corner the figure of fifty thousand dollars is circled. He hands it to Mick.

'Why's he staying here?' asks Drew.

'Renovations,' replies Jack, walking into the dining-room. 'They've spent a fortune on that place. I don't think they know what they're doing.'

'Oh, my goodness,' says Drew.

'My specialty. No big deal.'

He lowers a wooden tray with silver handles onto the table, unloading cups, coffee and a cake. The songwriters lean in to enthuse about the dark brown wall of crust holding a luscious pool of yellow goo.

'New York baked cheesecake. I made it for them. Let's partake, shall we?'

'We don't mind,' grins Mick.

'Didn't think you would,' says Jack. Picking up a knife, he starts slicing.

'When did he leave?' wonders Drew.

'Last night. He'd been away all of yesterday, off to see that roadie mate of yours. What's his name? Lofty? Gypsy?'

'Swifty.'

'Where's your plate? Quick.' The cake wobbles, landing on its side.

After a second slice and a refill of coffee, Drew asks if he can use the phone.

Three walls of the den – Jack's term for the windowless room at the rear of his house – are covered in bespoke floor-to-ceiling wooden cabinets, housing his record collection. On a set of drawers against the spare wall sits a record player flanked by two expensive speakers – a pair of puffy-eared headphones are plugged into the amplifier. Careful as he swings his legs around a low black table from the sixties crowded with pop memorabilia – a Barbie in go-go boots, a Batmobile in its original box – Drew plumps down onto the couch and dials.

'Hi, Swifty.'

'Holy fuck, what happened to you?'

'What do you mean?'

'Well . . .' puffs the roadie, 'everything.'

'You're going to have to be a bit more precise than that. But listen. Do you know Jack Mitchell's place? It's around the corner from Bingo's at 112 St Kilda Road. One, one, two, St Kilda . . .'

'I've found Bingo.'

'I know, Jack told us. One, one, two. It's a rundown shack between two office blocks. You can miss it, so drive carefully when you're close. Mick and I will be outside waiting.'

The roadie's spluttering and stuttering is let loose. Drew's interjections, *Bastard. Oh my God. Sorry about that. We're onto him too. What the hell. You're incredible.* Commas and semi-colons, punctuating the one-sentence summary of Swifty's last twenty-four hours.

Curious, browsing the shelves after the phone call, Drew, his fingers clicking as they trail over the stiff plastic sleeves, picks up the thread of the album cataloguing. It's alphabetical, not by genre. He goes to D. Daddy Cool, Dave Clark Five, Betty Davis, Miles Davis, Reverend Gary Davis, Doris Day, Dead Can Dance, De La Soul, Jackie DeShannon, Devo. Moving to Dylan, to see what goodies he's got there – mono pressings, a Spanish copy of 'Positively Fourth Street' with the different cover perhaps. Dolphy, Domino, Donovan, Do-Re-Mi. Pulling out an album he'd been given four days ago. *Oh, that's interesting.*

Mick and Jack, chatting easily in the lounge-room, have discovered a Northern New South Wales connection: an uncle and aunt of Jack's had run a family timber business on the Clarence River, outside of Yamba. Mick's family had holidayed at the beachside town in the caravan park. The talk hopped from fishing the river and boats and bait, to yabbies pumped on sandbanks, to crabs and a chilli crab cake recipe, when Drew returns from the den, hugging an album to his chest.

'We know him.'

'I bought it the day it came out. Seventy-one, it would have been.' Jack turns from Mick, coffee cup in hand. 'There's a couple of decent songs. It's of its time, of course. Lots of flutes and . . .' he smiles primly, 'other baroque touches.'

'He's a good writer,' admits Mick. 'We're thinking of doing one of his tunes on our next album. Not off that record – something he wrote a few years later.'

'He gave us a copy,' says Drew, marvelling at the cover. A young Russell Duggan in a cheesecloth shirt, his permed curls backlit by a flaming strobe light. Strange to have the younger version of the older man in his arms. 'We've got it with us.'

'He doesn't think much of it,' adds Mick. 'But people can be hard on their earlier stuff.'

'Do you think he'd have more?' asks Jack.

The songwriters laugh.

'He's got a box of them in his shed,' chuckles Drew.

'They go for money now.'

'Oh, he'll love that,' roars Mick. 'We're getting his career back together here.'

'If you gave me his address or a phone number, I'd contact him.'

'Okay,' nods Drew. 'I'll do that.'

'So what does he do now? Still gigging?'

'He washes houses for a living. We met him in Mount Drake – you know it? He's married to a lovely woman, she's an artist. They've got two kids. I don't think he does shows anymore.' Drew checks with Mick. 'He's doing alright?'

'There's a lot of interest from collectors,' notes Jack, dabbing the corners of his mouth with a white napkin. 'Late-sixties, early-seventies Australian stuff, particularly singer-songwriters. To give you an idea, a Hans Poulsen album – and not in good condition – recently went for forty dollars.'

'The great Hans Poulsen,' muses Drew. '"Boom Sha La La Lo". They don't write them like that anymore.'

'No, they don't,' says Jack in thought. 'Now that I've got two recording artistes here, I want to ask you a question.' Mick and Drew tense. 'What do you think of CDs?'

'They're the future, aren't they?' says Mick, relaxing. 'Not much.'

'Handy for selling on the road. Swifty can get eighty in a backpack.'

'So it's nothing to do with their sound?' remarks Jack. 'The issue is retail. Their advantage is their convenience and transportation.'

'I guess so. They're small.'

Ummm, hums the host.

Drew says they should go.

'Goodo. Nice to see you both. I hope I've been of some help in locating your wayward manager.'

'You have,' says Mick, standing. 'We appreciate it.' He gestures to the crumb-covered plates. 'And, man, that was good.'

'My pleasure. Love your albums, by the way.'

'Thanks.'

'Fine songwriting. Bingo brought them round.'

'That's sweet of him,' concedes Drew, as they walk past the kitchen. 'I didn't think to look.' The conversation drifting to his discomfort towards the borrowed and never returned John Phillips album. But then they're at the front door, bidding goodbye.

'It can be rather difficult to get to the road,' says Jack, gathering his dressing-gown around his shoulders like a cape. 'There's a path by the trees and scrub, or it's just easier to get through over there by the nettles.'

'Do you ever think of cleaning it up?' asks Mick.

'Landscaping?' A sly pout. 'I don't think so.'

*

They stand bow-legged, rocking on their heels, hands jammed in their pants, valiant against the cold main-street wind. Cars swish by. A bloke bellows obscenities from a passing window, a reminder to the songwriters – not that one is needed – they're creatures from another planet. The easy silence between them broken when Drew ventures, 'Nice to see Delilah.'

'Yeah,' Mick says lazily.

Drew decides to push. 'How did you know where she was?'

The glance from Mick is to ascertain whether this is light, funny Drew, or the serious version. 'We stay in contact through a few old friends. I know where she is. She knows where I am.'

'Oh.'

'She's got a job down here as a stylist on magazine shoots and stuff.'

'Good.'

'It's a start. She still wants to be a designer.'

'That can be a hard world to break into, I'd imagine. Not that I know much about fashion.'

'It can. But she'll make it. She's already selling some of her clothes to shops.'

'Right.'

'Boutiques.'

Drew wants to ask about the boyfriend. 'She looks good.'

Mick throws him a you-failed-the-test look. In a mocking tone, '*Yeah, she looks good.*'

'What I mean is . . .'

'She's doing what she wants to do, and so am I. I get it. Let's leave it at that.'

*

It's a stake-out. They haven't waited long – cramped in Swifty's white Volkswagen Beetle, their collective beady eye on Bingo's apartment – when they spot the approaching Saab.

'Give them five minutes,' says the roadie.

They watch the grilled roller-door slowly rise, the car glide into the underground parking.

'And no crazy stuff,' says Drew.

A grudging *Alright* comes from the back seat.

At the front door, Simone is welcoming. Perfect make-up, brown hair side-parted with delicate strands curling to the edges of her mouth. Over a black turtleneck, with a silver chain encasing an astrological sign, hangs a knitted orange-and-red poncho. Any surprise at the arrival of two road-worn musicians and a moon-faced, ginger-haired roadie on a late Sunday morning is not apparent on her face or in her manner. Kisses on the cheeks, she waves them in.

The lounge-room is painted white and not dissimilar to an exhibition space in a regional art gallery. Positioned against the walls are pieces of uncomfortable modern furniture and tropical plants in large ceramic pots. And while Drew and Swifty talk Adelaide with their host, the joys of the town's central market, Mick's eyes roam, catching the colours of the rainbow adjustments on Bingo's face as he enters the room carrying a green, plastic watering can.

'Look who's here. Plant Man.'

'Mick, I . . .'

'Actually, it goes with the jacket and the khaki boots, mate.'

'Don't.'

'Things look pretty comfortable here.'

'I panicked . . .'

'You did. Screwing us on money is one thing, but when we really needed you. If only . . .' Mick deep breathes, trying *so* hard to use words, not punches, 'If only for you to do what we pay you to do. Look after us. Care for us. Protect us. You're at Jack's place.' The level of his voice is ascending, percolating, about to burst through the spout and scald everyone. '*Hiding*,' he bellows.

That stills the white room.

'It's okay, darling,' says Bingo. 'It's something we can settle. A misunderstanding between the three of us.'

'No, that's not it. It's not a misunderstanding.' Mick eyes Simone. 'Your boyfriend's fucked us over. We're off to jail.'

'Alastair, what is this?'

'I should have called you. My big mistake. But I was checking with lawyers and the police. We had a solicitor ready in Rockhampton. I was trying to put it together. Build the picture . . . a case . . .'

Bingo puts down the watering can, a reassuring glance aimed at Simone's crumbling face.

'I should have, you're right. But I didn't know the car was stolen. Didn't Swifty tell you? Stan at Top Flight Entertainment –'

'Oh, fuck off,' says Drew. 'And the credit card?'

'You have to front up,' says Mick, advancing.

'Mick, don't,' Swifty warns.

'I'm walking out if this doesn't stop.' A crying tear in Simone's voice. 'Mick, are you crazy? What's he done?'

'Nothing. That's the problem, darling. You have to front up and tell the cops the credit card is you. The stolen car is you. And anything else bad we don't know about is definitely you too. And if you don't, we'll drag you there by your tongue.'

'I'll do it.'

Even with Mick inches from his face, a sour heat on his breath, Bingo feels he has weathered the storm. 'I've got a plan.'

'We want a confession.'

'It doesn't matter now.' Bingo braves eye contact.

'We thought you were with us,' glares Mick. 'You were one of us.'

Drew steps away from Simone and Swifty, to join his songwriting partner. Bingo hasn't seen them in a month. They always looked too big in a room. Tall, wild, charismatic, they fitted the stage.

'I remember us at your office years ago when we were getting the band together,' recalls Drew defiantly, 'and you saying that Mick and I were on the blurred crusade. Remember that? You were a believer . . .'

'Still am.'

'Telling us what you could do with our songs and how you'd protect and promote them, because we're geniuses doing something no-one else was doing, and you were going to be our link to the business world. It was a pact we had. That's what it felt like on those nights. So naturally, we thought we were in this together.'

'We are,' exclaims the manager. 'Just listen to me.'

*

The furniture has been dragged and grouped into a centre huddle around a coffee table, where two bottles of chilled Sauvignon Blanc are opened and being emptied quickly. Bingo and Simone are hand in hand on a small couch, while Mick and Drew lie prone on a long, cream Italian settee in need of back support. Swifty is snug, cross-legged on the polished floor.

'I met her on Friday afternoon at my office. We went for drinks and met up yesterday and that's when serious negotiations started. She's a publisher, and with a partner has a company called Green Thumb Publishing that's based in LA. Now, as you know, I've never sold the publishing rights to your songs, precious as they are. People have enquired. I've been holding out for the right deal to come along.'

'Is she a short lady?'

'Yeah,' says Bingo. 'I suppose so.'

'With, like, a boy's haircut?' Swifty smiles to himself. 'She's related to Nathanael from High Risk – they're second cousins. You see, that's the connection.'

'What the fuck are you talking about?' says Mick, to the head of ginger curls at his feet.

'Easy, mate,' mutters Drew, his neck aching on the couch.

'Remember the other day, when I was driving you down to St Kilda to Bob Burtell's place because we thought Bingo was staying there?'

'You thought I was *what*? At Bob's place?'

'Who's he?' Simone turns to Bingo. 'I don't think I've ever met him. Have I met him?'

'You have.'

'Can we stop this – I don't care,' says Mick. 'Who or where people were, or what they were doing on any day of the week or what they had for Christmas dinner last year, or the year before. I don't care about any of it. You were in the middle of telling us about this woman who works in publishing. Please go on.'

'Jason from Honeycrunch said he'd heard you were there.' The roadie tilts his head back to Mick. 'I said to you in the car I'd met this American woman. She said she was interested in touring Aussie bands. I didn't know about publishing and this other business stuff.'

'Thank you very much, Swifty,' says Bingo, like Mick eager to move on. He shuffles forward on the couch, pulling the cuffs of his leather jacket up his arms and cupping his hands. The satisfying clasp he feels in the locking of his fingers. As much as the songwriters' dream has been of gaining success, his has been the granting of it *to* them. 'So, for the rights to your songs on the first two albums, with an option on your next album included, she's offering an advance, payable in thirty days, of one hundred and sixty thousand dollars.'

Silence. The universe is still.

'*And* . . . and she said she can help us get a booking agent for shows in the US and a worldwide record deal. I've asked for Asylum.'

Mick closes his eyes, letting himself sink further into the soft leather folds of the settee. Like Drew, he immediately knows what this means. Normal life will stop. The vertical helicopter ascension out of reality is underway; its power able to momentarily nullify the threat of jail time.

When you add up this amount of money, anything over a hundred grand, with the words 'Los Angeles' and 'worldwide record deal' in the same sentence, he knows he's got the most precious thing any artist could ever hope for – career lift-off. It's everything he's ever wanted, and everyone who ever doubted, dismissed, or laughed at him was wrong. He and Drew. Well, well, well. It was time to walk tall. Not for them the measured words of The Successful. *We're not going to let it all go to our heads.* It *has* to go to your heads. After years of struggle and disappointment and career manoeuvring and stabbing other artists in the back – where else can success go? Your feet?

Seeing his charges temporarily narcotised by the news, Bingo lays out the next hours of their lives, while extracting a bulging envelope of cash from his jacket and passing it to Swifty. Their roadie will drive them to a hotel in town where they will get cleaned up, putting on clothes they have bought at David Jones. To meet Bingo and Ruth at the Captain's Bar at the Hilton at five, where they will sign a heads of agreement contract guaranteeing the money before she flies off to LA, to start knocking on doors, trying to get someone interested in their songs. Then, with her gone, he and the songwriters will front up to the police station on Tuesday, lawyered and cashed up, their stories straight.

There is resistance from the musicians to this last part of the plan: Bingo convincing them it has to be done. Trust me, he says, surrendering can only help.

'We have our own legal representation,' says Drew. 'Sophie Chabowski.'

'Sophie? Great. We'll use her. Sutcliffe and Howard' – he studies his wine glass, giving it a swish – 'are very reliable.'

*

Bishop thinks he is watching amateur hour. The roadie and the two musicians strolling to the car he has followed from the roadie's house. The question is when to pounce. He is beginning to rethink the manager's involvement – his sudden rapprochement with the musicians, smiling as they cross the street counting a wad of cash. Then there's the American chick. What's her deal? They've traced her to the Hilton, a place many a shonky character stays.

Look at them.

These two limp-wristed bastards drive him mad. His father, whom he met at twenty, was a muso. His mother's one mistake. He has to nail them. Every case cracked, every piece of police procedure followed, steps to his transfer back to Brisbane.

A newspaper exposé of a massage-parlour kickback scheme a year ago had him and a few colleagues sent to purgatory; sleepy country towns like Rockhampton, where he'd already put a few noses out of joint. He'd been watching the Durango Bar for months, and when the credit-card arrest notice came up, he'd gone to bust them on that and walked in on a drug deal. He was beginning to see the musicians' jailbreak as *his* lucky break. It had got him to Melbourne, and the case was growing by the day.

*

Mick and Drew know never to touch hotel bar-fridge alcohol. Everything in that sleek box of death is triple priced. Nobby's

Beer Nuts three dollars fifty a pack. Only occasionally will they indulge, adept as they are at emptying miniature vodka bottles, refilling them with water, and re-screwing the caps to appear unsealed.

They sip their Crown Lagers on Bingo's money, which is their money, but they don't think like that. Mick lying on his bed, Drew at the window spying on the silent city below. Trams the size of toys inching down Flinders Street. People grouped at traffic lights, some in pairs, others alone, all of them dots. Life can seem insignificant when viewed from a twelfth-floor window.

He and Mick are showered and shaved, their wet hair sleek on their necks, cheekbones sharp. And as practised as they are at living out of suitcases, they are now down to underwear and socks purchased a pair at a time. Got new shirts too – a struggle to find anything with flair or attitude in the department store. The meeting is in ten minutes. The beers are frosty, sending a gorgeous jolt to the brain.

'What ya thinking?' asks Mick.

'Nothing.' *Heather. What she's doing right now? How ten minutes with her could change his life.* 'What do you think of Bingo's plan?'

'Good. Easy for him, though, we'll be the ones doing time. And as Ron said' – he adopts an English accent – '"It'll be a proper fucking nick this time."'

'Ron does have a certain talent for storytelling.'

'He got Bingo's trickery right.'

'I can't do jail,' moans Drew, turning from the window. The street scene harder to watch. He can't be taken away from life. 'It would kill me.'

Mick is careful. 'We've got money now. Getting to Bingo was the right thing to do.'

'But it's not going to help us in the end. Breaking out of the facility may have been the worst thing we did.'

'Let's sign the deal. We don't know what tomorrow will bring.' A pause. 'That sounds like a song title.'

'Yeah, a corny folk song. I hate to be grim. Even if jail time is short. Six months. A year. Ruth is going to run. We're poison.'

A pillow is on Mick's chest. He's talking to the ceiling, or perhaps the sky. His voice is tender, off with the clouds. 'We've got songs and a manager. Never forget that.'

*

Ambling across acres of plush, grey-flecked carpet, the songwriters spot Bingo and a woman at a table. The bartender catches their eye; they point to their destination on the other side of the bar as they glide by. The Hilton is empty on a late Sunday afternoon, and Mick and Drew, no matter what happens tomorrow or the days after, are feeling like kings.

'Ruth O'Connor,' says Bingo, rising from his chair and with a delighted sense of formality, 'please meet Mick Woods and Drew Lovelock.'

'Thank you for coming to Melbourne,' beams Mick, dipping the handsome profile, extending full eye contact. 'Bingo's told us good things about you.'

'It's my nickname,' the manager says to Ruth, who is appraising the songwriters. LA won't overwhelm them. Ira will fall under their spell. 'Given to me by a guy called Jack Mitchell, who ran a record store in town. I used to buy records there after school. One day he said loudly, "Bingo! He's in here again." And it stuck. You can –'

'I never knew that,' says Mick, miffed.

'Nor did I.'

'You two don't know everything.' He smirks. Getting Ruth's eye, having shown his comfort with the songwriters. 'You can call me Bingo, if you want, although Alastair was nice.'

'I'll stay with Alastair.'

The bartender had followed the musicians, and as drink orders are taken, Drew watches the publisher – at ease with their manager, he can see – as she explains the ingredients and construction of a margarita to the puzzled barman.

She's vibrant, that's the first thing. Bird-like, dark eyes sparkling. Relief they haven't got a burly old guy filled with sixties music-business stories. She's fresh. That's good.

'When did you arrive?' asks Drew.

'Early Thursday. I'm not used to such long travel.'

'It's a long way,' nods Bingo to the songwriters. 'It really is.'

'I'm here,' she says triumphantly, lifting her arms. 'It's so lovely meeting the both of you. Alastair has been telling me of your career. The albums are great and you tour a lot.'

'He said you met through our roadie.'

'That's right, I did. Swifty was my contact to you guys. It was a bit confusing for a few days. I was trying to reach Alastair, he was out, I went to his office on the off chance, he was leaving. We had a little cat-and-mouse going there for a while.' She shines, a ring of red lipstick framing flashing teeth. 'We've had some good meetings, haven't we?'

'Ruth has done an incredible job in explaining the deal and knocking up a heads of agreement contract so quickly.'

Two sheets of typed paper and a gold pen are on the table. The songwriters and the publisher, relaxing into each other's company, are happy to let the manager do what able managers do – guide proceedings.

He draws Ruth on her beginnings in the LA music business. She explains the workings of radio station KCRW, her three years there in promotions and two years on air as an announcer. The step into music publishing suggested by industry friends, her abiding passion for songs and songwriters, which is when Drew and Mick engage more, interested to hear the mechanics of the publishing business and her brushes with famous musicians. She knows Dwight Yoakam.

The songwriters have heard enough. It's time for their manager to swing the conversation again.

'Ruth and I have done some work on the agreement between Open Door and Green Thumb, covering the sale of your songs and the fee.' He faces the songwriters. 'The terms are as I outlined at our previous meeting. With the signing of the contract, Ruth has agreed to pay half the hundred thousand American dollar advance in the next fourteen days. The rest of the money, and the finer details of the contract, the splits etc, we'll work out when she's back in LA.'

'I'm flying off tomorrow night,' she says. 'It was always going to be a short stay. Anyway,' she smiles, 'you'll be over soon.'

'They will,' says Bingo.

'Alastair tells me you want to play The Troubadour. That would be the right place for a showcase show and there's the club's connection with the seventies singer-songwriter scene. It will let everyone know you're in town and show them what you can do. So, we're going to have to get you a good booking agent.'

'That can be difficult, I've heard.' Mick and Bingo eye Drew, wondering why he is down-vibing. 'We know bands that have struggled to get shows in the US.'

Mick wants to say, *As if we've ever thought of ourselves as a normal band.*

'I have someone in mind.' She smiles again.

'There,' says Mick to Drew, satisfied.

'What will be your strategy with getting the songs to the people who would be interested, or potentially can do the most with them?' asks Bingo.

'As a first step, I'd get them to some key industry people. Also, we should release a track on an indie label before we approach major record companies. To let them know what we've got. "Easy Come, Easy Go" or "Lorraine It's Me" would work well on college radio to get that drum beating.'

Two of Mick's songs. Drew is cool with that.

'Having the song on a few key stations helps. WFMU in New York, for example. And to keep our thinking open. Do we, do you, want the songs pitched to other artists? To those that don't write their own songs, but sell a lot of records, earning you royalties?' She threads her fingers gracefully around the stem of her margarita, lifting the drink to her lips. 'Advertising? Appropriate products, of course. Or at all?'

Draining the glass, she returns it to the table. 'And there's movies. Film directors know their music these days. How a song can lift a scene, giving it a punch the screenwriter has been unable to land on the page.'

'The use of Roy Orbison in *Blue Velvet*,' says Bingo, turning his lit eyes to the songwriters. 'That was amazing.'

'When Dean Stockwell sang "In Dreams".'

'The look on Dennis Hopper's face.'

'Deranged.'

'And the glow of the lamp on Stockwell's face, as he sang it.'

'That's what I'd like our songs to do,' says Mick, 'Shit-scare people.'

'If someone could do that with our music,' says Drew, turning to Ruth, framing his hands in a square like a film director. 'To light up the screen.'

She has dropped from the conversation. *It's that guy*. The kind of features you don't forget. Stocky, with waves of thick, dark hair swept back from the forehead, a sleepy face and a pair of puffy eyes. Creepy voice too. He was in the elevator this morning. She asked him what floor: he said six with a slow drag. Walking towards her now, she thinks he'll veer to a barstool or a table. But no, he keeps on coming. The songwriters catch her stiff expression. Bingo swivels in his chair to find his face inches from a man's crutch.

'Who are you?' he demands, swinging his head further back to get a better look at the intruder.

'They know me.'

Mick and Drew have had the air pumped out of them.

'And you're Alastair Douglas-Smyth. The conniving manager.'

'Wait on . . .'

'So we know each other,' says Bishop. 'Who's the lady?'

'I'm going to repeat his question,' says Ruth, with steely patience. 'Who the hell are you and why are you following me around?'

'I'm sorry.' A slight bow of the head. 'I'm Detective Brian Bishop, currently with the Rockhampton Police.'

'*So?*'

The detective glances at the songwriters and manager. God, this is beautiful. Pay-off moments like these don't come often enough in a detective's life. The thrill sweeter still – he'd been told not to come to Melbourne. A waste of time. They won't make it that far. *They will*, he thought; *slipping from town to town, evading responsibility as they go, is what musicians do.*

Before he can say more, decapitating the songwriters' pitch at stardom in one sword-swish stroke, the bartender arrives.

Frozen mid-scene, they watch him lower a tray of drinks to the table with care; the songwriters thanking him with a sad lift of their eyebrows. He gathers a round of empty glasses.

'Menus?' he asks.

'No, thank you,' replies Bingo gallantly. He looks at Bishop, who shakes his head.

'A celebration?'

'A meeting,' corrects Ruth.

Then, like Bingo, Bishop gets to business; an eye on Ruth as payback for her cheek, and to gauge her reaction as the charges are delivered to the songwriters.

*

A peruse of the papers collected at the Hilton shows them to be music-business contracts. Woods and Lovelock through Open Door Management were about to sign a deal with Green Thumb Publishing – Ruth O'Connor as co-director, Ira Isherwood the other – for a sign-up fee of fifty thousand US dollars. Not only were the musicians partners in crime, they were a songwriting team about to get a big break.

Matching her arrival into Melbourne with the manager's movements, Bishop can now see that that's when the fun and games began. No-one wanted her to know. It explained the turnaround – when the hunted became the hunter – the manager suddenly wanting to contact the avenging musicians.

He'd start with the manager. Prior background checks turned up wealthy parents, indulgent of their only child. The mother, in particular, who had put money into a disco her son had run in the early eighties. They would finance a strong legal defence of him, and any damage a criminal case would inflict on their own social standing. He'd proceed gently; flattery and conviviality more likely to extract information from a bloke like this than the bare-knuckle approach. He was saving that for the roadie.

But why, he wonders, collecting the contract papers and returning them to a folder, were Woods and Lovelock convinced if they got to their manager all would be solved? 'Just give me one call,' Woods had pleaded to the desk sergeant in Rockhampton. The car was not yet off their charge sheet, and their manager would have seemed the fit for that and more.

That's why they'd panicked at the facility: two weird-looking musicians in hick town contemplating whether they should risk escaping or not. It was the credit card – and who'd push one way or the other on ownership of that piece of tomfuckery – that was the centre of it all. He'd wait and see; watch them incriminate each other and work out which way suited *his* way best.

*

Held together, their chairs spaced apart, Mick and Drew don't dare talk. Recording devices in the room most likely, clipped to the wings of the steel fan in the corner. Their glances to each other, telepathic messaging, calculating the enormous amount of trouble they are in. Compounded by imagining what would be happening in other rooms, who is saying what to who. Bingo would fold in minutes. Ruth is innocent – what will her fury and shock unleash?

Meaningful glances can only convey so much: the rest is playing out in their heads. The horror stuff. The heartbreaking collision of opportunity and disappointment – sunshine followed by torrents of freezing rain – they've just witnessed at the Hilton. The wreckage to be absorbed pacing a prison yard and enduring sleepless nights in a cell bed. Strange hands pulling at their blankets. Hot breath at their ears. They'd come out of jail changed men and not ones wanting to write songs.

*

Swifty was at home. There was no new work coming in yet. The tour with Mick and Drew would have had them in Canberra tonight at Tilly's. He'd checked the itinerary after dropping them at the hotel. He was restless; wasn't there an amp to repair or a guitar to restring? He'd done the washing-up – even though it wasn't his turn – and thought of walking Sue's dog. His consolation was anticipating tonight's party: Mick and Drew flush with cash, up for fun before bargaining their way out of jail. The loud rap at the front door; he knew it was serious from his room at the back of the house.

Weird thing, thinks Swifty, sitting opposite Detective Brian Bishop at Russell Street station. People's voices always fit their faces. Why is that? His mum and dad sounding any different: impossible. Imagine a squeak coming out of Mick or a gruff Aussie bark accompanying Drew's hand flutters. And here's the Rocky cop – frog-faced, his chat a sly croak.

'I'm going to give you a chance to save your own arse. You don't get that often, do you? The manager, who's a pretty sleazy character, and the musos, they keep you on a tight leash.'

'Sometimes. I *am* working for them, you know.'

'We've been looking around Brisbane. It's amazing how things are connected in the music scene – the *indie* music scene,' he corrects himself proudly. 'And they've found someone' – he checks his desk, pushing a sheet of paper aside – 'who drove up to Childers on the same day that Woods and Lovelock were there. And then she drove them over the border to a tiny town called Mount Drake. I've never heard of it, which is probably why they went there.'

The roadie's heart is a bass drum, beating triple time.

'Who told her to do that?' asks Bishop.

'I did.'

The detective isn't surprised often. 'Are you sure? Because if it was, that puts you and her in a rather difficult position.'

'What do you mean?'

'*Come on.*'

Swifty knits his brows. Goes a little cross-eyed.

'If the call came from Woods and Lovelock to' – he shuffles the papers again – 'Katherine Jane Burke, aged twenty-two, formerly of Bardon, now living at 16 Whynot Street, West End. Then the full force of the law would be coming down on the two musicians, wouldn't it? Not you and her.'

*

Drew, upright in his chair, noble, chin up, is quivering. Mick, wanting to look away, is presenting his best brave face when the door opens.

'This is a bit dark and dingy,' says Sophie Chabowski, gorgeous in a tight blue satin dress and heels, scanning the corners of the boxed room. 'A person could get depressed down here.'

'It's where they put us,' mumbles Drew.

She stands before the songwriters. 'So what's happened?'

'Game over,' whispers Mick.

'The Rockhampton cop who busted us at the club,' continues Drew, pronouncing the band's death sentence, 'is in town and tracked us down as we were about to sign a contract that would have transformed our lives.'

'The LA album,' says Mick, softly.

'That's Detective Brian Bishop and you were arrested at the Hilton Hotel this afternoon at . . .' Sophie glances down at a sheet of paper in her hand. 'I've forgotten my glasses, sorry for that. At . . . just after five pm. Five thirty-two.'

'Can he do that?' perks up Mick. 'Isn't it out of his, you know, jurisdiction?'

'A loophole?' peers Drew hopefully.

'He certainly can. And Bingo is being held here too, and an American woman. Who's she?'

'Ruth O'Connor. She was signing us to the deal. She's innocent, of course.'

'I was at Leo's and just walked in the door at home when you called. You're lucky. The girls have a Sunday lunch there once a month. Beautiful spaghetti marinara and chianti. It's on Fitzroy Street in St Kilda – you must know it.'

That's it, the songwriters have lost all faith. Their lawyer's tipsy.

'No, we don't,' says Mick with effort.

'I've just spoken with Sergeant Detective Frank Irvine. Fearless Frank. Not someone you'd want to cross.'

Drew begins hyperventilating.

'Aren't all cops like that?' reasons Mick.

'Let me go on,' says Sophie. 'All charges against you have been dropped, save the credit card, which will be a judicial matter – a minor court proceeding, I'd imagine, involving full repayment and a fine.'

Perhaps she's been too technical in her language. The expressions on the songwriters' faces have barely altered. 'You're not going to jail. You're free. He wouldn't tell me how, and as your legal representative I thought it best not to pursue the matter. You agree?'

'Free?' utters Drew. Like it's a word he's never heard. 'Free.'

'Yep.'

'We can walk out?'

'Sign out. There's a few formalities – get your keys, your car's in the police lock-up garage. I've never seen anything like it.'

'Oh my God,' exhales Mick, his face unlocking. Turning to Drew, he flashes the toothy grin.

'A guardian angel doesn't fit you guys. An *avenging* angel, that's better. Boys, you're squashing me.' The songwriters are hugging her. 'Someone showing great cunning,' she shouts over their nestling shoulders, 'and impeccable timing,' she proclaims in a theatrical courtroom flourish, 'is looking down favourably from the heavens upon you both.'

They walk with the expressions of those presumed lost, being slowly led back to civilisation after days away in a dark remote valley. The room they shuffle into not unlike the vaulted sandstone interior of a central railway station. Usually crowded and noisy, it is empty, save for a policeman behind a raised desk and a lone figure sitting on a pew-like bench against a wall. A guitar case at his feet.

Mick and Drew's attention has been drawn to the man who rose at their appearance. And as their lawyer and manager organise the returning of evidence and their car, Ruth and Swifty resuming their acquaintance, the songwriters move to the approaching stranger, who, without ponytail and beard, has the trembling vulnerability of a freshly shorn lamb.

Mick squints, like he's got dust in his eyes. 'What are you doing here?'

'I had to do it. I couldn't live with myself.'

'It was a ratty thing to do, you hippie bastard.'

'I know.'

'You put us through hell and back again.'

'I'm sorry.'

Ponytail is taking the serve he knew was coming, but daring to hold the suspicious, accusing gaze of the songwriters he admires so much. 'They were coming to get you anyway for the credit card. Tom had asked me to bring the grass along as a favour to you guys. A thank you for the music and the songs.'

'R-i-g-h-t,' says Drew, eventually.

'Bishop and Elroy couldn't believe their luck when they walked in on that.'

'You know them?'

'Well, I didn't then. I should have stayed in the dressing-room and taken the consequences. I know that now. I couldn't get caught.'

'We could,' Mick points out.

'That's not what I mean. You're going to find this hard to believe, but not staying allowed me to help in ways I couldn't have if I *had* stayed.'

'Hang on,' chuckles Drew. 'How did you pissing off help us?'

'I went to the police to admit to the dope. They told me you'd been taken to the facility and were coming back Tuesday. I thought that was odd. Then I heard you'd escaped.'

'That's my guitar case,' says Drew, pointing at the bench.

'Ron and Murray say hi.'

Ponytail can see he is running too fast. 'I know "Big" Bob Knowles. He's not a bad guy. My uncle and him went to school together. He's embarrassed about it all, actually. Bishop tore strips off him when he went out there.'

'Who the fuck *are* you?' interrupts Mick.

'Douglas Gordon Heywood the Third.'

Mick can't help it – he laughs into the guy's face. Spit flying everywhere.

Grinning, Drew says, 'And I thought my name was bad. Okay, Douglas Gordon Heywood the Third, what are you telling us?'

'It's simple. My family go back five generations in Rockhampton. Bishop has been there eighteen months – *that's* the difference.'

The songwriters hold their stare, while trying to unfold Ponytail's past and how it has afforded them their freedom.

Sensing their change, Ponytail continues.

'Lots of civic duty and good deeds done by the family through the years. There's even a bridge named after us. My grandfather and father keep up the traditions. I'm the black sheep. Only one with a PhD, though.'

'What in?' asks Drew.

'Asia and Pacific Studies.'

'So . . .' insists Mick.

'Bishop thought you'd run to Melbourne and try and find your manager. When he flew off on Friday, I knew you'd got there. I came down knowing what Bishop was up to. I was tipped off about the Hilton and came here.'

'Tipped off?'

'An influential friend in Rocky who knows influential people down here.'

'Let me get this straight,' says Drew, stepping back, his hands raised as if feeling for an invisible wall. 'If I'm understanding what you're saying here. It's a bit hazy. The jailbreak?'

'Forgotten.'

'The dope?'

'Is me.'

'The car, we know.'

'Gary Getty,' Mick and Ponytail chorus.

'Which leaves the credit card.'

'I can't help you with that.' Biting his lips. 'I don't have a spare eighteen grand.'

Mick pulls a trick. Stone-faced. He leans an arm on Ponytail's shoulder, drawing him in close.

'I do.'

*

Mick is driving; he drives on the big occasions. To pick up drugs. To see a friend's gig. Visit his dad. With his arms stretched gun straight to the wheel, he's pushed back into his seat as if to gain maximum distance and perspective on a golden future he and Drew are moving to. Voices are ricocheting inside the car, but he's not saying much, happy in his heart, while stealing glances at the gorgeous green gloom of the Botanical Gardens opening out as they cross the Yarra River. He remembers Jack Mitchell's casual prejudice for the city, and at moments like these . . . well, you have to admit, now Melbourne will always have a starring role in their story.

It was at the Hilton Hotel, where the Queensland cop walked in on the songwriters about to sign the Hollywood contract in the Captain's Bar with a gold pen that would forever change their career and the face of Australian music.

To Bingo's consternation, Ruth has chosen to travel with Mick and Drew in their car. He wanted to keep contact between the songwriters and their publisher at a minimum. God knows what they'll tell her, saying things they think are funny that aren't; saying things they think should be shared but shouldn't.

She'd wanted to go with them and the weird guy from Rockhampton, who had something to do with the miracle that had just befallen them at the police station. Leaving him and Swifty to retrieve the Saab from the Hilton car park and head off to the party Simone was assembling at the apartment. The roadie comfortable in the passenger seat recalling his days on the road with High Risk.

'That's the most astonishing piece of news I've heard since The Smiths broke up,' exclaims Douglas.

'It's a secret,' says Ruth.

'Staying between the four of us,' adds Mick.

'When it's announced in *Billboard*,' says Drew with a lofty inflection, 'then we tell everyone.' He can't help himself; he's joking anyway. 'And watch them cry.'

'I won't, honest,' laughs Douglas. 'Can I just say one thing and then it's done.' He turns to Ruth beside him in the back seat. 'Of all the Australian bands you could have signed – and there are plenty of them: some are terrible, a few are good, a couple are brilliant – you've chosen the best. Song for song, no-one can touch them.'

Mick and Drew have learnt, and it took them centuries, to say nothing when someone is complimenting you. Silence allows praise to echo *long*.

Ruth, guessing their tactic, prods. 'What do you think of that?'

'I think Doug is entitled to his opinion,' answers Mick, gracefully arching the car through a corner; down Dorcas Street towards Albert Park.

'I'm guessing the deal will also be advantageous for your next album,' remarks Douglas. 'You've mentioned in interviews the wish to record overseas.'

'That *may* be an option,' says Drew, cagey.

'Let's remember,' says Ruth, 'the first two records haven't come out in the States yet. No-one knows you. We'll have to see what happens with them, and where that puts you for the next one.'

The songwriters like the sound of that.

'Do you know who I think would be great covering you guys?' says Douglas. 'Elton John.'

Mick and Drew don't think much of that.

'I'm serious. Your songs are strong, but people think only a certain kind of artist, like an indie artist, could cover you. But they're classic in their construction. The lyrics are a bit adventurous for some, but it could work.'

'I agree,' says Ruth. 'I was thinking of some of the edgier artists in Nashville or Austin.'

'You could get our songs there?' asks Drew.

'Why not? I wouldn't have signed you if I thought that wasn't possible.'

Dream fulfilment. Shooting for the stars with their wily American publisher and a quirky, opinionated guy who may be credited on their next album as 'Guru': every great band needs one of them.

Drew digs into his trouser pocket. He unbuckles his seatbelt, digs more.

'Before I forget,' he says. They are approaching Bingo and Simone's address. 'Can you please give this' – he turns to face

Ponytail – 'to Ron and Murray, when you see them next. Put it in your pocket. Don't lose it.'

Ponytail takes the gold key with a dainty pinch, holding it to his eye.

'What does it open?'

'Never mind, just give it to them.'

The songwriters have thought of keeping it. A token. Something from their trip they'd guard tightly, only revealing it to dramatic effect in a *Rolling Stone* cover story or a band documentary.

'And I want you to tell Ron something. Are you listening? This is important,' calls Mick, not taking his eyes from the road. 'Tell him to pass the key on to the next person he meets that needs to escape the confines of their previous life.'

'Oh, that's good,' smiles Drew, turning back to the road. 'He'll get that.'

Ruth doesn't. 'Am I missing out on something?' she laughs.

*

'Harry . . . come on, Harry . . . *come on*, it's Brian. I'm in my office at Russell Street. Give us a call, will ya. Later, I'll be at the hotel. Bye.'

He clicks open a black leather attaché case on his desk, ready to fill it with sheafs of paper and plastic folders. Biros, pencils, a heavy stapler, amidst the mess. Two months' hard work. He's tempted to dump it in the bin. The phone rings.

'Hi, Harry.'

'What's up?'

'Good question.' His sleepy eyes trawl the bare, musty walls. Their smell had reminded him of a miserable week he'd had in

London one winter. 'I've been sitting here in my bunker for the last half hour trying to work it out. What I think happened is I got burnt at both ends. In Rocky *and* in Melbourne. If it had just been the one place, with the cops against me, I would have noticed it and still got the songwriters and their manager. But it's gone. It was weird, Harry. I couldn't see the logic.'

'It all added up from here. I don't get it. You never stumble on this shit. You're ruthless.'

'I missed something in Rocky. Something or someone I didn't know. It was a last-minute switch and it didn't come from the musos or the manager. They were scared. The manager was babbling.'

'And the roadie?'

'He was loyal. Soft on the girl, but loyal. Frank Irvine called me in. I had the warrants in my hand. He said the case was closed – I had to drop it. He apologised, but that was that.'

'I tell you, if I had to choose between a small town or a city for bullshit, I'd choose the small town every time.'

'Which is why I'm not going back.'

'Leave it with me, Brian. I'll get you transferred.'

'Don't.'

'Cairns or Townsville – your choice. Two years in one of them and you can sneak back to Brisbane a rehabilitated man.'

'I'm going to quit. That's what I've been sitting here reckoning.'

Harry's quiet. Bishop waits.

'You're rushing. Get back to work, take a deep breath . . .'

'I'm breathing, Harry, that's why I want to quit. I'm going to pack up and sell. You know I bought a new car? Traded the Honda for an '89 Commodore.'

'Flash, but I don't know about this.'

'First stop Tin Can Bay. I've got family there and they've always asked me to drop in.'

'Okay, and when you get to Brisbane? What makes you think there's something here for you?'

'They tell me the town's changed.' He snickers. 'The bad old days are gone.'

*

Mick is hungover. He partied long after Drew had slipped off to the spare bedroom, having knocked back one celebratory beer.

'Are you sure about this?'

Drew is determined.

'It's a long way, man.'

'I want the guitars back.'

Looking at his partner behind the wheel, he tries to suppress a grin. Drew kinda knows he knows. Both men have to play their parts in this goodbye scene. Not to do so would require them to enter emotional waters, personal intimacy waiting to bite them in the depths.

'Well, I'm glad you're picking them up.'

'Have to.'

'I know.'

'It's what I gotta do.'

That's closer to the truth, thinks Mick.

He gives the car roof a playful tap. 'Safe travels, and call me when you get there.'

'I will, my friend.'

Drew starts the car. Mick thinks he might even try and get there in one go.

'We're free!' shouts Drew suddenly.

Mick smiles too. 'How about that?'

Drew wants to add one more thing, but can't.

'Enjoy it,' says Mick, walking away.

*

Fog and inky darkness, owl hoots and a blanket of bats above a canopy of Norfolk pines, the blue Corolla slides side to side over the rocky hump of dirt to roll down into the car park. Ten hours the first day; up early, eleven today. Drew wonders if he'll ever be able to straighten out his body again. Pulling the keys from the ignition with effort, he feels like slumping onto the steering wheel for a quick twelve-hour nap.

The rush and brush of cold mountain air as he opens the door is a revitalising slap. Feet planted on Mount Drake. The muscles in his back feeling like they may one day realign. He's made it.

On the verandah, the blackboard lists many of the night's performers and their time slots of a week ago. A new name is Russell Duggan. Drew checks his watch: eight-thirty. Russell is on at nine.

Going through the front door, he can't resist a peek. She's not behind the bar. *Good.* He thinks of a drink and thinks not. Walking on, till spotting a full head of swept-back hair, he advances on a table, spinning a nearby chair and sitting in one graceful flourish.

'I love it up here,' he cracks blank-faced to Russell's astonishment.

'Oh my God!' the older songwriter shouts, his right hand falling in a knee slap. 'You're back.'

'Yeah, and you're playing.'

'Well, I thought I'd give it another go.' He takes a deep drag of his cigarette. 'And you'll be glad to know, I'm leaning on my seventies stuff. Even doing a song off my debut album.'

'Mick and I haven't had a chance to listen to it yet, but we will.'

'How is he?'

'In triumphant form.'

'I'm doing "Katie's Song".'

The look on Russell's face is endearing. He's the wide-eyed kid blowing his first bubble-gum bubble. Hard to believe he's back in the game – even if it is small time.

'The old stuff can be the good stuff.' It's corny, but Drew says it, anyway.

'Let's hope the audience think so. I'm lucky. I know I've got one supporter.'

Susan was smiling at Drew as she approached. A funny, look-who's-here, tilt to her head. They hug.

'What are you doing in town?' she says, sitting down.

'Seeing Russell play.' She knows why – he can see it in her face. A mischievous sparkle to her eyes. Russell has told her. 'And to get the guitars back we traded for the car.'

'Word's out about them,' says Russell. 'Andy has let it be known.'

'Really?'

'There aren't many secrets up here.'

Pop. Pop. The MC's tapping of the microphone sends gunshot sounds through the room. She introduces Stonewall Junction. The elderly husband and wife team carry their guitars and wide smiles onto the stage. In blue rhinestones last week, tonight they're in red.

'We can go over tomorrow,' says Russell, 'and pick them up.'

'That would be great.'

Russell watches the musicians intently. He's nervous, fiddling with his collar.

'How's the art show going?'

'It's coming along,' says Susan. 'We're thinking three weeks' time on a Saturday. I've just spoken to Heather.'

The band start up. 'Tie A Yellow Ribbon Round The Ole Oak Tree'. Their weakest song.

Drew leans into Russell. 'Let me get up with you?'

'And do what?'

'"Three Way Tie".'

'How do you know I'm even doing it?'

'It's a classic – you have to.'

Russell is uncertain.

'*Please.* I've got a harmony for the chorus. It'll really lift it.'

'If things are going well,' says Russell haltingly. 'If an encore is a possibility.'

Drew squeezes his arm in gratitude.

He sits with Susan through Russell's set; their applause and joyful shouts joining a swell each song receives. A few numbers into the performance, the back door of the bar opens and Heather walks in.

He watches her watch Russell. There's a nobility to her profile and an attentiveness to the music that he feels would extend to how she would view all things in life. He imagines standing at her side. Looking at what she's looking at, and through some kind of osmosis understanding what she sees. Thinking he could do this for some time. Years even. And then there's her erotic charge. Maybe it wouldn't be all standing and looking.

'That was "Katie's Song",' whispers Susan. Drew hadn't heard a word.

The show is going well. The old songs written in hippy Glebe and the first years up the mountain are strong – brought back from the dead to parade around in rude health. 'A good song never goes out of fashion,' Mick had whispered to Russell with whisky breath.

And like the sudden return of his old repertoire, stagecraft is finding its legs too. A remark when introducing a song gets a laugh. Rocking back on his heels while doing some serious strumming gets a cheer. A rueful shake of the head on a 'deep' line pulls heartstrings.

The reward is an encore.

Drew is aware of how good they must look. Older man, younger man, brothers in song. Their sweeping hair and strong profiles silhouetted in the single spotlight. Leaning into the microphone, Drew harmonises on the chorus.

The lady she must choose
Will it be sunshine or the blues
Will it be rainbows or rained-on shoes
I can no longer try
The hardest goodbyes
Are said at finishing lines
I'd looked across to find
We were caught in a three way tie.

A group of friends and new fans and the curious engulf Russell and Susan. The older songwriter is gracious in the throng. Packing away his guitar, he banters and bats back answers to questions on the meaning of his songs and his past. *Why haven't you played more often?* That's the question he doesn't have a quick answer for.

'Great songs, man,' a boy of about nineteen with a wispy moustache tells him, heading off into the night with a scruffy gang of Mount Drake youth.

Drew is watching Russell have his moment. A circle of women circling Susan. They are a charismatic couple drawing people to the flame that burns between them. He is about to go over and feel the warmth.

'Hey, you.'

'Oh . . . hello,' he says, turning.

His 'How are you?' and Heather's 'What are you doing here?' overriding each other.

'Good,' she says, out of the confusion. 'Juggling what I can. I've just booked Things Of Stone And Wood for later in the year. Do you know them?'

'Slightly.'

'I thought you were off playing one-off shows around the country under funny names.'

'There were no more shows. That was the last one.'

'Uh-huh.'

'When Mick and I played last week, we were in some trouble with the law. That's why the funny name, which . . . I didn't think was too bad. We went to Melbourne the next day and, through some kind of outrageous good fortune – our lawyer thinks we have an avenging angel looking after us – things got cleared up. I couldn't tell you at the time, although I wanted to.'

'I don't know how I would have reacted. I'm glad you didn't.'

'Oh, that's good.'

'I won't ask what it was,' she hints a smile. 'I'm assuming it's not murder.'

'No.' He laughs. 'Just silly stuff with our manager and being on the road. It's fixed.'

'Then why come back?'

'Well, to get to Melbourne we needed a car and we traded our guitars for one in "the blocks". I've come to get them back. That was part of the deal – return in a week, we can trade.'

'Just made it.'

'Yeah. The guitars mean a lot to Mick and I. They have a history and a . . . unique sound.'

'Uh-huh.'

'A special blend. One's a Gibson and the other's a Martin. I'm getting technical here, I know . . .'

'My camera's a Leica. I couldn't live without it.'

God, she's great.

'Also, I wanted to see Russell and Susan. He helped us with the car and' – opening his hands – 'I walked in on a fantastic show.'

'Susan had told me he played and wrote songs.' They look over at the couple. The throng is thinning. Susan catches their eye – they turn away quickly. Caught together. 'He was amazing. He can get more gigs on that.'

'And I wanted to see you. That's another part of it, a big part. Why I raced to get here in time.'

'That's very sweet,' she says carefully. 'I've got a secret to tell you.'

The house lights come on. The soft edges of her face are suddenly filled out and real. Her eyes are pink like rabbits; he hadn't realised that. They hold his stare.

'Jazzy and I are going back to London in a few weeks. She's got into a good school and I want to work from there again. I haven't told anyone in town yet.'

'Your sister?'

'She's fine. It's been lovely to have this time together with the children.'

'I'm happy for you. It's where you should be.'

'Oh, Drew.'

*

In Amsterdam, on one of his many nights of drunken stumbles through foreign cities while on tour, Drew had come across a corner bar by a canal. He'd gone in and sat with his beer and a cigarette, listening to the jukebox in the corner. 'Amsterdam Jukebox' was a song title or album title he carried around for a few years. Like the bar, the music was a trip back to the fifties – Billie Holiday, Sinatra, Jacques Brel – and it blended oh so perfectly with his world-traveller, world-on-a-string, tipsy, sentimental mood.

Heightening the experience was the room's nicotine-stained light, and here it flickers again, consoling him. A rustic wooden kitchen with candles – their glint catching the hanging pans over the stove, the brass latches on the windows, to settle in a series of refracting prisms, not unlike the brandy-coloured rays of morning sun, through a forest of empty wine and beer bottles on the table before him.

He's nestled between Russell and Susan. She's gathered the pouch of Champion Ruby reserved for nights like this and is rolling two cigarettes; one for herself and one for her husband, who, between drinks, is explaining the history of the mandolin in country music to Billy, a baby-faced giant in denim overalls.

Beside him is a young woman shelling nuts, whose name Drew hadn't caught. He'd been told she was an art student and the bass player for a folk band from Bangalow called Figs. At the end of the table is a youth with sleek, dark hair falling onto his shoulders and into his eyes. His name is Steve and he's the local boy wonder. Thrashing his Yamaha acoustic to within an inch of its life, he's just played two of his songs, the last a murder ballad with a body count Drew lost track of somewhere in the fifth verse.

'Why don't you play something?' asks Susan.

'Don't push him.'

'I'm not pushing,' she says to Russell. 'You're obstructing is what's happening with all your talk.'

'Hey, don't fight, you two,' slurs Drew. 'I haven't got a guitar for a start. Andy has –'

Russell hands him his and a plectrum.

Shifting in his chair, Drew bangs the head of the guitar on the table. 'Oops.'

He strums an E-minor chord. His fingers feel buttery on the fretboard and his tempo is uneven on his fledgling strum. Strumming more, Drew feels he has one song in him.

'It's a new thing,' he mumbles.

He's falling into a rhythm. There's a nice guitar riff at the start, but he's beyond playing that.

'A co-write. Mick did the music. I did the words.'

'Got a title?' asks the woman shelling pistachios.

'Yes, no, you'll get it.'

He glances at Susan for courage. It's the party version of her; a cigarette between her lips – drawing puffs, eyes at half-mast, the woman Russell must have fallen in love with.

They both broke out of jail, and walked quickly to the nearest hill,
Where they looked back upon the scale, of what they'd done to get to the hill

Floating out of the verse. Same three chords. The chorus.

And they had their songs packed away, no time to waste or lose,
And they had their songs to sing

When you're drunk, it's hard to do two things at once. The second thing cancels out the first and you can be left with nothing. He can sing the words and his fingers have a purpose of their own. But he's unable to sense the effect the song is having on those around him.

They made it to the nearest town, and found an empty house there to hide,

The guards were tracking them down, but they both felt
safe inside.
And they had their songs to sing, no time to waste or lose,
And they had their songs to sing

A small instrumental section sets up the third and final verse, which is double in length. The story gets resolved. He doesn't dare look up. No playing to the room. Not necessary.

They wondered where they should go, remembered a club that
they'd once played,
Run by a lady named Jo, who didn't mind if they stayed,
Because she had her heart upon, one of the men who played,
And as he sang his song, she saw, that he felt the same

There are no more lyrics. Just some sweet Mamas and Papas *da da da dahs* over the verse melody, to end on a resounding C-major chord that rings like crystal in the stillness of a cold mountain night.

'Fucking ace song,' says Steve, slow hand clapping.

'Ooooh, that's good,' rumbles Billy. 'Hey, hey, hey! Look what we got here, people!'

Looking down the table, it's smiles and cheers. It did sound good, thinks Drew. It's a keeper.

'Why didn't you tell me?' asks Russell darkly, the Western hero face jowly and withered from the booze.

'We couldn't,' says Drew, dry mouthed.

'I thought it was too good to be true. Two young songwriters walk into town and change everything in a day.'

'Oh, don't, Russ,' pleads Susan.

'We didn't want to drag anyone in,' says Drew, hurting. 'Not even you, who would have understood us the best.'

'What are you guys talking about?' smiles Billy.

'I must have missed something,' jokes the nut sheller.

'It doesn't matter,' says Russell, gruffly. 'What have you and Mick done?'

'Minor shit,' says Drew, relieved. 'Our manager, Queensland cops, forget it. It's over and we owe a lot of that to you.' He dares to place a hand on the big man's shoulder. 'Thanks, you saved us.'

Russell eyes him. Forgiveness coming slowly. 'I'm glad you boys came and it's worked out.'

'Yes,' says Susan firmly. 'But tell us next time. Alright?'

'There's a lot to this song, man,' says Billy, laughing. 'It's kind of like "American Pie". Open to a thousand meanings and, Drew, you don't have to tell us what they are, mate.'

'It's called "Songwriters On The Run", and it's a true song up until the third verse. That's where it goes off into make believe. Wishing what you want to happen to happen.'

'"Songwriters On The Run"?' remarks the woman. 'Criminals on the run or . . . gangsters on the run. But *songwriters*.'

Steve shakes his mane. His cute-boy face earnest. 'It's clever.' He begins to fingerpick the song's three-chord melody, Billy joining him, blowing low notes on a harmonica he has cupped in the glove of his hand.

'I talked to Heather and it was great to see her,' says Drew. 'We picked up from where we were, whatever that was. It was nice, but it's not like anything is going to happen.'

'The song was what you wanted,' ventures Susan.

'Yes, but it wasn't real.'

'Did you tell her? That's the important thing,' says Russell.

'In as direct a way as I could, and she got my meaning.'

'Funny . . .' muses Susan, stubbing out her cigarette. 'We had an art-show meeting during the week and Heather asked about you. I thought there was more there than what you say. Just hints. But things can change.'

'When was the meeting?' asks Drew, pulling himself into focus.

'It would have been just under a week ago. Wednesday. The day after you left.'

'What did she say?'

'Oh, I can't remember exactly. Did I know you? She'd heard you and Mick had left the club with Russ and stayed with us.'

'The day *after* I left, she asked.'

Russell, glass in hand, is swaying. 'You see. She likes you. I still think you're in with a chance.'

'This can't be told to anyone.' Even as Drew says it, he knows he wouldn't say it if he was anywhere near sober. 'Heather and Jazzy are leaving here in a few weeks to go back to London. Jazzy's got into a school and Heather wants to work from there again. That's what's happening. She told me.'

He stands up and hands Russell his guitar. Announcing to the room his gig is over. 'I'm off to bed.'

From his head hitting the pillow to snores is a short time. On his back, his arms and legs spreadeagled, his body a star, the room's four walls spin around him like a wheel. A coloured wheel. The bedside lamp on, he sees something he missed a week ago.

Susan's birds are flying. A pattern he'd overlooked as they moved from frame to frame. Eyes drooping, he understands the artist's intent. Parakeets in a rainforest going round and round and . . . round . . . and round . . . always returning.

DAYS AFTER

Drew's bedroom is at the end of the hall. A room built onto the back of the family house for his grandmother who moved in when ill in the early seventies. After she passed away, it became his room. At nineteen, he was ready to haul armloads of vinyl, his record player, his amp, and his first electric guitar – a black Ibanez Les Paul copy – out of a cramped middle section of the house, to the relative seclusion of his nanna's room and get down to some serious songwriting while failing university.

He'd returned to the place of his first songs through the years. It had been kept as he'd left it, save for one significant change. The strips of wallpaper, a forest scene that covered one bedroom wall, had vanished sometime in the eighties. It had featured in *The Man Who Fell To Earth*: the Bowie character in the movie, playing table tennis with an autumnal forest plastered behind him. In a nice touch, leaves were scattered at Bowie's feet, and Drew had gathered foliage from the backyard to lay across his grass matting floor – his parents having come to some accommodation of their son's more harmless eccentricities.

Thankfully, everything was as it always was on his arrival from Mount Drake. Russell dropped him off, charming his parents, to drive away and attend to errands in the city. And although Drew craved change in life and art, he'd walked wearily down the hall, suitcase and guitar in hand like so many times before, back to a beginning story he cherished.

Over the next days he did little but sleep and eat in shifts; waking in time for the midday movie on TV, catching up on family news with his mum and dad over dinner. His sister had a new boyfriend; the Davidson house two doors down was up for sale. The relief at having access to food he didn't have to buy or prepare, and slipping on clothes he hadn't washed, was immense.

Knowing he'd reached a particular point in his recovery, dressed in old jeans, black shoes and a flannelette blue shirt to ward off the gorgeous Brisbane June chill, he left the house one afternoon to walk to the local shopping centre. It was a single strip of shops when he was a boy, to suddenly become a shopping mall one year. Like the removal of the Bowie wallpaper, no-one had asked him. Change – you only notice it when you return home. Past the high school, he stops and stands at the gates of his old primary school.

He is still capable of reaching out and connecting to his younger self. And as appreciative as he is of sixties music and culture, he's glad he passed that turbulent golden decade doing nothing more than running around an oval, knees tucked under a desk, listening to a teacher. Gazing at the school rooms, the name of every kid in his Grade 7 class still in his head, he feels like a returning hero on leave from rock and roll duties. Someone who ventured off the path the school had prepared him for, and done great deeds: two albums with Mick, foreign tours, and – with the trapdoor entry of Ruth O'Connor into his life – a US publishing deal.

His parents knew nothing of the music business. There was crazy logic to it – Drew earned the least amount of money of anyone in the family, yet had all the attention and fame. Friends of his mother would telephone at daybreak: '*Have you seen it? Drew's in this morning's paper.*'

Publicity, not record sales, had changed everything. It had begun with the Toy Crime single; John Peel playing it on BBC radio and the articles and media attention hadn't stopped since. His parents were proud of him, and had come to realise music had saved their son. They also saw the gaunt figure stagger through the front door home from tours or cities, to fatten and freshen up, a quick dose of family love, to head off for another round in the ring.

They worried. He knew that.

Drew and Russell had driven to Andy's the day after Russell's show. Approaching the house, they'd heard the sound of guitar playing. Someone picking out fine blues figures and licks. Russell had lifted his eyebrows in appreciation.

The drop in Andy's face at the front door told the story.

'Hi, good to see you,' said Russell from the bottom stair.

'You can keep the car. I'd be good with that.'

Russell looked at Drew, as if the thought of Andy reneging on the deal had never entered their minds. 'You want the guitars back, don't ya?' declared the elder songwriter.

'I've come with the cash,' added Drew. 'Fifteen hundred dollars.'

Andy's eyes zeroed in on a faraway spot. Somewhere above Russell's shoulder. 'Come in.'

The house was spare and clean. No great character to the place and Andy lived alone. A bachelor pad with no loving touches.

'You want something to drink. Water? Beers?' Glancing at a plastic dish on the table. 'Got some local bananas, if you want.'

'No, we're fine, thanks,' said Drew.

'How was the car?' asked Andy affably. The three men grouped in the middle of the lounge-room.

'Oh, really good, it handles beautifully.' Drew pulled a pointed finger from his hip like a gun. 'The brake pad on the left front wheel may need a little work, but besides that . . .'

'Eighty-three Corolla and it was a fair price. You were in a spot of bother, Mick told me that.'

'He was right.' Drew doubled down on Andy's dig. 'We were definitely in a spot of bother.'

'He wants to trade,' said Russell evenly.

'Sure. No, I'm just thinking aloud. You could keep the car and I'd throw in five hundred bucks on top.'

Drew feigned considering the offer, to shake his head.

'You're sticking to the law,' joked Andy, undermining the musician's outlaw poses.

'You made a grand out of it,' said Russell. 'Which isn't bad for a week's work, when all you're doing is sitting around at home.'

'Then the deal must be honoured,' acknowledged Andy crisply, a stretch to his smile. 'I'll go get them.'

'No, I'll go,' said Drew. 'Let me collect them.'

*

'You've *got* to get down here.'

Drew laughs, and in that moment he recognises only Mick can zonk him like that – so hard on a first line.

He's on the back verandah, the telephone line taut, running from inside the house through the sliding door to the phone cupped at his ear. Two-and-a-half-thousand kilometres away, his songwriting partner could be at his side, spilling his glee.

'I'll get there. Just give me a little more time.'

'Oh, man!'

'Tell me.'

'Word *is* out and people are going crazy. Everything's changed. Bingo's saying we don't have to chase things anymore; people are chasing us now.'

'I thought we were keeping it a secret.'

'It's Melbourne. No-one –'

'So what are they saying?'

'They can't believe it. I mean we've *really* pulled something off here. American record executive comes out and signs just one band. No-one else. Just us.'

'Does Troy know?'

'We've jumped the queue. I think so.'

'Oh.'

'He'll get his turn, and if he doesn't, fuck him.'

'That's very charitable of you.'

'I was at a party the other night at Angela's. Tom. Sean from the Models. That DJ guy. Honeycrunch people. Tracey was there, Swifty too. What's that band? Forgotten.'

'Good band name, Forgotten.'

'Yeah, it is. Stacey and Lisa. A few people from Greville Records. And you could just tell, by the way people were, that they knew. It's like a fire jumping from one side of the road to another. You've *got* to get down here.'

'I will. I'm relaxing and writing. How's Swifty?'

'He's got himself a girlfriend.'

'Oh my God, what's she like?'

'Nice. You know, one of those ethereal types. They seem to get along well. She's an actress – a drama student at Swinburne.'

'Let's hope it lasts.'

'Have you spoken to Bingo?' wonders Mick.

'No, I've been meaning to call.'

'So you don't know.'

Mick takes a drag of something. 'A movie.'

'Uh-huh.'

'He said he'd call you when he knows more.'

'What kind of movie?'

'A Hollywood movie.'

'Oh, that kind. Anything more?'

'Ruth's pitching our songs to the director. A South American guy named Carlos. There's some interest, evidently.'

'I got to go. Mum's just arrived.'

'Say hi to her from me. What's for dinner?'

'Homemade spring rolls. She cooks them in a wok.'

*

That night, borrowing the family car – a gold 1986 Ford Falcon – Drew goes to a gig; a band with some hype on them playing at a corner pub in the city. He creeps into the show and hangs against a wall, scanning the room for familiar faces over the brim of his beer. There's a quick turnover to the Brisbane scene: few people from the early eighties are still going to gigs in 1991. They've either left town – London or New York, some of them, Sydney others – or are bedded down in the suburbs. Still interested in music, but not the roughhouse local venues.

The band are four young guys throwing themselves around a tiny stage. Their instruments hung ridiculously low, three of them, their long hair flaying across their backs, are in knee-length baggy shorts and work boots. To Drew, in slacks, a black V-neck sweater, white shirt and tie and polished shoes, they look less like a band and more like a gang of landscape gardeners.

Thank goodness he's out of rock and roll. Towards the end of The Shells, when The Pixies and Dinosaur Jr. were coming through, he knew they were good, but he couldn't go another round. He'd been listening to rock music with dedication for twenty years. At thirty, he'd heard enough. It was time to leave the noise and the buried-in-the-noise lyrics in search of something new.

Out into the blackness and empty streets of 10pm Brisbane. To drive home, come softly up the back stairs and settle into the lamp-lit reverie of his room. Here in the rear of the house was his longtime laboratory. He was a scientist mixing up the medicines of his songs. Books he'd read. Lyric ideas, song titles, life-on-the-road mush scribbled into his diary. A few treasured cassettes. Recently, his feelings as he stood at the school gates, the aches and pains of passing time. Stirred and boiled, intoxicating fumes and test-tube bubbles in his head, playing guitar for hours each day, the house his, his parents at work during the week, hoping for that magic click of the code – a new song. Like a newborn baby, unique to the world. To add to what he already has for an album he and Mick are to record in LA at the end of the year.

On Asylum.

Bingo had phoned yesterday, his mum and dad overhearing the call in the lounge-room. Celebrations after. He hadn't realised what financial security would do to his nerves – quelling them in a euphoric rush. The movie was real. Had a title. Had stars. Expected to gross a hundred million plus. Five of his and Mick's songs in the script and slated for the soundtrack album.

A young woman named Ariel Garland has changed their lives. While LA waited for an earthquake, she has set one off in his and Mick's career. They're going to get a shot at the big time. Be stars, probably. Which puts even more pressure on what he can dream up in his bedroom.

In pyjamas, lying on the single bed by the windows, his nanna's bed, made of iron – like her – a secret ministry of frost forming on the back lawn, he ponders his greatest dilemma: what to do with the third verse of 'Songwriters On The Run'.

Mick would hoot and holler, sarcasm and disbelief aplenty, if he heard it.

Because she had her heart upon, One of the men who played
And as he sang his song, she saw, That he felt the same

She didn't feel the same. Her heart was not upon him. She was leaving for London with her daughter. If only love and life could be written like a song. What had been inspired prophecy when scribbled on a service-station napkin while driving away from Mount Drake was shown to be insipid fantasy and foolishness when returning to Mount Drake. Songs, they can fuck ya.

He runs some alternate lines through his head, starting with the two he has, to kick off ideas.

They wondered where they should go, remembered a club that they'd once played
Run by a lady named Jo, who didn't mind if they stayed

To then jump to . . . the truth?

And then they got a car and drove as far away as they could
And they were never heard of or found again

The second line doesn't work. What rhymes with 'could'? Wood, good, should, neighbourhood . . . ah, here it is.

And then they got a car and drove as far away as they could
Then they took a turn, and found themselves parked in Hollywood

Or . . .

They drove so far, they found themselves in downtown Hollywood.

Oh dear.

He can see the problem. As a break-out-of-jail song, the twist of a romance in the third verse works as a neat wrap-up to the narrative. Without it, and if he is to mirror his and Mick's true adventures, the song would have to be at least ten verses long. Like some kind of sea shanty or traditional folk ballad. Is that what they want on this album? No. And even that might not catch sufficient detail. By the time he got to the Hollywood punchline, anyone who was listening would have died of boredom. Songs, they can . . .

His mother is at the door. 'There's a letter for you.' She puts it on his desk, beside a knife opener that used to belong to his nanna. His mum's mum. A tiny sword that could have been from the eighteenth century. Ideal for ramming aristocrats. 'I'm off to the shops. Do you want anything?'

'Are Dad's clubs under the house?' asks Drew. 'He wouldn't mind me borrowing them?'

'Nah.' She swats his concern away. 'When's Charles coming over?'

'At two. We're teeing off at two-thirty.'

'I'll be home by then. I can give you a lift.'

'Okay, that's great. I'll bring the clubs up.' He flexes his shoulders. 'Let's see how the old swing is going.'

'You'll probably hit the first ball into the creek,' his mother cracks.

'You'd chip down to the creek, and go over with your second shot.'

'Don't get nasty.'

'I'm only joking.'

Her teasing humour, something else he's fallen back into with ease.

She'd said 'letter'. It feels like a birthday card, stiff and two-sided. He turns thirty-three in two months. Tearing the envelope, he takes out a card: an invitation to the Bakers Dozen Arts Show. The date and details drawn in a delightful artsy and craftsy style. On the back is handwriting.

Hey Drew,
I hope this finds you well – your folks taking good care of you. Songs? They spring to life like tropical waterfalls, my friend. The art show is on this Saturday and it would be good to see your good self here. We could do with some star power, says Susan, who sends her love. Heather dropped the invitations off and brought along a photo she asked me to enclose. Please say hi to Mick. He's welcome anytime too.
Stay Groovy,
Russell

The photo. Cheekbones sharp. Hair good and out of the eyes. His hunched shoulders hugging the Gibson. His glance, falling full onto, into, all over, the photographer. He's trying very hard to impress her. And he's relieved.

She knows it's funny, too much, and sent it along as a challenge or a kind of peace offering or both. Holding the photograph in his old bedroom, he can feel how far he has travelled since bundling into Mount Drake with Mick. He's not that guy anymore – no longer on the run, and his fortunes have flipped. He'll go see her and say goodbye.

He'll see Winston too – what song was he going to play as he leapt on stage in the Listening House? And Allen, he'll walk outside his car-repair shed, and he'll run his hands along the rust and stand back and take in the breaking waves on the distant beach, the swirling yellows and blues, the blazing ball of sun.

With his new money he'll buy the Kombi and bring it back to Brisbane. Parked under the house, his dad will complain. It will stand as a steel monument – a beautiful twisted piece of junk sculpture on wheels, celebrating the first thirty-two years of his life.

Later that night, a silky stillness descending on suburbia by 9pm, just the ghostly flickers of television sets glimpsed in dark lounge-rooms as signs of life, he unpacks his guitar – it is the playing hour. E minor. The tricky intro lick he came up with that first night out of jail by the campfire with Mick. He sings his song. The three verses and he'll keep the third as is. 'Songwriters On The Run' is done.

It's true to its moment. Don't change imperfection if it has a perfection of its own. If he ever taught songwriting, that would be his first rule.

He can see the song's future. They'll record it in a cathedral-sized LA studio with famous session musicians, who will compliment him and Mick after nailing a perfect first take. Maybe the song will become the album title.

And when he sees Heather in London or Rimini, they'll laugh about it. His silly moment. That he could ever believe she'd fall for him instantly. Those things don't happen. That's fantasy stuff. It takes time.

ACKNOWLEDGEMENTS

Thank you to Patrick Mangan, editor extraordinaire. His musical knowledge, his patience, his wanting the book to be the best it could be. He was a constant.

Thank you to my publisher, Beverley Cousins, for her steady hand and encouragement. If Beverley liked it, I knew I was making good progress.

Thank you to Justin Ractliffe for his judgement and support. He signed me to Penguin on a plot-driven first draft. To then wisely ask: 'Where is the poetry in this?'

Thank you to Karin Bäumler. My wife and collaborator. She read drafts of the book, heard me pace and groan, to listen and advise as only she can. Danke.

Thank you to Bernard Galbally, my Australian manager, who has guided the book, as he has me, to better things.

Thank you to Bob Johnson, my overseas manager for forty-one years, who can calm troubled waters, allowing me to do what it is that I do.

Thank you to Pete Paphides, a good friend, who read the first draft and was encouraging. It helped.

Finally, thank you to Christian Ryan, who read the stars back in 2005, and showed enormous bravery in signing me up as music critic for *The Monthly*; gifting me a life as a writer.

SONG CREDITS

SONGWRITERS ON THE RUN
Words and music by Robert Forster

HEART OUT TO TENDER
Words and music by Robert Forster

DARK SIDE OF TOWN
Words and music by Grant McLennan

I WRITE THE SONGS
Words and music by Bruce Johnston

INSIDE AND OUTSIDE THE **GO-BETWEENS**

GRANT & I

'The truest and strangest poet of our generation'
NICK CAVE

ROBERT FORSTER

Grant & I is the story of the friendship and collaboration of Grant McLennan and Robert Forster, who gave Australia The Go-Betweens, one of our best and most influential bands. It was named Book of the Year 2017 by *Mojo* and *Uncut* magazines.

The Go-Betweens, one of Australia's most talented and influential bands, very nearly wasn't. Grant McLennan didn't want to be in a group, and couldn't even play an instrument. That didn't stop the singer-songwriter duo of Forster/McLennan becoming one of the most acclaimed partnerships in Australian music history.

Just as The Go-Betweens always defied categorisation, *Grant & I* is like no other rock memoir. At its heart is a privileged insight into a prolific artistic collaboration that lasted three decades, and an extraordinary friendship that rode out the band's break-up to remain strong until Grant's premature death in 2006.

Unconventional in lineup and look, noted for near misses and near hits, always a beat to one side of the mainstream – the band's unusual beginnings were followed by twists that often confounded its members as well as fans and record companies. The story of The Go-Betweens is also the story of the times, and *Grant & I* is a wonderfully perceptive look at the music industry and a brilliantly fresh take on the sounds of the era.

As distinctive a writer of prose as he is of songs, Robert Forster is wise and witty, intimate and frank, astute and knowledgeable. There could be no better tribute than *Grant & I* to this partnership and band who remain loved and revered.

'The truest and strangest poet of his generation.' Nick Cave